MW00941196

THE TIME HUNTERS AND THE BOX OF ETERNITY

CARL ASHMORE

THE TIME HUNTERS AND THE BOX OF ETERNITY

Carl Ashmore

FOR LISA, ALICE AND WILL
– *as everything is.*

1

CHAPMAN'S CHOICE

Wandsworth Prison, London. April 6, 1903.

A gas lamp flickered outside George Chapman's cell door, tinting his black eyes orange, and he heard a distant bell ring a quarter to midnight. He wrapped a blanket round his shoulders and watched a spider scuttle down the damp stone wall.

Then a bitter realisation struck. The spider would outlive him.

Teeth-gritted, Chapman swelled with rage - he wanted to destroy it, to crush it in his fingers. But then, as it scurried onto the floor, he felt an unexpected emotion, one he'd never experienced before in his thirty-seven years.

Mercy.

For three weeks, since a jury convicted him of murdering his wife, the spider had been his only companion in this filthy box of a room. Perhaps it should live.

Turning to face the barred window, Chapman thought

about the day ahead, his last on earth, the day of his own execution. And the same recurring question crept into his mind: how would he feel when death finally came? For so many years, he'd seen so much of it, more than anyone could possibly imagine. And it was this fact that afforded him his greatest thrill. His true identity remained secret.

No one knew who he really was.

He was about to laugh, when a sudden chill swept the air. Confused, he glanced round, seeking its source. At once, streams of dazzling crimson light shot all around – twirling, crackling, spitting. Momentarily blinded, Chapman clamped his eyes shut, smothering his head with the blanket. Then - *BOOM* – the light vanished.

A voice sliced the darkness. 'Severin Klosowski?'

Dazed, Chapman threw the blanket off. 'Who – who is it?' he said. 'How do you know my real name?'

'I know many things.' A besuited sallow-faced man stepped out of the shadows, holding a two-handled black leather briefcase. 'You were born in 1865 in Nagorna, Poland. You arrived in London in 1887, and changed your name to George Chapman in 1895. Shall I elaborate on that heart-warming story?'

'No!' Chapman snapped back. 'But I - I don't understand.'

'I would be astonished if you did,' Emerson Drake replied calmly.

Chapman's face flushed red. 'What narcotic have you given me? Which hallucinogen? Regardless, I shall tell you nothing of my secrets, my - '

'Silence! You've been given nothing,' Drake cut in, 'other than the prospect of a lifeline. My time here is short ... so let me ask you a question: Do you want to live?'

'What do you mean?'

'At two o' clock tomorrow afternoon you'll be taken to a room they call the Cold Meat Shed and met by William Billington, who will proceed to hang you by the neck until you are dead. Now that is one possible chain of events - the other is up to you. So I shall ask one last time - do you want to live?'

'Yes.'

'Very well,' Drake replied without emotion. 'So be it. However, you shall not live as you have lived. You shall be mine. You will do my bidding. Is that acceptable?'

'I'm confused.'

Drake's cold blue eyes met Chapman's. 'Let's just say, I am a great admirer of your work and I believe you can offer much to my organisation. In return, your loyalty will be rewarded. Do we have a deal?'

Chapman took a moment to survey his tiny cell and an incredulous smile arched on his mouth. 'I shall do whatever you wish.'

'A wise decision,' Drake replied, offering him the second handle on the briefcase. 'Take this handle.'

Chapman eyed the briefcase suspiciously. 'What is it?'

'This is a *Portravella*, a portable time travelling device.'

'Time travel?'

'I shall explain later.' Drake glanced at his wristwatch. 'A warden named Gordon Bridge will make his rounds in precisely sixty-seven seconds. I would like to have left by then.'

'As you wish,' Chapman replied eagerly.

'However, just one more question,' Drake asked. 'How does it feel being the most infamous monster in the history of mankind?'

Chapman looked startled but composed himself at once. He noticed the spider scuttle past him. Then he crushed it beneath his bare foot. 'I don't know what you mean, Mister Drake.'

Precisely a minute later, Gordon Bridge found the cell deserted.

2

THE RETURN OF THE TRAVELLER

'Haven't you finished packing yet?' Joe Mellor said, his eyes flicking from his sister's half-packed suitcase to the mountain of clothes on her bed. 'We'll never leave at this rate.'

'Nearly,' Becky replied. 'Besides, we can't go anywhere until Uncle Percy gets here, so shut your -'

'Why are you packing so much, anyway?'

'Unlike you, I like to change my underwear on a daily basis.'

Joe ignored the comment. 'But we're only going for a week.'

Becky gave a low growl. 'I'm aware of that, pimple brain. Now why don't you go and play with your bow and arrow and bog off.'

'Because I'd rather stay here and annoy you.'

Becky rolled her eyes. 'The reason I'm packing so much is because who knows where we'll end up?' She lowered her voice to a murmur. 'Can I remind you that Uncle Percy is a time traveller and this is the first time we'll have seen him since the summer *without* mum being there.'

'So?'

'So he might take us on a trip?'

'Yeah, I know that,' Joe replied. 'But I don't see the point in packing all those clothes for a day trip to Stone Age Coventry, do you? Not unless you're trying to pull a caveman.'

Becky shot him a ferocious glare. 'Oh, just get lost and go and do whatever it is *little* boys do.'

A triumphant glint flashed in Joe's eyes. 'Little?' he snorted. 'I'm taller than you now, haven't you noticed?'

Becky felt nauseous. Joe had struck a nerve. Since his recent twelfth birthday something terrible had happened. Joe had grown an extra foot in height and, even worse, developed an irritating streak of self-confidence, particularly when talking to her. 'Yeah, well, as your limbs have grown, so your brain's shrunk. It's now roughly the size of a chicken dipper.'

Joe tilted his head as if studying Becky closely. 'I'm not being funny, Becks, but have you put on weight?'

Becky looked dazed, confused even, as she took a few moments to mull over Joe's words. Then, she erupted. 'No … I have not!' she roared. She scooped up a trainer and hurled it at his head, missing it by a whisker.

Joe sped from the room and leapt down the stairs, three at a time.

Becky powered after him, narrowly avoiding Mrs Mellor who emerged from her bedroom and said, 'What's all the shouting about?'

'It's him,' Becky yelled, her fists clenched. 'This time, he's … dead!'

'Calm down, young lady,' Mrs Mellor said. 'Joe. Get up here, please ... now!'

Joe shuffled back up the stairs. When he reached the top, Mrs Mellor turned to face them both. 'Now, will somebody tell me what on earth has prompted World War Three?'

'He called me fat!' Becky snarled.

'I didn't,' Joe replied. 'I asked if you'd put on weight. I didn't say you had.'

Becky scowled at him. 'Don't be such a smart ar -'

'That's enough, Becky!' Mrs Mellor turned to Joe. 'If you ever say anything like that to your sister again, you'll be in serious trouble. Do you understand me?'

'But –'

'No, *buts*... I mean it. And I would've thought you both had something better to do considering Uncle Percy is due here in ten minutes.'

Becky glanced at her watch. Ten minutes! Straight away, her desire to rip Joe's head off vanished, replaced by a wave of anticipation. She was returning to Bowen Hall and, more importantly, to its astonishing residents: Uncle Percy, the eccentric but brilliant inventor; Will Shakelock, groundsman, real life medieval action hero and all round hunk; Maria and Jacob, housekeeper and butler, the friendly elderly couple from nineteen thirties Germany; Milly, the Sabre-tooth tiger and her cub, Sabian; Gump, the baby Triceratops and, perhaps most incredibly of all, Pegasus, the snow-white winged foal.

Becky dashed back to her room and continued to pack. Throwing a final sock ball onto the pile, she felt her lucky pendant roll against her neck. She stopped for a moment and cradled it in her fingers. The pendant had been the last gift from her dad before he supposedly died, and was by far her most beloved possession. Recently, however, it had taken on a new level of significance. Only a few months ago, she had discovered he'd been a time traveller and, even more astonishingly, was still *alive* – imprisoned somewhere in time by a rogue traveller, Emerson Drake.

It had been the most extraordinary revelation and had taken all of her resolve not to tell her mum but, on Uncle Percy's recommendation, she and Joe had chosen to say nothing, at least until he'd been found and rescued.

And Uncle Percy had promised to do just that. Ever since Drake had boasted of his celebrated prisoner, Uncle Percy had worked tirelessly, night and day, following clues, chasing leads, using each and every one of his countless resources to find him.

Becky just knew one day he'd succeed.

SUNLIGHT SPILLED THROUGH THE WINDOW, illuminating Becky's long wavy black hair as she coiled it into a ponytail. She heaved the suitcase to the door and lugged it downstairs, placing it beside Joe's at the front door. She glanced at her watch again.

Uncle Percy had agreed to collect them at eleven and, being a time traveller, he had a tendency to be exceptionally prompt. In fact, she'd never known him to be late for anything. Not once.

Becky pulled on her duffel coat and listened out for the crunch of a vehicle pulling onto the graveled driveway. Hearing the kitchen clock toll, she entered the lounge, and stared out of the wide bay window. As the clock sang its eleventh chime, she knew something was wrong. And when Joe joined her, she could tell from his expression he thought the same; any grievance they had vanished at once.

'Where is he?' Joe asked.

'I don't know,' Becky replied.

Seconds became minutes. Becky rang Uncle Percy's mobile but got no answer. After the fifth attempt, she gave up and paced the room, with Joe sitting on the couch, rapping the arm nervously and gazing into space.

Mrs Mellor watched them both with a bemused look on her face. 'What's the matter with you two? He's allowed to be late.'

'You don't understand, Mum,' Becky replied anxiously. 'Uncle Percy is never late.'

'I'm sure he isn't,' Mrs Mellor replied. 'But if he's coming on the M6, he's probably stuck in traffic. You know how busy it gets.'

'He won't be coming on the M6.'

'How on earth do you know?'

Becky wasn't about to say he'd almost certainly be arriving in a time machine. 'I just do.'

'Even if he hasn't come on the motorway,' Mrs Mellor said, 'he could've still broken down.'

'He's the best inventor in the world, Mum. Anyone that can invent the Fuzzbagatron can fix a car.'

Mrs Mellor's face creased. 'What's a Fuzzbagatron?'

'A tubey thing that pings a lot.'

Joe looked up. 'Becky's right, Mum. He won't have broken down.'

Mrs Mellor gave an exasperated sigh. 'Personally, I think you're both overreacting. However, if you're so worried then give Maria a ring. I'm sure she'll know what's going on.'

Becky spent the next ten minutes holding the phone away from her ear as an increasingly frantic Maria fretted about Uncle Percy's whereabouts. By the time Becky hung up, Maria had become a hysterical wreck.

'Maria said he left three hours ago,' she whispered to Joe. 'He was wearing his best suit, carrying a bunch of Stephanie Roses and was going on a quick trip before coming to collect us.'

'A quick trip? Where to?'

'She wasn't sure.'

Joe pondered this for a moment. 'Okay, still, that's great.' He looked relieved. 'He's travelling. That's why he's late.'

'Don't be thick. The fact he's time travelling means he can pinpoint to the second when he gets here. No, something is definitely wrong…'

As the hours passed, Becky felt consumed with fear. Where was Uncle Percy? When was Uncle Percy? And what could she do about finding him? She phoned Bowen Hall repeatedly, but abandoned the idea when Maria's words became little more than incomprehensible howls, punctuated by great stuttering breaths.

It was six in the evening when a somber looking Mrs Mellor lowered a bubbling lasagne onto the kitchen table. 'Come on,' she said softly. 'I know you're worried, but you should both try and eat something.'

'I'm not hungry,' Becky replied.

'Me neither,' Joe agreed.

Becky was about to ask if she could be excused when the most wonderful idea burst into her head. She knew exactly what to do!

Uncle Percy registered his trips with GITT (The Global

Institute for Time Travel) precisely for situations like this. If only she could contact Annabel, the GITT receptionist, then she could find out exactly where and when he was. She also recalled Uncle Percy had mentioned a highly trained division within GITT called 'Trackers' that specialised in rescuing travellers in distress.

She leapt up excitedly and seized her phone when a number of things happened at once: a terracotta vase sat on the fridge rattled violently; the back door swung open as if struck by a fierce gust of wind; and a ball of light appeared, bright against the starless sky, above the oak tree that filled the garden.

Panicking, Becky glanced out of the window.

She knew precisely what was going on.

The light swelled – crackling and fizzing – as thin torrents of electrical charge shot out, coiling round the tree's branches like shimmering silver ringlets. Then – *CRACK* – a whip-like noise split the night. Then silence.

Becky didn't know whether to laugh or cry. She raced outside and stopped dead in her tracks, struggling to grasp the astonishing sight before her. Perched in the tree's branches, like a gigantic bird's nest, was a green and white Volkswagen campervan.

Time crashed to a standstill.

Only when Becky heard a high-pitched squeak from behind, did she tumble back to reality. Blood froze in her veins. She turned quickly to see Joe, his head cupped firmly in his hands, and to his left, her mother, her mouth opened so wide it nearly touched her knees.

Mrs Mellor had seen everything.

3

MEMORASING MUM

Horrified, Becky's eyes flicked from her mother to the campervan and back again. Then the campervan's door opened and Uncle Percy leaned out, waving cheerfully. 'Good - ' He glanced up at the coal-black sky, before shifting his gaze to the bewildered group. '- Evening, everyone...'

Becky stood there, unable to find a reply.

Uncle Percy climbed out. As he did his foot caught on a branch and, before he could stop himself, he plunged forward, landing face down with a *splat* in a puddle of mud.

Becky forgot about her mother and rushed to his side. 'Are you okay?'

Uncle Percy pulled a silk handkerchief from his breast pocket and dabbed his face clean. 'I'm fine. How embarrassing!' he said. 'How are you, Becky?'

Becky was about to reply when she noticed his long silver hair was matted with blood. 'You're bleeding.'

'Oh, it looks worse than it is. Had a bit of an incident at

Mammoth Gorge.' Uncle Percy stood up and flattened out the creases in his suit. He waved at Mrs Mellor and Joe. 'Hello, Catherine. Hello, Joe. Sorry I'm late.'

Mrs Mellor's jaw had now dropped so far it threatened to fall off altogether.

Uncle Percy patted down his hair in a vague attempt to look presentable. 'I do hope it's still the right day.' He whispered in Becky's ear. 'It is, isn't it?'

'Yes.'

'Good,' Uncle Percy said. 'Gosh, Catherine, I bet you're wondering what on earth is going on, aren't you?'

Mrs Mellor gave a shaky nod of the head.

'Okay,' Uncle Percy said. 'The thing is ... I'm a time traveller. And Becky and Joe - well, I suppose they are, too.'

'What are you doing?' Becky gasped, before being silenced by a shake of Uncle Percy's head.

'Becky and Joe discovered my little secret when they visited in the summer. In fact, they caught me performing some rather crude dentistry on my Sabre-tooth tiger, Milly, and I couldn't really talk myself out of that one.' He chuckled. 'Anyway, we had a jolly fine time, visiting Ancient Greece, finding the Golden Fleece, meeting the Argonauts and befriending a Minotaur named Edgar. Crikey, it was a fun adventure, wasn't it?' He grinned at Becky and Joe, who looked dumbstruck but forced a nod.

'Anyway, I'm telling you this because I've been on a trip today and was unfortunately involved in a Mastodon stampede. As you can see from the state of Bertha, my time machine, it was – rather like a Mastodon - somewhat hairy.'

For the first time, Becky noticed that Bertha's bodywork was a collage of cavernous dents and scratches, much of the paintwork having been scraped away.

'I believe the Terriflexor Condenser has been damaged,' Uncle Percy continued, 'which would explain why I've returned to this Time Point and not the one intended. It would also explain why I regrettably materialised in a rather splendid oak tree.'

'I-I don't understand,' Mrs Mellor stammered.

'Of course you don't, my dear woman. But your face does look quite the picture. In fact, why don't we preserve this moment for prosperity?' At once, he produced what appeared to be a small digital camera and - *click* – took her picture. However, instead of the usual white flash, a thick torrent of navy blue light shot from the lens, encircled her head like a mist, and then faded away.

Becky gave a little squeal. Her mother had become as solid as granite, her eyes vacant, her breathing thin and shallow.

'W-what have you done to her?' Becky panted.

Uncle Percy flicked his hand. 'Oh, don't worry, she's been *temporalised*. No biggie!'

'No biggie?' Becky barked. 'You've frazzled her brain!'

'This – is - so - cool,' Joe said, waving his hand in front of his mother's face, but not getting any reaction whatsoever.

'Oh, it's hardly frazzled,' Uncle Percy replied. 'In fact, it's perfectly safe. I'll *Retemp* her in a bit and she won't be any the wiser.'

Becky wasn't convinced, but knew Uncle Percy well enough to know he would never harm anyone, especially not her mother. 'If you're sure.'

'I am. Anyway, I'd better repair Bertha and straighten out this mess.' A moment later, he'd clambered up the tree and could be heard tinkering with the van's control panel.

Then something else occurred to Becky. 'And will being temporalised make her forget the last ten minutes?'

'I'm afraid not.'

'Then how will you explain the campervan in a tree thingy?'

'She'll have to be Memorased.'

Becky felt a flush of panic. 'And what's that?'

'Oh, it's nothing,' Uncle Percy said. 'I'll use a close-range Memoraser to send a nanowave into her archicortex, planting a timodifier that'll remove short-term recall for a specified period of time.'

Becky sighed. 'Stop being - well ... *you*, and remember I don't speak geek. What does that mean?'

'It means she won't remember any of it.' Uncle Percy frowned at Joe. 'I don't think you should be doing that, young man!'

Becky looked over and saw that Joe had folded down Mrs Mellor's bottom lip, inserted two pebbles up her nose and stretched out her ears so she looked like a monkey.

'Oh, but Uncle Percy ...' Joe's eyes twinkled mischievously. 'This is a once in a lifetime opportunity.'

Becky snorted. 'So is death, and that's precisely what'll happen to you if she finds out you've done that.' She paused for a moment. 'On second thoughts, let me get my phone and I'll film it.'

'I don't think so,' Uncle Percy said. 'Joe, restore your mother's dignity, please, or I'll temporalise you and hang you from this tree like a Christmas decoration.'

Joe complied at once.

'Now, Bertha's Terriflexor Condenser is fixed, so let me find a quiet spot nearby to materialise and I'll be back in two ticks and half a jiffy.' Seconds later, the time machine had disappeared.

Five minutes passed before Becky heard Bertha pull up at the front of the house. Racing to the door, she flung it open to see Uncle Percy, beaming from ear to ear. 'Shall we start again?' he said, embracing her. 'Lovely to see you again, my dear.'

'And you,' Becky replied, returning the hug twofold.

'Now, shall we retemp your mother before Joe does something we'll all regret?' He strode through the hall, into the kitchen and on to the patio. Then he stopped and gave a loud, exasperated sigh.

Mrs Mellor was stood there, as stiff as a board, her arms clamped to her side, and a plant pot set upon her head like a lampshade. Joe's eyes were fixed innocently on the sky, as if it had nothing whatsoever to do with him.

'That is not funny,' Uncle Percy said, shaking his head, although Becky wasn't entirely sure he meant it. He removed the plant pot and scowled at Joe. 'Can you do something useful for a change and see if you have any lemonade. It'll help the retemping process.'

'I'll check,' Joe said, racing into the kitchen.

Uncle Percy turned to Becky. 'Shall we get her inside?' At once, he hoisted Mrs Mellor onto his shoulder like a roll of carpet and carried her into the house. Entering the lounge, he propped her against the mantelpiece and took out the Temporaliser. With a mixture of dismay and amusement, Becky watched her mother sway slightly as Joe joined them, carrying a glass of dark brown liquid.

'We haven't got any Lemonade,' he said, holding up the glass. 'Will Dandelion and Burdock do?'

'I don't see why not,' Uncle Percy replied, adjusting a

large shiny dial on the Temporaliser. 'Now, we'll have to retemp and memorase her almost simultaneously.' He produced what looked like a small black torch with a series of numbers etched on its casing. 'I think a fifteen minute memorase should do the trick.' He trained the Temporaliser on Mrs Mellor and - *click* - a shimmering emerald haze surrounded her. At the same time, he switched on the Memoraser. Humming lightly, it sent a narrow ray of silvery light into her eyes. Uncle Percy gave a satisfied smile and pocketed both gadgets.

Becky watched, her heart thumping. What if it didn't work? What if she couldn't be revived? However, before she had time to worry further, her mother stirred slightly and gave a low moan. Then, with a start, her eyes snapped open and she snatched at the air, colour returning to her cheeks.

'There, there, Catherine...' Uncle Percy said softly. 'You're fine now.'

'P – Percy?' Mrs Mellor gasped. 'What happened?'

'You bumped your head. Here, sit down.' Uncle Percy steered her gently on to the couch and took the glass from Joe. 'Drink this. It'll help.'

Mrs Mellor drained the glass. 'I – I don't understand!'

'Of course you don't,' Uncle Percy said. 'But I've given you a once over and you're perfectly fine. There's not even a lump.'

'I don't remember a thing.'

Uncle Percy gave a sympathetic nod. 'That's just a spot of amnesia. You'll be right as rain in a few minutes.'

Mrs Mellor looked confused. 'When did I bang my head?'

Uncle Percy blushed slightly. 'Er, during the tornado.'

'T – Tornado!' Mrs Mellor exclaimed.

Uncle Percy nodded. 'I'm afraid so. It's done some terrible damage to the tree in your back garden. But no one was harmed and that's all that matters.'

'That's good.' Mrs Mellor sank into the chair as she processed this strange news. 'And why were you so late, Percy? Is everything all right?'

'Ah, sorry about that. Yes, I'm fine. I was involved in something of an accident and had to be towed to a garage. I've been there for hours. It was a *mammoth* job, apparently.' He winked at Becky. 'Anyway, my mobile phone was damaged in the accident, so may I use your landline to call Maria to say we'll be leaving shortly?'

'Of course.'

Uncle Percy left the room.

Becky joined her mother on the couch. 'You sure you'll be okay, Mum?'

'Oh, yes,' her mother replied distractedly, her fingers probing her scalp. 'I've never lost my memory before. What did I bang my head on?'

Becky hesitated for a moment. 'A plant pot.'

'Really?' her mother replied. 'I must say this whole thing is very odd.'

When Uncle Percy returned, Becky knew from his brow-beaten expression he'd been given a serious ear-bashing even before he mumbled, 'Maybe I should buy some flowers on the way home? Maria's not in the most forgiving of moods…'

Over the next ten minutes, as Uncle Percy patched up his own injuries, Becky and Joe finished dinner, loaded their suitcases into Bertha and gathered on the driveway. Rain cracked against gravel and a bitter wind whipped Becky's face as she approached her mother, only to see her eyes were dampening.

'No crying, Mum,' Becky said. 'We're only going for a week.'

Mrs Mellor gave a loud sniff. 'I know. I'm just being stupid.' She hugged Becky before turning to Joe. 'You take care of each other. And remember, Uncle Percy shouldn't have to tolerate your squabbling, so please behave.'

'We will, Mum,' Joe said.

'They always do, Catherine,' Uncle Percy said, giving Mrs Mellor a kiss on the cheek. Then he looked at Becky and Joe. 'Anyway, shall we make tracks? There's a German lady who is rather keen to see the two of you again, and equally keen to smash my face in with a Königskuchen pan.'

Becky and Joe clambered into the campervan as Mrs Mellor stared anxiously at Bertha's exterior. 'Are you sure that's fit to drive, Percy?'

'Of course,' Uncle Percy said, with a casual flick of his hand. He climbed in and rolled down the window. 'Besides, we'll be avoiding any busy roads.' And before Mrs Mellor could say anything else, he had reversed on to the road.

'What she doesn't know -' Uncle Percy whispered to Becky, '- is that shortly we'll be avoiding roads altogether...'

Becky felt her stomach quiver as she stared at the Victorian terraced houses ahead, their brightly lit windows veiling the simple, ordinary lives within. Bowen Hall, on the other hand, was as far from ordinary as you could get. And as Uncle Percy pulled away, she knew the moment she had longed for had finally arrived.

She was going home.

4

THE TRAVELLING TIMES

Uncle Percy steered Bertha out of Lyndon Crescent and on to the main road. Passing a betting shop, a launderette and a Greek takeaway named *Abra-Kebabra*, they turned down a side street that led to a sprawling park, bordered on all sides by iron railings.

Becky watch Uncle Percy push a switch on Bertha's dashboard and with a soft whir, the speedometer flipped over, replaced by a map of the immediate vicinity; a tiny green and white triangle seemed to be edging away from a cluster of purple rectangles. 'What's that?' she asked, intrigued.

'It's an Alto-radar,' Uncle Percy said, bringing Bertha to a halt on a deserted stretch of scrubland to the left of the park gates.

'And that's how you know when other cars are nearby?' Joe asked.

'Cars, boats, aeroplanes - any type of vehicle, Joe. We're the green and white triangle ... other vehicles are represented by different shapes and colours. For instance, an orange circle would signify a wind-propelled boat, whereas a blue rhombus would symbolise a twin-engine bi-plane. A purple rectangle represents your run of the mill car, all of which, as you can see are moving away from us. The Alto-radar can also indicate any human or animal presence in the area. After all, we don't want just anyone witnessing our little vanishing act, do we?'

'I guess not,' Joe agreed.

Uncle Percy watched as the final rectangle left the screen. Then he typed something on to Bertha's time pad. 'Anyhow, I think I'd better go and face Maria's music, don't you?'

Becky's insides churned as the campervan grumbled and shook. At once, streams of blinding light poured from Bertha's dashboard, reaching every corner of the time machine. She barely had time to close her eyes when – *BOOM*.

Even when she knew it was over, Becky couldn't bring herself to look, partly for fear that Bertha had malfunctioned again. Her concerns vanished, however, when she heard Joe say, 'I'd forgotten just how totally awesome that is!'

For some reason, Becky had expected them to materialise in Uncle Percy's laboratory, The Time Room, hearing the bleeps and hums of the workstations, its tall, brilliant-white walls alive with the soft ticking of countless clocks, each reading different times from a range of timelines. She was surprised, therefore, to discover that Uncle Percy had plumped for something else entirely.

They were on a curved path, opposite the ivy-covered

boathouse on the banks of Bowen Lake. Only when Becky arched right, did she understand why Uncle Percy had brought them here. In the distance, majestic against the velvety black sky, like something from a fairytale, stood Bowen Hall.

'You know,' Uncle Percy said, 'it's nice when your favourite building is also your home.' He started the campervan and they drove off.

Before they reached the Hall, however, the front door crashed open and a short, portly figure raced out. Dressed in a black and white housekeeper's uniform, Maria resembled a well-fed penguin. 'My angels ...' she squealed. 'My angels are here!' A moment later, her husband, Jacob, limped into view, his kindly face revealing a wide, generous smile.

Maria continued her charge, her arms flapping manically. Powering towards Bertha, she hurled the passenger door open and heaved Joe out with the force of a mountain gorilla. Then she planted wet kisses over every visible patch of his face.

Joe knew better than to resist. 'Hi, Maria.'

Maria's eyes widened as Joe stood to his full height. 'Look how Master Joe has grown! I knew it. The first time I saw him, I said he would be strong ... strong as a lion and with a heart to match. And I was right. Maria is always right.' Then, with equal vigor, she hauled Becky out of the van. 'And Miss Becky...' She clasped Becky's face in her stubby fingers and her eyes moistened. 'You grow more beautiful with each moon. She looks like a princess, doesn't she, Jacob?'

'She does, indeed,' Jacob said.

'Thanks, Maria,' Becky replied, hugging her.

Then Maria's eyes fell darkly on Uncle Percy, who appeared to be tiptoeing towards the door. 'And you? What have you to be saying for yourself?'

Uncle Percy smiled feebly. 'Sorry I'm late.'

Maria's face grew scarlet. 'Late? Late, is what he says! You are not late ... You have been missing! Jacob has been worried sick.' She gestured at Jacob, who looked like he was about to contradict her but thought better of it. 'Poor man! Look at him. You have taken years off his life.'

Uncle Percy looked guilty. 'I'm really sorry, Jacob.'

Jacob gave an indifferent shrug. 'There is nothing to be -'

'Bah! There is much to be sorry for!' Maria interrupted.

Uncle Percy raised his hands in a gesture of peace. 'Maria, I'm sorry you were worried, but like I told you on the phone the stampede was just an unfortunate accident.'

'An accident that would never have been if you were not there at all.' Maria's voice cracked. 'You should live for the now and not for what has passed. She has -'

Unexpectedly, it was Jacob's stern voice that cut her down. 'That is enough, Maria. This is not your business!'

Becky grew alarmed. She'd never heard Jacob raise his voice before.

'It is my business, Jacob,' Maria insisted. 'I love him. I want him safe. I want him here, for me to look after until I am in the ground. If he is angry with me then ... pah! That is better than losing him.' And with that, she turned and dashed into the Hall.

Jacob stared at Uncle Percy. 'I apologise for my wife. Her intentions are good.'

'I know they are.'

Jacob gave a half-smile and followed his wife into the Hall.

Becky was lost for words. 'What's going on?'

'That is a very long story,' Uncle Percy said. 'And it is certainly not one for tonight.'

Becky was about to press the matter, when a soft voice floated on the air. 'And what is the cause of this disorder?' She spun round to see Will approaching them.

'Will!' Joe raced over and shook Will's hand.

'How be you, young sir?'

'I'm ace,' Joe replied. 'How are you?'

'I am better for seeing you again.'

Becky looked at them together and felt an unexpected pang of envy. A unique bond had formed between them, one she could never share. Teacher and student. Before she had time to dwell on this, however, Will had embraced her.

'Miss Becky,' Will said. 'It does me good to see you.'

Becky smiled back. 'Great to see you, too.'

Will's gaze shifted onto Bertha for a moment before finding Uncle Percy. 'One can surmise you've had an eventful day, my friend.'

'That's one way of putting it.'

Will's eyes narrowed. 'Should I know more?'

'Not really,' Uncle Percy replied. He turned to Becky and Joe. 'Anyway, let's get the two of you settled into your rooms.'

After unpacking the campervan, they climbed the Hall's front steps. All the while, Becky couldn't take her eyes off Uncle Percy, who looked strangely distant; his hazel eyes, usually so full of life, appeared dull and troubled. She knew something was wrong. However, the second she stepped into the Entrance Hall, all thoughts of this disappeared as, with a high-pitched yelp, a bundle of sandy-coloured fur sped across the floor and zigzagged excitedly between her feet, trailed by the identical but considerably larger outline of his mother.

'Sabian!' Becky beamed, scooping up the Sabre-tooth tiger cub and pressing his head against hers. She felt a delicious shiver as his whiskers tickled her nose. It was then she saw the morning room door stood ajar. Maria was sitting on a chair, her body shuddering as she wept into Jacob's shoulder.

Uncle Percy had noticed, too. 'If you'll excuse me, I believe I must have a little chat with Maria. Will, would you be so kind as to show Becky and Joe to their rooms?' He took a heavy breath and entered the morning room, closing the door behind him.

After a few uncomfortable seconds, Becky said, 'What's going on, Will?'

'I believe Maria is upset because of your uncle's disappearance today. She has lost many in her life, family and friends. I believe she feared she would lose him, too. After all, he is her family now.'

Becky nodded. 'I can see that, but what did she mean about not living in the past?'

Will's expression darkened. 'I did not hear that. And if I did, it would not be for me to comment.' He picked up her suitcase. 'Come ... let us settle you in your chambers. These events will be all but forgotten in a short while.'

But Becky didn't want to forget anything. She wanted answers. And as she trailed Joe and Will up the left hand flight of stairs, a stubborn silence amplifying the howling wind that had picked up outside, she couldn't help but feel disappointed her return to Bowen Hall wasn't quite as magical as she'd hoped.

MINUTES LATER, Becky stared out of her bedroom window at the angry sky, thinking about Uncle Percy and their eventful arrival at Bowen Hall; the feeling that something was deeply wrong clawed at her like a headache. She flung her suitcase on the four-poster bed and began to unpack, when her eyes were drawn to a folded newspaper on the writing table. Looking closely, she saw the banner *The Travelling Times* and below the masthead, a six-word headline that sent her head spinning. Dashing over, she picked it up and flattened it out on the bed.

THE SEARCH FOR JOHN MELLOR CONTINUES ...

MAY I, in my position as Institute president, and on behalf of all members of the administration committee, thank the hundreds of you who continue to search so diligently for TT114 John Mellor. I have never known such a collective effort! Every single member of the organisation has submitted an exploration record looking for John and, to my knowledge, eighty two timelines and three hundred sectors have been eliminated from our investigations. Granted, we have had little success so far, but stay optimistic (as John always was) because your next trip could be the one that matters. However, the committee has asked me to remind you to stay vigilant. Emerson Drake (and please excuse my language) may be a snivelling bloody toe-rag, but he is a devious, deceitful, and highly dangerous snivelling bloody toe-rag. So if you see or hear of anything suspicious on your travels then please contact TT98, Percy Halifax or Tracker one, Charlie Millport, and they will take the necessary measures to investigate further.

I would, however, like to draw your attention to some recent notable but amusing failures in our search for John. TT104 Keith Pickleton was convinced that John occupied a six by four cell at Alcatraz in 1936 under the alias, Freddy 'The Toad' Wiggoni. TT170, Mustapha Khan believed him to be imprisoned in Sitting Bull's camp in South Dakota in 1869, under the assumed Native American name, Sunkmanitu Tanka Ob Waci. And my personal favourite was TT145 Phyllis Crawberry's belief he was being held captive by the German monarch, King Charles the Fat in 885AD. Sadly, upon investigation, all of these theories were found to be utter twaddle. Still, one day we shall succeed and a good friend, devoted father and husband, and committed time traveller will be with us once more.

Again, I thank every single one of you for your efforts.

Timing out,

TT86 Charles Butterby.

Oh, and can I remind you that Annabel Mullins, our much loved daytime receptionist, has organised a Bring and Buy Sale at St Barnabus Church, Fudgington on the 11th December and would appreciate donations of prizes for the tombola (nothing pilfered, stolen, swiped or nicked from history, please.)

BECKY READ the article again and again. After the fourth

time, she folded up the newspaper carefully and held it to her chest. Her hands were trembling. Of course, Uncle Percy had mentioned that other travellers were searching for her dad, but seeing it in black and white, knowing that so many were involved made it all the more real. Surely, it had to be a matter of time before they had a breakthrough.

Then the door burst open and Joe rushed in, panting, his face flushed cherry-red. 'Have you seen this?' He held up an identical copy of The Travelling Times.

'It's great, isn't it?' Becky said, and before she knew it, had raced into Joe's arms and was giving him the strongest hug she could.

Joe looked like he'd swallowed a wasp. 'What are you doing?'

'Hugging you.'

'Well ... don't.'

'Why not?'

'It's disturbing.'

'Why?'

'We don't do that. You hit me, you don't hug me.'

'But I don't want to hit you. I'm happy.'

'I thought hitting me made you happy.'

'It does. But I'm not in a hitting mood.'

'I prefer it when you are...' But it was clear from Joe's tone he didn't mean it.

Suddenly, a peculiar tapping sound followed by a loud squawk came from the corridor. She released Joe and glanced at the doorway. A stumpy grey bird with a very fat, green beak, a plume of snow-white feathers to its rear, and short, stubby wings, waddled into the room.

Becky's eyes nearly popped from their sockets.

Joe moved to her right, puzzled. 'What type of bird is that?'

And for once, Becky knew. She'd been fascinated by them ever since her primary school teacher, Mrs Ebrey, had shown her pictures in a tattered history book. 'It's – it's a dodo ...'

5

A ROSE BY ANY OTHER NAME

It certainly is, Becky.' Uncle Percy appeared at the door. 'Her name's Deirdre.' He looked drained, but an unmistakable spark had returned to his eyes.

Utterly fearless, Deirdre brushed herself against Becky's shin.

Becky crouched down and ran her fingers over Deirdre's curved beak. An enraptured smile crossed her lips. 'Where's she from?'

'Mauritius ... Fifteenth Century. I was there a month ago investigating a lead on your father. A predator must have attacked her. If I'd left her she would've died, so I brought her back and nursed her back to health. She's made quite a home for herself down by the lake. I don't think she'd let me take her back to her own time zone now if I wanted to.'

Deirdre gave a tiny squawk as if to say she agreed.

Joe waved the newspaper. 'And thanks for this.'

'Yeah,' Becky said. 'It's brilliant. Really brilliant.'

'I just wanted you to know that the travelling community is doing all it can to find John. And we won't stop looking either. We will find him.'

'We know.'

Uncle Percy drew a deep breath. 'Now, let me apologise for the earlier scenes with Maria. I'm sure you're intrigued to know what it's all about, but for once, would you do me the favour of not pursuing it. I think we should just put it behind us and have a wonderful week.'

His words were so heartfelt Becky had no intention of challenging them. 'Sure,' she said, as Joe nodded his agreement.

Uncle Percy smiled. 'Thank you. Now why don't we go downstairs and begin our holiday? Tonight, if you'll indulge me, I thought we'd have a Victorian evening...' And with a wide grin, he picked up Deirdre and left the room.

The moment he disappeared from sight, Becky glanced at Joe and whispered, 'Victorian evening? L-A-M-E ...'

To HER SURPRISE, Becky found she enjoyed the night enormously. Will ensured the parlour's stove blazed with kindling, while swapping stories with Jacob about their former lives; Maria appeared in fine spirits, her round face flushed from the swift consumption of two goblets of cowslip wine; and Uncle Percy seemed in a particularly mischievous mood, dressing Milly and Sabian in matching Deerstalker hats, and tying a lace bonnet to Deirdre's head, as she toddled around the parlour feeling thoroughly self-important. When it came time for supper, Maria laid on

Lemon cake, imperial gingerbread and soft crullers, washed down with ginger ale punch.

It was halfway through her second helping of gingerbread, when Becky turned to Uncle Percy and said, 'Is it okay if I take Peggy for a walk round the grounds tomorrow?'

Maria giggled. 'That is if her fancy fellow will allow it.' She tottered precariously on her chair, before belching. 'Verzeihung! You will be pardoning me, please.' Amid the laughter, Becky and Joe swapped confused glances.

'Fancy fellow?' Becky asked.

'I didn't tell you, did I?' Uncle Percy replied. 'Apparently, love is in the air at the Hall. Peggy appears to have found herself a boyfriend.'

Becky looked shocked. 'Who?'

'I'll give you a clue: four legs, thick, armour-plated hide, three horns, and a somewhat clumsy demeanor.'

'Gump?' Becky said.

'Indeed.' Uncle Percy grinned. 'Our little Triceratops turns out to be quite the lothario. He sleeps next to her stable each night; they go out walking together during the day. He even leaves a mountain of grass outside her stable door for when she wakes up. It's quite sweet really.'

Becky broke into laughter. 'Really?'

'Go Gumpy!' Joe said, clapping his hands.

'Well,' Becky said, feigning concern. 'As I am officially her keeper then I might have to have a little word with him.'

Uncle Percy smiled. 'I do believe his intentions are entirely honourable.'

'Let's hope they don't have kids,' Joe quipped. 'Just imagine a white Triceratops with wings...'

It WAS midnight when Becky flopped into bed. The wind had dropped leaving the Hall and grounds eerily quiet. For a moment, she just lay there thinking about the strange events of the day and then the scene changed. She was standing beside her mother on a twisting lane. Rain pelted down from a muddy sky, slashing her face. She pulled her scarf tight around her neck and looked up to see her mother smiling kindly back. Then, in the distance, two silvery eyes appeared in the distance; horrifying, wicked eyes. A spine-chilling roar shattered the night. *The monster had found them.*

She seized her mother's hand and ran, her heart hammering in her chest. But the monster was gaining; its poisonous breath filled her lungs. And, with a triumphant howl, the monster was upon them.

Becky woke up with a start. The clock read 3 am. For the next twenty minutes, she tried to get back to sleep, but with no luck. Fully awake now, she decided to check her Facebook messages but had left her phone downstairs so she switched on her bedside lamp, threw on her dressing gown and left the room.

Becky's footsteps clacked against the Entrance Hall's marbled floor as she entered the passageway that led to the kitchen. To her surprise, she saw an orange glow coming from the parlour and heard the crackle of the stove still burning away. Entering the parlour, she was surprised to see Uncle Percy staring blankly at the fire, a thick patchwork quilt stretched over his legs, a half-filled glass of whiskey in one hand and a photograph in the other.

'Uncle Percy?'

Uncle Percy jolted with a start. Looking flustered, he

quickly slid the photograph beneath the quilt. 'B-Becky? What are you doing up?'

'I left my phone down here and -' But she couldn't finish the sentence. Staring into her uncle's eyes, she saw they were bloodshot.

She knew at once he'd been crying.

BECKY'S HEAD REELED. She didn't know what to do. She hadn't meant to interrupt this most personal of moments and felt like dashing back to her room, pretending she hadn't seen a thing. At the same time, she wanted to comfort him, to discover why he was upset, to do what she knew he would do if the roles were reversed.

Uncle Percy wiped his eyes. 'Deary me. I must look quite a state.'

Becky pulled a chair over and sat down. 'What's wrong, Uncle Percy ... is it to do with that photograph you're trying to hide?'

Uncle Percy gave a sober chuckle, pulled the photograph into the light and passed it over to Becky. 'You don't miss a trick, do you?'

Becky looked down to see an attractive young woman wearing a mauve dress that met her ankles, her long auburn hair curly and wild; her blue eyes shone like sapphires. 'Who is she?'

'Her name's Stephanie Calloway.'

'She's beautiful.'

'She was. I'm afraid she passed away a long time ago.'

'I'm sorry.'

Uncle Percy drained his glass. 'Yes, it was very sad.' He stared at the picture. 'She was one of those extraordinary people in that everything she touched was the better for her touching it.'

'How did you know her?' Becky asked.

'We were students at Oxford together. She, along with Bernard Preston and Emerson Drake, were part of the time travelling society I told you about at Mammoth Gorge.'

Becky cast her mind back. 'The Otters.'

'That's right. Anyway, although I didn't realise it at the time, she had something of a crush on me. Of course, I was too preoccupied with travelling to even notice.' He gave a mirthless chuckle. 'And besides, I always thought she would go for someone like Emerson. He was so confident, so self-assured, and believe it or not, so very handsome in those days. He also seemed quite keen on her.' His tone grew bitter. 'I find it difficult to talk about the two of them in the same sentence. Steffers was truly good, perfect in every way. And Emerson ... well, it turns out he was the antithesis of everything she stood for, everything she believed in. Evil personified...'

'Anyway, after university we began to spend an increasing amount of time together. She would stay at Bowen Hall, sometimes for weeks on end. It was then I realised I was falling in love with her. And, incredibly, she felt the same way. I'd never been so happy. Anyway, I decided to ask her to marry me. Can you guess where I popped the question?'

Becky smiled. 'Mammoth Gorge?'

'Correct. Anyway, I asked and she said no. She then proceeded to tell me about her illness. I was confused, angry. The doctors told her she only had a matter of months to live.' His voice cracked now. 'I couldn't believe what I was hearing. After that, I went off the rails. I even tried to do something I said I'd never do...'

'And what was that?'

Uncle Percy's expression changed. Becky couldn't tell if it was one of regret or shame. 'I tried to build a time machine to take me into the future,' he said. 'I devoted all my time, my energies to it. I became obsessed. I thought if I could learn their medical advancements, I could cure Stephanie. I didn't care about the potentially disastrous consequences of my actions. Anyway, I came close to achieving it, but just as I was about to make what I believe was the final breakthrough, I stopped my experiments and destroyed my research.'

'Why?'

'She asked me to,' Uncle Percy said simply. 'She said that if it was her time, then so be it. She had accepted death.' He gave a tremulous sigh. 'Therefore, reluctantly, I accepted it, too. I still wanted to marry her but she told me to wait, that one day I would find someone else and that if there was to be a wedding then that should be my first.'

Becky fought back the tears. 'I am so sorry.'

'That's quite all right, my dear. It's important you know why Maria reacted in the way she did. You see, yesterday was the anniversary of Stephanie's death. And each year, on that day, I return to Mammoth Gorge to spend time with her. I think that Maria thought perhaps I wouldn't come back ...'

Silence descended over the room.

Slowly, Becky leaned over and cupped her uncle's face

in her hands. 'And I know you always will.' Then she kissed him softly on the cheek, stood up and silently walked away.

She never did get her phone.

6

THE WILD WILD WESTBROOK

Becky tossed and turned for hours before falling into a restless sleep. It was nearly nine when an ear-splitting squawk sounded in her ear, followed by a familiar giggle. She shot up to see Joe fleeing the scene, a disgruntled dodo in his arms. Growling, she crawled out of bed, and jumped into the coldest shower she could bear. Ten minutes later, she entered the kitchen to see Uncle Percy, Jacob, Joe and Will sat at the kitchen table.

'Good morning,' Uncle Percy said.

'Morning,' Becky croaked back.

Maria stepped away from the oven, waving a sizzling plate of sausages in her gloved hands. 'You be sitting down, please, Miss Becky. Maria wishes to feed you until you're as large as a walrus.'

Becky pulled out a chair, deliberately whacking Joe's shin with the chair leg as revenge for his earlier prank.

'Oww,' Joe cried out.

'Sorry,' Becky mumbled.

From then on, breakfast turned out to be quite pleasant.

Uncle Percy, much to Becky's relief, acted like the previous night's conversation never happened, as he explained something called Heisenberg's 'Uncertainty Principle' to Will, who appeared so bored he looked ready to eat his own face. Maria had never looked happier, barking orders at Jacob and skipping round the kitchen, replenishing empty plates with food time and time again. Milly and Sabian tucked hungrily into a towering stack of pork chops and Joe ate so eagerly that Becky thought he might finish his food and start eating the plates.

'So are we going on a trip today, Uncle Percy?' Joe asked, a half-eaten sausage dangling from his mouth.

'I'm afraid not, Joe. I have some important work to finish in my laboratory today. Tomorrow, however, I think we shall certainly go somewhere. Where and when would you like to visit?'

Joe thought hard for a moment. 'You know where I'd really like to go - to the twelfth century, to Will's time ... Medieval England.' He beamed at Will, whose face seemed impossible to read. 'I want to see Sherwood Forest and meet the merry men.'

'Medieval England?' Uncle Percy said, turning up his nose. 'I've never been that keen on Medieval England. No offence, Will.'

'And none shall be taken. Twas a dangerous age, Joe. I would imagine you safer elsewhere.'

Joe shrugged. 'Every time period is dangerous, if you don't treat it with the respect it deserves. Isn't that what you're always telling us, Uncle Percy?'

'To some extent, yes,' Uncle Percy replied. 'What about ... erm ...sixteenth century Florence, we could watch Leonardo Da Vinci paint the Mona Lisa, which I assure you is quite amusing as his model was a twenty stone man with a hair lip.'

'It's not that exciting though,' Joe replied. Then his eyes gleamed as another idea popped into his head. 'What about that place in America where that flying saucer crashed in the nineteen forties. I read about it on Wikipedia.'

'Roswell, New Mexico.'

'Yeah. Didn't they find a couple of aliens with heads in a spaceship?'

'Oh, they weren't aliens,' Uncle Percy replied. 'And there was no spaceship.'

'But something happened?'

'Oh, something happened, all right,' Uncle Percy chuckled. 'But I'm afraid the supposed spaceship was, in actual fact, a 1985 Delorean DMC 12 sports car driven by an Australian time traveller Emmet Lloyd. Apparently, it had a similar problem to the one Bertha had, a malfunctioning Terriflexor Condenser, which caused it to crash-land quite spectacularly in the desert. Unfortunately, the materialisation and subsequent crash were witnessed, and therein lies the birth of the Alien theory. Anyway, as Emmet lay there, unconscious, somebody contacted the authorities and both Emmet and his time machine were taken away. Anyway, when Emmet came round he triggered his pagidizor and was rescued by Charlie Millport.'

Becky thought for a moment. 'Hang on, wasn't there a film with a Delorean time machine?'

'Was there?' Uncle Percy replied. 'I haven't seen it. I'm rather surprised you haven't noticed, but Bowen Hall doesn't have a television set...'

Once breakfast was over, Becky and Joe made their way to the stables. Frost glittered like sugar on the surrounding fields and an icy breeze chilled Becky's nose. As they neared their destination, Becky's heart fluttered. Of all the amazing creatures at Bowen Hall, it was Pegasus she missed most when she wasn't here. After their adventure and until the end of the summer holidays, Becky had spent each day taking care of her, feeding and grooming her, helping with the vaccinations, and most of all playing with her, until they had forged a solid, unbreakable bond. Her pace quickened when she spied the paddock. Then she spotted a large, powerful creature, three curved horns protruding from its giant head, lying guard beside the nearest stable door. Gump had grown considerably taller and wider since they'd last seen him and now resembled an armoured car.

'Gumpy!' Joe said. He raced over and patted the Triceratops' beak-like nose. 'Jeez, Gumpy! You need to cut back on the pies, mate. For a baby, you're massive.'

'I'd say he was officially a toddler now,' Becky said.

As her voice hung in the air, a snowy white head popped round the stable door, puffing excitedly. Pegasus cantered out of the stable into daylight.

'Peggy!' Becky squealed, wrapping her arms round the foal, feeling her little wings flutter with joy.

Joe smiled. 'Is it me or has Peggy grown a fair bit, too?'

Becky stood back and took a long look. 'I think you're right,' she said, crouching down and kissing Peggy's nose. 'So have you missed me?' Then she glared at Gump. 'Now what's this about you fancying Peggy? Just remember, if you mess with her you'll have me to -' She didn't even finish her sentence, when a sudden cool gust of wind blew back her hair; goose pimples shot up on her neck. She cast

Joe a fearful look as a tiny ball of light appeared above them, growing in size.

'Oh, no!' she breathed.

Just then, lightning bolts shot all around, disappearing when an almighty *boom* ripped the air. When Becky's eyes adjusted, she saw a gigantic motorcycle had replaced the light, its wide chrome handlebars gleaming. An enormous man sat astride it wearing a heavy black leather jacket, his long bushy brown hair, speckled with grey, was tied in a ponytail beneath a wide-brimmed coal-black Stetson hat.

'Well, well … what a nice surprise …' the biker growled in a slurred American drawl. 'If it ain't little Becky Mellor.'

Becky was about to turn and run when the biker's face split into a smile. 'You sure are as pretty as a peach.'

Confused, Becky replied, 'Erm, thank you.'

'Now where's that brother of yours?' He looked round and his eyes found Joe. 'Ah, there he is. Hell, boy, ain't you gettin' as big as a mustang! Howdy to ya.'

Joe looked stunned. 'H-howdy.'

'And you are?' Becky asked.

'Where are my manners?' The biker whipped off his hat, flung his massive legs over the bike, stood to his full height and bowed. 'I'm Bruce, missy. Bruce Westbrook.' Fixing his hat back on his head, he walked over to Becky, his hand outstretched. 'I'm an old pal of tha' dogoody uncle of yours.' Then his gaze fell on Pegasus. 'I'll be a wood rat's auntie. The famous Pegasus. Your uncle told me she was a beauty, but I had no idea.' He walked over to Peggy and knelt before her.

'She doesn't take kindly to strangers,' Becky warned quickly.

Bruce traced his hand gently across Peggy's back and

spoke in a soft, rhythmic tone. 'She's a horse, ain't she? What I don't know 'bout horses ain't worth knowin'.'

Joe stared wide-eyed at the motorcycle. 'Cool bike!'

'She's a honey, that's for sure,' Bruce replied, getting to his feet. 'This here is Sweet Sue. She's a 1983 FLHS Electra Glide Sport Harley Davidson. In my opinion, the finest ride ever built.' His gaze lingered on the motorcycle before he turned to face Becky and Joe. 'Is your uncle around?'

'He's working in his laboratory,' Becky replied.

'Okay dokes,' Bruce said. 'D'you guys wanna climb aboard Sweet Sue and we'll go and have ourselves a little pow-wow with him.'

'He said he didn't want to be disturbed,' Becky said.

Bruce's expression turned grave. 'Oh, he'll be fine bein' disturbed by what I gotta tell him. You see, yesterday I was swilling grog in a pirate bar in eighteenth century Tortuga, and who should mosey in, surrounded by his bullyboys, but an old sparring partner of his. And from what I heard, you may know the scumbag, too?'

'Us?' Becky asked, confused.

'Sure. The name Otto Kruger mean anything to you?'

7

A FISTFUL OF DOUBLOONS

Becky's blood turned cold. Otto Kruger was Emerson Drake's enforcer, Adolf Hitler's ex body-guard and one of the most cold-hearted killers in history. 'What was he doing there?'

'That, little lady, is a mighty long story,' Bruce replied. 'And one I don't have all the answers to. However, let's go and see that uncle of yours. Maybe, together, we'll find us some...' Bruce mounted the bike and gestured for Becky and Joe to climb aboard.

Ordinarily, Becky would have been thrilled to ride on a motorbike, the breeze whipping her hair, fields blurring as they passed, but memories of Otto Kruger crashed into her head, leaving an ugly knot in her stomach.

Bruce steered Sweet Sue to the side of the Hall, where they stopped before a windowless outbuilding. Although she had only visited the uppermost floor, The Time Room, Becky knew that beneath it lay a multi-levelled complex where Uncle Percy kept his time machines (he admitted to having five), and who knew what else? She jumped off the bike, moved to the thickset steel door and gave it a shove. It didn't budge. 'Locked!' she said, before rapping three times. She looked at Joe. 'And if he's working in the Lower Levels he'll never hear us, even if we use your head as a battering ram.'

Just as the words left her mouth, a shrill bleep sounded and a small, very ordinary looking brick morphed into a screen. The screen flicked on and Uncle Percy appeared at its center, wearing a pair of thick-rimmed glasses that magnified his eyes to the size of apples. 'Hello, Becky. What can I do for you?'

Bruce stepped forward. 'You can get your butt out here and give some lovin' to the Arizonian wildman.'

Uncle Percy looked surprised. 'Bruce?'

'In all my beautiful glory, old buddy.' His tone grew serious. 'And we got ourselves some business to attend to, my friend.'

'Have we?' Uncle Percy replied. 'Very well. If you would just wait there a jiffy, I'll send my latest project out to collect you.' His face shone. 'I've literally only just finished her.'

Becky and Joe exchanged intrigued glances. *Her?*

A few moments later, Becky saw the circular pad to the right of the door flash green and she heard the jarring crunch of a hundred bolts twisting free. As the door inched open, Becky had the surprise of her life. A metallic figure stood there, gleaming beneath the strip lights. Barely meeting Becky's waist, it had a distinctly feminine quality about it with soft, rounded features, a friendly oval face and a large pink bow fixed to the side of its head.

'It's a robot!' Joe blurted out.

'Good morning, Master Joseph. I am, indeed, a robot,

although I prefer the term Electroic Cognivated Gynoid.' The robot gave a little bow. 'If Miss Rebecca, Master Joseph and Mister Westbrook would kindly follow me.' And the robot swivelled round, and with short, jerky movements stepped away from the door.

Becky, Joe and Bruce trailed the robot to the far end of the Time Room, where a translucent door slid open on their approach. Entering a tiny box room with a handrail on all sides, they lined up behind the robot as she said, 'Floor minus 6, Room 1A. The Knick-Knack Room. Oh, and Mister Halifax suggests you hold onto something.'

As Becky seized the handrail, the floor vibrated and – *whoosh* – the lift plummeted down at a dizzying speed. Becky's stomach lurched. Bruce and Joe took it in turns to see who could give the loudest whoop. Then with a sudden jolt, the lift stopped, before speeding sidewards, room after room blurring before their very eyes. Then it shot upwards and stopped again for a moment or two, before another sheer drop and a crashing halt, which threw Becky roughly against the door. Rubbing her shoulder, her groans were drowned out by Joe and Bruce high-fiving each other.

Disorientated, Becky looked out to see Uncle Percy standing beside a circular table in a large room filled with high shelves, stuffed with various objects. 'Welcome,' he said, his arms outstretched.

The lift door slid open and they all stumbled out.

'That was ace,' Joe said. 'Can we do it again?'

'I thought you might appreciate that, Joe. The Ectolift has an ultra-booster very similar to the one fitted to the Silver Ghost. I don't normally use it myself but I thought you might enjoy a little ride.'

Bruce's enthusiasm equalled Joe's. 'You wanna get that sold to Disneyland.'

Uncle Percy chuckled. 'I don't think so, Bruce.'

Becky couldn't quite see the funny side. 'You could have warned us.' She growled, smoothing down her hair, which now resembled a disheveled hedge.

'And where would the fun in that be?' Uncle Percy replied.

'Fun is not having a broken neck!'

Joe looked around. 'This place is massive.'

'It is certainly sizeable, Joe,' Uncle Percy agreed. 'I forgot you'd not been down here. There are six floors and forty-two rooms in total. There's even a swimming pool some-where, but I haven't used it in a decade. You should bring your costumes one time and we'll all go for a dip sometime. That reminds me ...' He stared at the robot. 'Barbie, if you could clean the pool for me when you have the chance. I think it's on floor minus three.'

The little robot gave a jerky nod. 'Certainly, sir.'

Becky laughed with disbelief. 'Barbie? You've named her Barbie?'

'After the doll?' Joe said.

Uncle Percy looked baffled. 'The doll? What on earth do you mean? She's named after Barbara McClintock.' Becky and Joe looked at him, puzzled. 'You know, *The* Barbara McClintock who won the Nobel Prize for Physiology and Medicine in 1983?' He tutted. 'What on earth do they teach you in schools, nowadays?'

'You can't expect the kids to be as nerdy as you, good buddy,' Bruce said. 'Now come for some big man lovin' you freaky brainpot.' He walked over and gave Uncle Percy a hug.

'Great to see you again, Bruce,' Uncle Percy replied. 'To what do I owe the pleasure?'

Bruce face turned grave. 'You got any bourbon?'

It's a little early in the day for me but – '

'If it's daytime, it ain't too early.'

'Barbie, would you get Mister Westbrook a glass of -'

Bruce gave a dissatisfied grunt.

' – A *bottle* of bourbon …' Uncle Percy continued. 'And a jug of lemonade for the rest of us. Thank you, my dear.'

'Of course, sir.'

Becky watched as Barbie stomped through a door on the left. 'Where did she come from?'

'I've been planning her for some time. She really helps me down here, fetching and carrying, cleaning, working on the time machines; she's proving to be very useful, and in time I'll bring her into the Hall. She can even bake a Lemon Meringue that would rival Maria's, not that I'd ever let Maria know that.'

'You'd better not let Maria know about her full stop,' Becky added. 'She'd kill you. I mean really, literally, actually kill you.'

Uncle Percy shuffled uncomfortably. 'That would be her first thought, yes. However, Maria's part of the reason I've built her in the first place: whether she likes it or not, both she and Jacob are getting older. We all are. And, in due course, Barbie will be an asset around the Hall with the more manual jobs, the jobs Maria may not be physically capable of doing. I think Maria will be fine with it in a couple of -'

' - Decades,' Joe interrupted.

'I was about to say *days*.'

Becky looked unconvinced. Just then, Barbie reappeared

carrying a tray of drinks, which she promptly placed on the table.

'So can she do any cool stuff?' Joe asked.

Uncle Percy grinned. 'Cool stuff? Isn't it cool that she responds and interacts independently, that there is cognitive reasoning. She isn't just one of Emerson Drake's Cyrobots, you know. Barbie is perhaps the first true example in the world of Strong Artificial Intelligence. She can plan, learn, problem solve and she's self-aware. In a nutshell, Barbie is very *cool* indeed.'

Joe shrugged. 'That sounds great, but can she turn herself into a car like a Transformer?'

Uncle Percy looked baffled. 'Why would she want to turn herself into a car? That sounds rather silly. However, although she may not be able to do that, she can do plenty of other 'cool' stuff, can't you, Barbie?'

'I hope so, sir,' Barbie replied.

Uncle Percy gestured towards the gigantic chandelier above them. 'Barbie, I do believe there's a cobweb on the far side of the chandelier. Would you get rid of it for me, please?'

'Certainly, sir,' Barbie said, as a bright blue feather duster shot from her index finger.

Suddenly, Becky heard a soft drone and, without warning, the little robot powered upward, flying through the air like a rocket, circling the chandelier twice before stopping, giving it a quick polish and soaring back, landing at precisely the same spot she had stood before. 'The web has been removed, sir.'

'Thank you, Barbie.'

'Knock me down with a Bison's hump!' Bruce exclaimed.

'She can fly?' Joe gasped.

'She can do more than fly, Joe,' Uncle Percy replied. 'Barbie, I believe I left a cup of tea in my chemistry lab on Floor minus 2 at 9.30am. Would you be so kind as to get it for me, please?'

Just then, an electrical charge engulfed Barbie and - *pop* - she vanished. Becky didn't even have time to process this when Barbie reappeared, clutching a cup of tea, thin slivers of steam coiling from its surface. She passed it to Uncle Percy. 'Just as you left it, sir.'

'Thank you, Barbie.'

'S-she's a time machine?' Becky stammered.

'She's many things, Becky. She has knowledge beyond human comprehension, she can speak every recorded language, she knows every mathematical equation, she can lift up to four tonnes in weight, she never tires, never complains. And she's charming company.'

Barbie curtseyed. 'Thank you, sir. I do hope Master Joe thinks I'm cool enough for him now.'

Joe nodded. 'Barbie, you own cool.'

'You sure are somethin' else, Percy,' Bruce said. 'If only the world knew what a doggone brainbox you were, you'd win that Nobel Prize every year.'

Uncle Percy chuckled. 'I like things just the way they are, thank you, Bruce. Anyway, shall we take a pew and you can tell me what's up?' He sat down and poured a round of drinks.

Becky settled into her seat and watched Bruce's expression turn solemn as he pulled out a small brown leather pouch, tied at the top by a length of twine. Hesitantly, he emptied it and two gold coins rolled on to the tabletop.

'I heard about your experiences with the Golden Fleece,'

Bruce said in a low voice. 'Well, I believe you might have another problem. Heck, the entire world might have a problem.'

'What do you mean?' Uncle Percy said.

'Pick one up,' Bruce insisted.

Hesitantly, Uncle Percy leaned over and his fingers curled round the coin closest to him. The instant flesh touched metal, his face changed; his eyes blazed with fury, his body tensed, filled with a sudden, blistering rage.

Becky couldn't believe it. 'Uncle Percy ...Drop it!' she cried, seizing his hand and forcing it open. The coin clattered to the table. Terrified, she stared at him to see his usual colour return; all trace of his shocking metamorphosis had gone.

'Oh, no,' Uncle Percy exhaled, slightly disorientated as though waking from a bad dream. 'This is bad! This is very bad ...'

8

THE BOX OF ETERNITY

B ruce looped off his neckerchief, draped his hand in the material until no trace of skin was visible, and picked up the coins, sliding them back in the pouch. Then his eyes met each one of theirs in turn.

'That rage you just felt ...' He nodded at Uncle Percy. 'You don't have to be in contact with the coins either for it to take over you. If I'd left them out long enough, we wudda all been affected. Those coins ... they radiate evil, sure as my Momma's cornbread was as tough as snakeskin boots.'

The words lingered in the air. Eventually, it was Uncle Percy who spoke, 'How did you get them, Bruce?'

Bruce sat back in his chair. 'Well, I ain't ashamed to admit I've got a soft spot for gamblin'. And outside the great gamblin' towns of the old West – Tombstone, Dodge, Virginia City - my favourite haunts are the Pirate ports of the Caribbean. Those buccaneers just 'bout love their gamblin'. A few days ago I was in Fat Annie's bar in Tortuga, playin' a few rounds of Bone Ace, when this grizzly old sea dog, Gilbert Threepwood, pulls up a chair at the table and whips out the coins. We played a few hands and I won them. To be honest, and I only found this out later, he was glad to get shot of 'em. After they were mine, he told me the whole strange story...' His gaze fell on the pouch before he looked up again. 'And it ain't a pretty one.'

'And what's that?' Joe asked.

'He said he cut them outta the belly of the nastiest Hammerhead to swim the Seven Seas.'

'Hammerhead?' Becky said.

'It's a shark.' Bruce gave a weighty sigh. 'But here's the rub: accordin' to Threepwood, this shark shouldn't have been alive at all. Half of its body had been eaten away. It shudda been dead. And if that don't give you the heebie jeebies, check this out ...' He leaned in as if reciting a ghost story. 'Threepwood believed it was already dead when they fished it outta the water ... dead but alive!'

'A zombie shark?' Joe said skeptically.

'Hey, I ain't sayin' I believed it... just what I been told. Anyway, the crew had to bash its brains to mush before it finally stopped moving.'

Becky's face creased. 'Urghh!'

'I said it wasn't a pretty story. Anyhows, the coins were passed round the crew, but like what happened with your Uncle Percy here, the ones holdin' them became enraged. Threepwood said it was about all he could do to stop them tearing each other apart. Anyway, when the ship docked in Tortuga, Threepwood moseyed over to Fat Annies and that's when he lost them to me. Still, word must've got out because who strolls into Fat Annies the very next night asking about the coins but Otto Kruger ...'

Uncle Percy's face dropped. 'Otto Kruger?'

'The very same. But he weren't callin' the shots.'

'Emerson Drake was there?'

'Nah,' Bruce replied. 'Not Drake. This was some gangly dude with a thick walrus moustache. Strange accent. At first glance, he looked all hat and no cattle … pale-faced, no meat on his bones, a bit of a dork, but I tell you, his eyes wudda scared the devil himself. Black eyes. Soulless eyes. Even Kruger seemed to be treading carefully round him. Anyway, moustache man had obviously heard 'bout my winning the coins and came over. A second later, he pressed a scalpel to my throat and demanded I pass them over. But I got buddies in Fat Annies, and before moustache man knew what was goin' on, he was smack dang in the middle of an old-fashioned pirate brawl. Anyway, after landin' a couple of good punches on Kruger's goons, I got outta there and returned to the twenty first century. And that's when I get thinkin' 'bout you, Perce, and your little summer adventure.' He looked darkly at Uncle Percy. 'Just now, when you touched them coins, is that how it felt when you touched the Golden Fleece?'

Uncle Percy took a moment to reflect before he answered. 'No… And yes. When I touched the Fleece, it was – well, otherworldly, divine, like some higher power had personally touched it.' He nodded at the coins. 'These feel like they've had contact with something powerful, something like the Fleece, but merely echo its power, like a scent that hangs in the air even after the wearer has gone.'

Bruce took to his feet and began to pace up and down. 'That's exactly what I thought. That's why it's taken me twenty-four hours to come and see you, Perce. You see, I did some research of my own and discovered a curious story that might tie in with all of this. It tells of an English

Galley ship, The Whydah, which, under the command of Captain Lawrence Prince, had been navigating the Windward Passage when it was attacked and taken by a pirate, Black Sam Bellamy. Anyway, The Whydah was allegedly carrying a magnificent chest, which was being transported to England as a gift for King George. Anyhow, the story goes that this chest had been in a remote African village for thousands of years, and had never been opened. You see … the villagers believed all the evils of the world were contained in that chest and if opened, would be released to destroy everyone and everything. Now, Perce, does that remind you of another famous story?'

'You're talking about Pandora's Box?'

'Yes, Sir,' Bruce said, sitting down again. 'That I am.'

Becky's mind raced. 'I've heard of that,' she said. 'It's another Greek myth, isn't it?'

'Yes, Becky, it is.'

'Tell me about it then,' Joe said to Becky

Becky searched her memory. 'It's about a woman called Pandora, who was given some kind of box by a God - Zeus, I think - but was told not to open it. Anyway, after a while she got curious and opened it anyway. Unluckily for her, the box contained all kinds of nasty stuff, which got released into the world.'

'Or as Hesiod wrote,' Uncle Percy said. "All of the burdensome toil and sickness that brings death to men."'

'So Pandora's Box exists?' Joe said. 'And Drake's looking for it?'

Uncle Percy's body deflated. 'Let's not jump to conclusions, Joe.'

Bruce shook his head. 'You're wrong there, Perce. I think

you should jump to conclusions ... because I think that's precisely what's goin' down here.'

'Great!' Joe said. 'Then we'll have to go and get it.'

'Now, now ... let's not get ahead of ourselves,' Uncle Percy said. 'You're supposed to be enjoying a relaxing half-term break.'

'Stuff that,' Joe replied. 'We want to stop Drake getting his hands on Pandora's Box, don't we, Becky?'

Becky hesitated for a second. 'Yes.'

Uncle Percy ignored them and turned to Bruce. 'You said that Black Sam Bellamy had acquired the chest. Have you any idea what happened to it?'

'Well ...' Bruce's voice dropped to a whisper. 'This is where the tale gets as cloudy as a sandstorm, but I do know for sure that Black Sam owed a debt to another pirate - a pirate no one, not even the hardiest buccaneer messed with. A debt he supposedly paid with a chest full of gold coins. Does the name Edward Teach mean anything to y'all?'

Uncle Percy's face turned a dull white. 'Crikey.'

Becky could see Uncle Percy recognised the name. 'Who's Edward Teach?'

'My knowledge of the Golden Age of Piracy is scant to say the least,' Uncle Percy said. 'However, I do know that Edward Teach was supposedly the most feared, most infamous pirate of them all. You may know him by his cognomen ... Blackbeard.'

9

THE MAGPIE INN

'Blackbeard?' Joe gasped. 'How cool is that, Becky?'

Becky returned a half-smile, but couldn't bring herself to agree. She longed for another adventure, but she also knew the dangers involved. They had been lucky to survive the last one, and what with Otto Kruger, a mysterious scalpel-wielding stranger, zombie sharks and Blackbeard already thrown into the mix, she didn't exactly feel confident of an easy ride.

'It may sound cool, kid,' Bruce said, 'but let me tell you, and be under no illusion 'bout this ... Blackbeard's bad news. I've heard stories from some tough hombres that'd make a rattlesnake lose its rattle.'

Joe didn't appear to hear him. 'Hang on a minute ...a box ... Blackbeard ... gold coins ...' Realisation flashed in his eyes. 'Pandora's Box *is* Blackbeard's Treasure Chest?'

Becky's mouth fell open.

A cheerless smile inched on Bruce's mouth. 'You're as sharp as a tomahawk, kid. That's 'bout what I was thinkin' ...' He looked at Uncle Percy, who groaned miserably. 'So what's your plan, Boss? This kinda thing's your party. I'm just the gatecrasher.'

Uncle Percy looked uncomfortable. 'Plan? I don't have a plan. I'm a scientist, not Allan Quatermain. I get excited about combustible flidgebangers and vector-wave calculus, not sword fights and treasure hunting.' He stood up and began to pace in a circle, his eyes fixed on the floor; round and round he went, seemingly engaged in a bitter internal struggle. Eventually, his face grew resigned and he sat back down. 'Very well. If what you suggest is true, Bruce, what choice do I have?' He exhaled heavily. 'If Pandora's Box exists, and Emerson Drake is searching for it, I consider it my duty to at least try and find it before he does.'

'Me, too!' Joe slapped the table enthusiastically. 'So how do we go about it?'

'I'm not sure it should be a case of *we*, Joe.'

Joe huffed. 'Aw, let's not do this again, Uncle Percy. We have to go with you. I mean, if it wasn't for us -' He waggled his finger in front of Becky's face and went cross-eyed. ' - Well, Becky's eyesturningwhitelikeademon-witchthingy - Drake would have scarpered with the Fleece and who knows where we'd all be then. That's right, isn't it, Becks?'

Becky didn't appreciate Joe's way of putting it, but he did have a point. Somehow, while Drake had been escaping with the Golden Fleece, she'd had a strange episode, one she could still only vaguely recall, when the Fleece had broken free from Drake and flown into her arms. She couldn't explain it, she knew it made no sense, but it had happened. 'First of all,' she snapped at Joe. 'I did not look like a demon witch.' Then she turned to Uncle Percy. 'Secondly, for once, the dweebling's right. We do have to come with you.' She looked serious. 'Dad's a part of all this, which means we are, too.' She smiled sweetly. 'Besides, Edgar said I was the Fleece's guardian, maybe I'm the guardian of Pandora's Box, too?'

'So that's that,' Joe said as if that was the end of the matter. 'What do we do next?'

Uncle Percy looked defeated. He pondered for a moment and tented his fingers. 'Mmm, I think we ask Barbie if she would be so kind as to upload, gather and collate everything she can on Edward Teach, as well as any historical evidence of the existence of Pandora's Box. Would you do that for me Barbie?'

'Certainly, sir.'

'And, meanwhile, we pop into Addlebury for a pub lunch at The Magpie Inn.'

Becky looked confused. 'A pub lunch … why?'

'Because that's where Reg Muckle will be.'

'Who's Reg Muckle?' Becky asked, convinced she'd heard the name before.

'Reg is a traveller. At least, he was. Now he's a publican. Still, in his travelling days, he and his wife, Mabel, would regularly be found wandering the Caribbean ports of the seventeenth and eighteenth centuries. They loved it there and I doubt there's a person alive who would know as much about that era as old Reg.'

'He stopped travelling to run a pub?' Becky asked, intrigued.

'Mabel became very ill,' Uncle Percy replied. 'He gave up travelling to look after her. Sadly, she died and he swore he'd never travel again. Personally, I don't think he's ever recovered from her passing.' He seemed to avoid looking at Becky as he injected some enthusiasm into his voice. 'Anyway, let's not get too maudlin … it'll be nice for you to visit the Magpie Inn. It's something of a landmark in these parts and has a fascinating history in itself. More importantly, Reg serves the most delectable Cheshire cheese and onion flan …'

AFTER SETTING Barbie's search parameters, Uncle Percy retired to Bowen Hall library clutching a weathered copy of Captain Charles Johnson's book *A General History of the Robberies and Murders of the most notorious Pyrates*. At the same time, Bruce departed for his holiday ranch in Wyoming where it was decided he would wait for Uncle Percy to contact him; not a conventional ranch, it was located in the Miocene Epoch and boasted a thousand-strong herd of Hipparions (a twenty million year old horse).

Becky and Joe spent the rest of the morning cleaning the stables, the tedium of which only lifted when Will joined them with two jugs of apple juice. He listened intently to the Pandora's Box theory and seemed as eager as they were for another adventure, although Becky got the impression it had more to do with meeting Otto Kruger again than anything else. After Will left to tend to the lawns, Becky and Joe remained to finish their chores.

'This is awesome…' Joe said, emptying a bucket of fresh water into a trough until it slopped over the sides. 'Another relic quest!'

'At the moment, we're only going for a pub lunch,' Becky said. 'It's hardly Raiders of the Lost Ark.'

'Yeah, but that's how it starts,' Joe replied. 'Before we know it … it'll be cutlasses and X marks the spot and - '

'Have you actually given any thought to the fact that it's dangerous?' Becky snapped.

Joe scowled. 'What's up with you?'

Becky shot him a prickly look. 'This isn't one of your Xbox games. If it wasn't for the Minotaurs, Uncle Percy and Will would be dead, and we would be used as bait to get dad to talk. And once dad does that, he's dead for sure. It might sound fun, but people can get hurt or worse…'

Joe didn't reply. For a moment, it looked like he was giving this serious consideration, until he blew a raspberry. 'Nothing's going to happen to anyone. And I can't wait to meet Blackbeard… maybe I should give myself a cool pirate name.'

'Bumfluffbeard?'

'Ha ha,' Joe replied. 'Come to think of it, Becks, it looks like you're growing a bit of a beard yourself.'

A second later, a lump of Pegasus dung was flying at his head.

AT MIDDAY, Becky lined up beside Joe at the front of Bowen Hall. A chill settled in her bones as she watched Uncle Percy, his overcoat collar curled high, swing the Rolls Royce Silver Ghost to a halt. Staring at the roofless car, she pulled her pom pom hat tight around her ears and considered asking Uncle Percy to ultra-boost them to Addlebury.

Fortunately, it wasn't really necessary, as within ten minutes they were trundling down Addlebury High Street, passing Bunkle and Sons, a family-owned butchers and a large village hall with a rain-damp poster on its door that read *Kendo classes every Tuesday'*; a pair of ancient stone crosses covered in strange markings stood like ice sculptures beside a freshly mown green. Looking to the far end of the street, Becky saw a rickety Tudor style public house with an angular thatched roof, streaked with lichen and moss. Constructed over three floors and painted black and white, it leaned notably to the left, giving Becky the impression that a strong gust of wind could blow it over.

Uncle Percy brought the Silver Ghost to a stop in the pub's car park and leapt out, trailed by Becky and Joe. 'Actually,' he said cheerily, 'I'm delighted we've come today. You see, The Magpie Inn is actually one of the few genuine Tudor –' Before he could finish, however, a snapping sound from the pub's rear stopped him in his tracks.

Becky glanced at Uncle Percy, who appeared somewhat puzzled. 'Was that a time machine?'

'It certainly sounded like one, didn't it?' Uncle Percy replied.

'I thought Reg had stopped travelling?' Joe said.

'He has,' Uncle Percy said. 'But I suppose travellers still visit him, if only to stock up on his home-brewed real-ale 'Olde Noggin.' He chuckled. 'A pint of that and you don't need a Memoraser to forget what you've done.' And with three long strides he disappeared into the pub.

Inside, Becky was surprised to see a huge shaggy brown dog snoring before a raging fire which crackled and popped; wooden tables, each with a brass candlestick in its center, were dotted across the timber floor, the tops of which were coated in thick clumps of dried wax like icing on a cake. The oak beamed ceiling was so low that Uncle Percy had to stoop to avoid banging his head as he spied a thickset grey-haired man sat in the corner, drinking bitter from a pewter tankard.

'Sid,' Uncle Percy said. 'Sidney Shufflebottom?'

The old man looked up. 'Bless my soul…if it isn't Percy Halifax,' he said, surprised. 'Don't see you in the boozer too often, nowadays. How you keepin', son?'

Uncle Percy shook the man's hand vigorously. 'Not bad at all, Sid. Good to see you. How's Irene?'

'She's very well, ta.'

'And young Zak?'

'Oh, he's an angel,' Sid replied. He looked over at Becky and Joe and flashed a welcoming smile. 'And who are these two?'

'This is Becky and Joe Mellor, my niece and nephew,' Uncle Percy replied proudly. 'We've come to see Reg… is he around?'

'Think so,' Sid confirmed, his eyes flicking over to the deserted bar. 'Doreen!'

A young woman with a heavily made-up face, popped up from beneath the counter, chomping noisily on a piece of chewing gum.

'Reg about, Doreen, luv?' Sid asked.

Doreen paused, surveyed the group coolly, then tilted her head back and screeched, 'REEEEGGGG !' Then she gave a disinterested yawn.

Sid leaned into Uncle Percy and whispered, 'Sorry about Doreen. She's new and between you and me might be in the wrong job … she appears to hate people.'

A door behind the counter creaked open and a short, grizzled man appeared, wearing a loose-fitting brown jacket, patched at the elbows with uneven scraps of material; his chin showed at least three days of stubble and his eyes looked swollen as though he hadn't slept in some time.

'Thanks, pet,' Reg muttered. He looked over at Uncle

Percy, and for a brief moment his face displayed shock, before flashing a welcoming smile. 'By 'eck, if it ain't me old chum, Percy Halifax.'

Uncle Percy smiled back. 'How are you, Reg?'

'I canna complain. 'Bout yourself?'

'I'm well.'

Reg looked at Becky and a twinkle lodged in his eyes. 'Now if that ain't that the prettiest face starin' back at me. John's girl, eh? Becky, if I ain't mistaken.' He turned to Joe. 'And Joe, too. Good lookin' lad, no doubt. My, I ain't seen either of you since you were bairns.'

'Hello,' Becky and Joe said in unison.

'Is there any chance we could have a little chat, Reg?' Uncle Percy asked. 'In private ...'

'Sure,' Reg replied. 'Come round the snug. Doreen ... giz a shout if you're rushed off your feet.'

Doreen grunted something back at him before resuming her chewing. Reg pulled open the counter top and gestured for them to follow.

A moment later they were in a tiny room that smelled of pipe tobacco and stale food; half-drunken coffee mugs littered the floor and piles of unopened post threatened to topple from a dusty mantelpiece, above which hung a portrait of a middle-aged woman wearing a cream dress and holding a parasol. It was the portrait that caught Becky's eye.

Reg noticed and moved to her left. 'Believe it or not, that there's one of the most valuable paintings in the world.'

'Really?'

'Look at the artist's signature.'

Becky lowered her gaze to a man's name in the bottom right hand corner: *'Vincent.'* Immediately, she recalled an art project she did for school the previous year. 'Is… is that -?'

Reg smiled. 'Vincent Van Gogh painted that for me in 1887. It was the first painting he ever sold. And to be honest, he only ever sold one other in his lifetime, so that's what makes this one pretty darn rare. 'Course, no one knows that. I tell most folks it were painted by Vincent Buggins, an old army mate of mine.'

'It's a lovely picture,' Becky said.

Reg's smile grew. 'Aye, it is. Quite fitting, coz my Mabel were a lovely woman. In fact, there were none lovelier.' He seemed to hesitate for a moment, before moving to a chest of drawers on the right hand wall. Pulling open a drawer, he withdrew a small gold ring with a glittering crimson stone set in its bezel.

'Here, child …I'd like you to have this.' His hands trembled as he passed the ring to Becky. 'It's very old and was my wife's favourite, aside from her weddin' ring, of course.'

Becky's looked down and gasped. 'I can't - '

'No,' Reg insisted. 'She woulda wanted it. I really don't know any women 'cept Doreen out there and she wouldn't give it the care it deserves. I hope you'll do that for me … and my wife.'

'I shall,' Becky replied. 'Thank you.'

'Allow me.' Reg took Becky's finger and slipped it on.

'That's very kind of you, Reg,' Uncle Percy said.

Reg gave a casual shrug. 'It just sits in a drawer, Percy. As you know, every now and again the past should be allowed to breathe again. And that can only happen in the present.'

'I understand.'

'So why've you come to an old man's pub?'

Uncle Percy's face grew serious. 'Can I assume you heard about our little adventure in the summer?'

'Aye. I still have my ears to the ground. Why, just before you got here I had a visit from one of the old GITT crowd.'

'Ah, we thought we heard a time machine,' Uncle Percy said.

'They still pop in from time to time to rob me of my Olde Noggin.' Then Reg shook his head with disgust. 'Emerson Drake, eh? I mean, I never trusted him, always thought he was a weasel myself, but I never thought him capable of all that.'

'Well he is. And a whole lot more. And now it looks like he's searching for another relic, which means we have to try and beat him to it. Now, this is speculation, but it appears the legend of Pandora's Box might, to some extent, be true. It also appears that at some point in history it may well have fallen into the hands of one, Mister Edward Teach, who may have used it as a treasure chest...'

Reg gave an audible groan. 'Blackbeard!'

Uncle Percy nodded. 'Indeed.'

'What do you know about Blackbeard?'

'As for the man, only what history books tell me. Supposedly born Edward Teach in 1680, he joined Benjamin Hornigold's sloop as a pirate. He acquired his own ship, The Queen Anne's Revenge in 1717 and was known from then on as Blackbeard. He was killed by Lieutenant Robert Maynard of the Royal Navy in the winter of 1718.'

'Most of that is true,' Reg replied. "Cept for the bit about Robert Maynard. He never killed Blackbeard. Not at the Ocracoke inlet on the 22nd November 1718, which is what you'll have found in those history books of yours. Sure, the

Royal Navy captured his crew, but they didn't get Black-beard, that's just navy propaganda, just like the story of how Blackbeard's severed head was impaled to the bowsprit of Maynard's sloop as a warning to other pirates. It didn't happen. Nah, Blackbeard escaped, with his head firmly attached to his neck. And I know that for a fact.'

'How do you know?' Uncle Percy asked.

'Because I was there, at Ocracoke, and I saw the whole damn thing.'

'Then what happened to him?'

Reg's face darkened. 'Well, that's the thing, ain't it? I don't know. And if anyone does, then I ain't heard of it. There are stories, sure ... some say he drowned in a violent storm, some say a Great White tore him limb from limb, others say something terrible happened when he returned to Mary Island. None of it's proven though. All I knows is that from 22nd November 1718, he was never seen or heard of again. He just disappeared from the seas...'

10

ISRAEL HANDS

A hush descended as everyone took time to
consider this. Then Uncle Percy asked a question.
'You mentioned a Mary Island?'

'Aye,' Reg replied. 'Mary Island was Blackbeard's base,
his headquarters.'

Uncle Percy's brow furrowed. 'I know there are thousands of islands in the Caribbean, but I've not heard of that
one.'

'You wouldn't have,' Reg replied. 'It doesn't exist, at
least not on any official charter or map. It's the name Blackbeard gave it, named it after his fourteenth wife, Mary
Ormond.'

'Fourteenth?' Becky gasped.

Reg grinned sourly. 'He liked the ladies, did Teach.
Anyway, Mary Island was where he stored his plunder, his
treasure, in caves deep underground, piled so high it
reached the heavens, so they say.'

Joe's eyes glittered. 'And it's never been found?'

Reg gave a sharp shake of his head. 'No one's ever known where to look. As I said before, no one knew which island was Mary Island. However, if legend is to be believed there were two markers, each crafted by Israel Hands, Blackbeard's sail master, showing the location of Mary Island. He was also supposed to have left instructions as to where on the island the treasure could be found, but *if* these markers exist, they've never been found either.'

'Israel Hands?' Uncle Percy said. 'As in the character in Robert Louis Stevenson's 'Treasure Island'?'

'The very same. But Hands was real enough, all right, and one of the few that Blackbeard trusted. Never met him myself, but from what I hear he was an interesting fella - tough, merciless, but also principled, educated, a musician, and an excellent painter. I've never looked into it myself 'cause I've never had a mind to.' Reg's gaze shifted slowly to the portrait of his wife. 'But if this Pandora's Box is one of Blackbeard's treasure chests, then you might want to see if those markers are real or not ...'

———

TO BECKY'S SURPRISE, the food at the Magpie Inn tasted every bit as good as Uncle Percy said it would, and by the time it came to leave, the top button on her jeans threatened to pop off. As she left the pub feeling twice as wide as she'd entered, she watched Joe who was hopping around like an excitable puppy.

'This is brilliant!' Joe said. 'I mean, not one, but two trea-sure maps.'

'Markers, Joe, not maps,' Uncle Percy said.

'Still, it's great fun,' Joe replied. 'I'm thinking we go back in time, find Israel Hands and get Will to hit him until he tells us where the treasure is. We don't even need the markers then.'

Uncle Percy shot Joe a disapproving look. 'You do know, Joe, that violence is invariably the worst way of solving a problem.'

'But Will is really good at it.'

'That's the sort of thing Emerson Drake would do, surely you wouldn't want us to embrace the same moral compass as him, would you?'

'No,' Joe replied truthfully. 'So what are we going to do?'

'I do agree we hit something,' Uncle Percy replied. 'We hit the books...'

Bright sunlight poked through broken cloud as Becky settled herself onto the Silver Ghost's backseat. Without thinking, she rolled Reg's ring around on her finger and felt a sadness well inside. The ring had belonged to a well-loved woman, a wife, a daughter, perhaps even a mother, but it was a woman who no longer existed, a woman who could no longer enjoy the ring's beauty as she could. And then a vision crept into her head, of Uncle Percy and Stephanie, of the pain that filled his eyes whenever he mentioned her.

Getting old sucks, she thought to herself as she heard Uncle Percy's voice.

'Barbie, we're on our way back to Bowen Hall.' He spoke into an unseen microphone. 'Would you please compile an optomediaphibic folio of Blackbeard's sail master, Israel Hands, and join us in Bowen Hall library. Oh, and please make sure a stout German lady doesn't see you, or neither of us will survive the day. Thank you, my dear.'

Becky leaned forward 'What's an optomediathingy?'

'An optomediaphibic folio,' Uncle Percy corrected her. 'It's a little application I've inserted into Barbie's control panel. I've not tried it out yet. Between you and me, I'm quite excited to see how it looks.'

'So what is it?'

'Oh, you'll have to see for yourself. We'll be there in ten minutes.'

Joe's eyes gleamed. 'We'd be there even quicker if you pressed the ultra-booster.'

Uncle Percy gave a playful grin. 'Joe, you really are quite the scoundrel.' He paused. 'But then, so am I...'

A second later, they were travelling so fast Becky nearly threw up her lunch.

———

Soon, Becky and Joe were watching a nervous Uncle Percy tap softly on Bowen Hall library door; his gaze flicked left and right as if on lookout for an unseen enemy. 'Come on, Barbie, open up ...' he pleaded under his breath.

'Are you really that scared of Maria?' Becky asked.

'Yes,' Uncle Percy replied without a hint of shame.

A key turned on the other side of the door. Swiftly, Uncle Percy heaved the door open and disappeared inside. 'Come on ...quick!' he ushered Becky and Joe inside, before quickly locking the door behind them.

Bowen Hall Library looked precisely how Becky remembered it: coated in a light dust and musty, with soaring shelves that bowed under the weight of thousands of books and parchments. The circular table in the centre of the room, however, was barely visible beneath the tall stacks of computer printouts and dozens of leather bound volumes which covered its surface.

'Nice to have you back, sir,' Barbie said.

'No sign of Maria then?' Uncle Percy asked anxiously.

'No, sir. Barbie has checked her Alto-radar on a recurrent basis. Madame Maria has remained in the kitchens for the last forty six minutes, preparing what Barbie believes is a Shepherd's Pie.'

Uncle Percy looked visibly relieved. 'Excellent. She really would take a tin opener to both our heads if she found you in here. Anyway, did you manage to compile the folio?'

'Yes, sir. Barbie has now uploaded, categorized, and cross-referenced all available information and constructed the optomediaphibic presentation as requested.'

'Then, as they say in the theatre, break a leg, Barbie.'

Barbie paused. 'Sir would like Barbie to break her leg? Very well.' She raised her tiny metal fist high, and was about to bring it crashing down on to her leg, when Uncle Percy held out his hand to stop her.

'No,' he said. 'It's just an expression. I'm sorry. I mean on with the show …'

Barbie tilted her head and looked confused.

Uncle Percy sighed. 'Just start the presentation.'

At once, a slight click sounded and Barbie's skull-cap flipped open. Then a thick shaft of brilliant shimmering light burst from her head, filling the ceiling.

Becky gasped loudly as the light swirled in front of

them, before forming clear, distinct, three dimensional images. A young boy, dressed in tattered rags sat beneath a willow tree, drawing the most detailed picture of a ship ... the same boy (older now) standing proudly on the bridge of a Royal Navy frigate waving at a small crowd as it set to sea.

Becky looked gobsmacked.

The story moved forward as the boy became a man, the naval officer became a pirate, and suddenly a fully grown Israel Hands was standing beside a hulking man, with raven-black hair that seemed to cover every inch of his face.

'Israel ...' Blackbeard growled in a deep, rasping voice. 'My trusted friend. I make you sail master of my flagship: The Queen Anne's Revenge...'

The image of a colossal forty-gun pirate ship filled the library.

Joe gave a delirious whoop and clapped enthusiastically; Becky's mouth nearly hit the floor; even Uncle Percy looked quite pleased with himself.

For the next ten minutes, and using all manner of information sources - Barbie recounted every known fact about Israel Hands: how he'd lost his leg to a cannon ball on a raid in Charleston; how he had fathered a son he'd never met. Then, surprisingly, the presentation shifted two hundred years, to an article from The Chicago Daily News, dated 15th February 1929 which read:

BLACKBEARD PAINTING BRINGS IN THE BOOTY ...

· · ·

YESTERDAY, in the prestigious Grand Ballroom of the world famous Palmer House Hotel, Chicago was at the centre of a second history making incident. Thankfully, on this occasion, the only bang that mattered came from a gavel. In a Charity auction of Pirate Memorabilia, hosted by the world-famous auctioneers, Christie's, a painting of the notorious buccaneer Blackbeard, by his second in command, Israel Hands, was sold for an unprecedented one million dollars to an unknown buyer. Art experts are really quite baffled at why this painting garnered such astounding interest. Timothy Cheeseman, chief auctioneer for Christies said ....

THE ARTICLE WAS ACCOMPANIED by an image of Blackbeard sitting on an enormous golden throne. Then, abruptly, the images dissolved as, with a soft *click*, Barbie's skull-cap flipped shut.

'What – was - that?' Joe gasped, staring wide-eyed at Uncle Percy.

'It did look rather good,' Uncle Percy said proudly, 'even if I do say so myself. An optomediaphibic folio is an audio-visual montage drawn from every online digital media resource - every museum, library, art gallery, film archive - across the world, including, would you believe it, something called YouTube ...' He winked at Becky. 'See, who says I'm not *with it*?'

'You are with it,' Becky said, stunned by what she had just seen. 'You're most definitely with it.'

Uncle Percy smiled. 'You just wait until I install the optohistophibic folio application, but that's for another day.'

'What was all that about an auction?' Joe asked,

intrigued. 'A million dollars for one of Israel Hand's paintings. Reg didn't mention that.'

'I can only assume he didn't know,' Uncle Percy replied. 'Fascinating stuff, eh? I mean, that was nineteen twenties America. A million dollars then was like seven million now.'

'But who would pay that kind of money?' Becky asked.

'I have no idea,' Uncle Percy said, thinking carefully. 'I can only assume that *we* will....'

'What?' Becky fired back.

Uncle Percy drummed his fingers against his jaw. 'Frankly, I doubt it's a serious art collector. No, it seems to me that someone wants it for a reason, other than its artistic merit.'

'Like what?' Becky asked.

'I don't know. Perhaps, we should ask ourselves whether there may be another reason that an Israel Hands painting might be worth a million dollars?'

A light flickered in Joe's eyes. 'It's one of the markers,' he panted.

'It could be, Joe,' Uncle Percy replied.

'So let's get to nineteen twenties Chicago and buy it,' Joe insisted.

Uncle Percy threw him a look of concern. 'Im not sure it's quite as straightforward as that.'

'Why not?' Joe replied.

Uncle Percy hesitated. 'There are a few things we must consider first.'

Becky snorted. 'Yeah, like where are we going to get a million dollars from?'

Uncle Percy didn't flinch. 'Oh, it's not the money. I can get the money.'

'Then what is it?' Becky asked.

A distinctly solemn look appeared on Uncle Percy's face. 'Well, in order for the bidding to rise to a million, it's clear there must be at least two very interested parties. And if we are, indeed, one of the bidders, then who is the other?'

11

MARIA'S FLASHBACK

Dinner was a particularly fraught affair. Joe had let it slip to Maria they were travelling to nineteen twenties Chicago in the morning and she had exploded like a grenade. 'Chicago?' Her eyes bore into Uncle Percy. 'Verrückter! Crazy man! Is your brain fallen out?'

'I do hope not,' Uncle Percy smiled feebly, avoiding Maria's glare by nudging peas around his plate. 'I really don't know what your problem is, Maria. Chicago is a marvellous city and we're only going to an auction. I'll pick you something up if you'd like? How would you like a nice vase?'

'A vase?' The words oozed out of Maria's mouth like burning oil, brimming with menace.

Jacob cringed as Maria's face ballooned red and she screamed, 'A VASE?'

'It was only a suggestion,' Uncle Percy mumbled.

'I have no need for a vase! And this Chicago is not a

marvellous city. It is a sewer. Gangsters .... Liquor ....
Tommy Guns ... You forget, this was my time. I remember
the newsreels. Even in Berlin, we knew all about Chicago.'

'Sounds great to me,' Joe quipped.

'It's not great.' Maria turned on Joe angrily. 'It was a
violent city, with stupid, bad men firing guns at each other
nilly willy.'

Uncle Percy chuckled. 'I think you'll find the phrase is
willy nilly.' At this, he was met by such a frenzied glare he
retracted his statement at once. 'Actually, 'nilly willy' is
much better. Anyway, I am one hundred percent confident
that we'll be quite safe in Chicago, Maria. I doubt any gangsters will be at an auction for pirate memorabilia. And I
have made sure certain safety precautions are in place.'

'You're not strapping bombs to yourself again, are you?'
Becky asked, recalling the Tracker Pack that Uncle Percy
had smuggled to Ancient Crete.

'I don't think that's necessary this time.' Uncle Percy
glanced at Maria, who looked like steam would spurt from
her ears at any moment. 'If I may reiterate ... we're only
attending an auction.'

'Yeah,' Joe said, 'but we all know Otto Kruger will probably be there.'

'OTTO KRUGER?' Maria shrieked. 'Otto Kruger will be
there?'

'We don't know that for sure,' Uncle Percy said quickly,
looking in Joe's direction for support. 'Infact, there's no real
reason to think he will be. Is there, Joe?'

'Er, no,' Joe lied. 'I was joking. He won't be there No
chance!'

Maria's gaze locked on Joe suspiciously. When she

spoke it was in a slow, measured, ominous way. 'I shall be telling you something, Master Joe. Maria has a clothes mangle, a very old, very rusty clothes mangle. If Maria finds out you lie to her, then she hunt you down and use her mangle to squash things that ought not be squashed.'

'He's lying,' Becky said at once. 'Squash whatever you want.'

Joe looked terrified. 'No, I'm not,' he protested. 'Really, Maria, there's no reason for Otto Kruger to be there. No reason at all. P - Please don't mangle my unsquashables...'

Becky couldn't remember the last time she'd enjoyed a meal quite as much.

AFTER DINNER, everyone's spirits improved. Maria's rage had subsided, and she and Jacob attempted to teach Becky and Joe a traditional Bavarian dance. Gump and Pegasus were allowed the run of the house and, much to Joe's delight, Sabian chased an increasingly ill-tempered Deirdre around the parlour, until she turned round and gave him a nasty nip on the nose. At seven thirty, Will joined them, bringing with him a Katana sword to show Becky, a gift, he told her, from a Japanese samurai warrior he'd met during the third crusade. Becky, however, seemed much more interested in what role he played in the crusade (about which he seemed surprisingly vague) than in the sword itself. At eight, and despite Maria's objections, Uncle Percy decided they should play indoor football in the Entrance Hall. All passed without incident, until Joe miskicked the ball, shattering a six hundred year old Murano glass vase.

The next morning, Becky emerged from a deep, untroubled sleep feeling energised and ready for the day ahead. As she lay in bed, cocooned in her duvet, she tracked the misty sunlight that streamed through the curtains to a shimmering object that hung on the wardrobe door. Her heart sank.

'He's done it again!' she mumbled. 'He's trying to *girlify* me!' With a huff, she flung her duvet to the floor and stomped over to an elegant bubblegum-pink satin dress. 'Oh, no.'

The bedroom door burst open and Joe thundered in, wearing a blue pinstriped suit, white tie and gleaming patent leather shoes. 'Are you ready?' His eager expression turned to one of disappointment when he saw she was still in her pajamas. 'You're not even dressed yet?'

Becky stared at his outfit in horror. 'But you look okay.'

'I look pretty cool, I reckon.' Then Joe caught sight of her dress and he grinned. 'You're wearing that? Wicked! You'll look ridiculous.'

Becky agreed, but wasn't about to show it in front of him. 'Do you want me to get Maria to mangle your unsquashables?'

Joe didn't tease her after that.

Thirty minutes later, Becky emerged from her room, a sullen expression on her face. She felt like a fool. The dress clung to her like cellophane and a pair of flat, pointed shoes rubbed uncomfortably against her ankles. Worse still, Uncle Percy had chosen a bell-like cloche hat to complete the look.

She gave a heavy sigh. As far as she was concerned, the only redeeming factor in all of this was that they were travelling again, and to America in particular. Other than the visit to Mammoth Gorge, she'd never been to America, and had always wanted to go. Shuffling down the corridor, she avoided anything with a reflective surface, then turned down the left flight of stairs to see Uncle Percy waiting patiently for her at the bottom. He was wearing a white tuxedo, black bow tie and held a Stephanie rose in his hand. At seeing Becky, his face melted with pride. 'Becky, you look dazzling.'

'I look like a dwoob,' Becky replied.

'And what exactly is a dwoob?'

'One step down from a dweeb.'

'Ah, that would explain everything.'

'I used to think you were a dweeb.'

'I think I'd rather enjoy being a dweeb. It sounds fun. Oh, this is for you.' He passed over the Stephanie rose.

'Er, thanks,' Becky replied, not really knowing what to do with it.

'Now, may I have the honour of accompanying you to breakfast?' He held out his arm.

Becky pushed it aside. 'Now you're being a double dwoob ...' And she barged past him and across the Entrance Hall.

Uncle Percy watched her clomp down the passage that led to the kitchens. 'A double dwoob, eh? My life is complete.'

BECKY ENTERED the kitchen to see Joe sitting at the table; fidgety, he chewed his toast at double speed. Becky was about to say something, when his eyes gave the swiftest flick to the far wall. Looking over, Becky saw Maria, her hands firmly positioned on her ample hips, her face cherry red. Becky knew immediately she'd still not come to terms with them going to Chicago.

However, as Maria stared at Becky, something unexpected happened: her glare softened and her skin drained of colour; her bottom lip trembled and she took a series of great, juddering breaths.

'Maria, are you okay?'

Just then, Uncle Percy breezed into the room. 'Now, what I think is –' His words were lost as a deafening wail echoed all around. Exploding into tears, Maria hurtled across the room, throwing her arms around Becky and speaking incoherently in German.

Becky stood there, astonished. *Something was very wrong.*

It was clear, however, from Uncle Percy's expression he knew exactly what had made Maria so upset. 'Oh, crikey,' he said, dashing over and comforting Maria. 'My dear lady, please forgive me. I never thought.'

'Please, sir, no. There is nothing to forgive, 'Maria replied, tracing a shaky finger down Becky's cheek. 'You look beautiful, Miss Becky … like an angel.'

Becky felt confused. What was going on? She was about to say something, when Maria dashed out the room. Uncle Percy sighed heavily, slumped onto the chair, and buried his head in his hands.

'What was that all about?' Becky asked, her head whirling.

'I am a stupid man,' Uncle Percy replied. 'An absolute fool.'

'Why?' Becky asked.

'What's going on?' Joe asked, disorientated.

'Idiot!' Uncle Percy berated himself.

'I – I don't understand.' Becky replied. 'Uncle Percy, please tell me what's happening.'

Uncle Percy's gaze slowly locked on Becky. 'You reminded Maria of her late-grandaughter,' he said. 'Your dress, your hat, your shoes, would have been quite fashionable in Maria's time. And Maria's grandaughter was only a few years older than you. It's the kind of outfit she may have worn. I just never thought.'

'I didn't know,' Becky said. 'I should go and apologise.'

'Of course you didn't,' Uncle Percy replied. 'But this is my fault. And it is I who will make the apologies.'

'What happened to her?' Joe asked. 'Maria's grandaughter, I mean.'

Uncle Percy's brow creased. 'It's a very painful story, Joe … one that involves humanity at its very best, and at its very worst. You see, as you know, Maria and Jacob lived in Germany in the nineteen thirties. And for all decent German people it was a hugely difficult time. You see, as I'm certain you are aware, there were some Germans who were as bad as can be, as bad as mankind has ever seen. Unfortunately, some of these men were in positions of great authority. Anyway, Maria and her family did something in their eyes that was unforgiveable, and Maria's son, his wife and their daughter paid for it with their lives.'

Becky shivered. 'What did they do?'

'They offered protection to those who needed it most. I don't think now is the time to go into specifics, but I will say that Maria's family did a noble, courageous, merciful thing … something few others would have done, particularly at that time and in that political climate.' Uncle Percy hesitated before continuing. 'And I will say one more thing, just so you understand Maria's reasons for acting the way she does from time to time ...'

Becky and Joe swapped anxious glances.

Uncle Percy struggled to find the words. 'It was Otto Kruger that did it. It was Otto Kruger that murdered her family...'

12

A HACKNEYED APPROACH

B ecky couldn't eat after that. Dazed and shell-shocked, she stared at her empty plate, unable to find any words that could begin to make sense of the situation. Even Joe had lost his appetite, and together they sat in silence, while Uncle Percy left to talk to Maria. He returned ten minutes later, wearing a somber but satisfied expression. 'She's fine,' he said. 'I think it was as much the shock as anything else.'

'Should I get changed and go and see her?' Becky asked.

Uncle Percy shook his head. 'She's all right, really she is. In fact, she's asked me to apologise to you, Becky, for scaring you ...'

'That's daft,' Becky replied. 'She didn't scare me. I was just ...well, shocked.'

'I told her that. You see, I know she hasn't known you long, but she really does care for you both dearly, and perhaps now you have some context as to why she worries so much. In her life, Maria has suffered more than her fair share of loss; I doubt she could function if she endured anymore.'

'We understand,' Becky said. 'Don't we, Joe?'

'Course,' Joe replied. 'But no one's gonna lose anyone.'

'How right you are, young man,' Uncle Percy said. 'However, as we know Maria is feeling better, perhaps we should concentrate on the other matter at hand: Chicago. I genuinely don't expect any trouble at the auction, but I do feel we must have our wits about us.'

'Agreed,' Joe said. 'Is Will coming? If there is trouble, we'll need him.'

'He certainly is,' Uncle Percy said. 'He's suited and booted and waiting for us in the Time Room. He's been helping Barbie make a few adjustments to Beryl.'

Joe cast Uncle Percy a look of surprise. 'Beryl?'

'Indeed. I've not had the opportunity to do a full service on Bertha, so I thought we'd use another one of my time machines. Her name's Beryl. Besides, if we do find ourselves in the Caribbean at any point, I think she could be quite useful given the right circumstances.'

'What do you mean?' Joe asked.

Uncle Percy smiled mysteriously. 'Let's just say I've made some *major* modifications to Beryl.'

By MID-MORNING the sky had turned bruise-black with thick clouds that hung ominously like burnt marshmallows. Becky trailed Joe and Uncle Percy into the Time Room, feeling both excited about the trip, but somewhat embarrassed by her outfit. Once inside, she was surprised to see

Barbie hovering high above them, her fingers buried in a small, silver circuit box in the ceiling.

'How are we doing up there, Barbie?' Uncle Percy shouted up.

Barbie soared to the ground, landing with a soft *clink*. 'All done, sir,' she replied. 'The Resceptor Forax has been recombobulated.'

'Thank you, my dear,' Uncle Percy replied.

At that moment, a low hissing sound could be heard from their left. Becky spun round to see Will emerge from the Ectolift, wearing a stylish, sheer-black dinner suit, his long brown hair looped in a pony-tail. He was carrying two objects – one that looked like a bicycle pump, and the other, a tanned leather pencil case.

'Check out James Bond,' Joe grinned.

'James Who?' Will replied.

'James Bond,' Joe repeated. 'Surely you've heard of James Bond?'

Will shook his head. 'I have not. Is that a compliment?'

'I should imagine so, William,' Uncle Percy said.

'Then I shall take it as one,' Will said to Joe. 'I thank you.'

'No sweat,' Joe said, staring at the objects in Will's hands. 'What are they?'

'They, young man, are a couple of my creations,' Uncle Percy said as Will slipped them into his jacket pocket. 'And let's hope we don't have need for them.'

Joe was about to press the matter further when Uncle Percy said, 'Anyway, would you like to meet Beryl?'

'Deffo,' Joe said, as Becky nodded.

'Follow me then.' Uncle Percy strode over to the stair-case which led to the raised platform above. He approached a workstation and spoke into a tiny microphone. 'Percy Mathias Halifax, TT98...'

A computerised voice responded, 'Embarkation Procedure activated. Today's password ...'

'Cumbersome Cucumbers.'

Immediately, the familiar face of a middle-aged woman with long, rust-coloured hair and rather gaudy make-up appeared on the monitor. When she glimpsed Becky and Joe, she gave an earsplitting screech. 'Becky! Joe! Oh, what a lovely surprise. Get out of the way, Halifax. I don't want to stare at your ugly mug.'

Uncle Percy stood aside, smiling. 'Charming.'

'Hi, Annabel,' Becky and Joe said at the same time.

'Look at the two of you ... I can't believe how much you've grown. Joe, you're as tall as a tower. And Becky ... Becky -' Her eyes misted over. '- I could cry, really I could. You look stunning.'

'I look like a stick of Blackpool Rock,' Becky replied flatly.

'Nonsense,' Annabel said sincerely. 'You're quite the young lady now.'

'Whoopee,' Becky muttered, making sure Annabel didn't hear.

'Now let me guess from your beautiful outfits when your destination is... Mmm, the nineteen thirties?'

'Nineteen twenty nine,' Uncle Percy said.

'Very nice,' Annabel replied, turning again to Becky and Joe. 'I can't begin to tell you how pleased I was to hear about your father. We will find him, you know. It's all the TT's talk about. I've never seen them so determined. They're searching everywhere for him.'

'We know,' Becky replied. 'And we're really grateful.'

'Oh, don't be silly,' Annabel replied. 'We all love John. In fact, if I remember correctly, one or two of the girls in the office used to have a crush on him. He really was quite charming. And very handsome.'

Becky arched her eyebrows. 'You think?'

'Oh, yes,' Annabel replied. She winked at Uncle Percy. 'Mind you, I've only ever had eyes for your uncle.'

'Stop it, you'll make me blush,' Uncle Percy said.

'You know it's true,' Annabel pressed. 'And you just wait until the Christmas party, Percy Halifax. I'm bringing the mistletoe and I'll be showing you that old feelings never die.' Her mouth formed a circle and she blew him a kiss.

'I think your husband may have something to say about that.'

'Knowing him, I doubt it. Anyway, where and when are we going today?'

'Timeline 3. Sector 9. Coordinates: 9 – 7 – 09'

'Chicago, eh?' Annabel typed something on her keyboard.

A buzzer sounded and a cube of Gerathnium fell into the slot below the computer. 'Indeed.' Uncle Percy said, picking it up. 'We're off to an auction.'

'An auction, eh? It's not a livestock auction, is it?' Annabel asked suspiciously. 'I mean, we don't want any, er, I don't know, *winged horses* bringing back, do we? Or dodo's for that matter ...'

Becky recalled Uncle Percy mentioning it was Annabel's responsibility to complete the mountain of paperwork necessary to register any animal brought from the past to the present. She could also tell from Uncle Percy's reddening face he hadn't been the one to mention Pegasus or Deirdre.'

'I-I don't know what you mean,' Uncle Percy said, staring fixedly at his feet.

'You never do, Halifax,' Annabel smirked. 'Anyway, on a serious note, please be careful. All of you.' Her tone turned serious. 'Time travel has changed. Emerson Drake has seen to that. And we must all change along with it. Please, watch your backs.' She forced a smile. 'After all, I'd like to see you all safe and sound at the *Enchantment beneath the sea dance* at Christmas. Remember, I'm bringing mistletoe ...' And before Uncle Percy could offer a response, she'd gone. The workstation fell still.

'What's the 'Enchantment beneath the sea dance?' Becky asked.

'It's the fancy dress theme for this year's GITT Christmas party. Traditionally, it's quite the shindig. Just imagine two-hundred travellers dressed as various sea creatures, getting festive fuelled by Reg's Olde Noggin'.'

'So it's the ultimate *geek-fest* then?' Becky said.

'It may well be,' Uncle Percy nodded. 'I just have no idea what that means.'

'And we can go?' Joe asked eagerly.

'I don't see why not.' Uncle Percy smiled warmly. 'But for now shall we return to the matter at hand? Would you like to meet Beryl?'

'Yes, please,' Becky said.

'Very well.' Uncle Percy arched forwards to the computer's microphone. 'Activate Beryl...'

A groaning sound came from below. Becky and Joe raced to the banister as the floor below gradually vanished into the wall, to be replaced by a revolving platform, on top of which stood a coal-black car. Gleaming beneath the Time Room's lights, the car's curved bodywork and orange sign,

TAXI, made it one of the most recognisable vehicles in the world.

'It's a London Black cab!' Becky said.

'A 1958 Austin FX4 Hackney carriage, to be precise,' Uncle Percy said. 'And I do believe that she is the perfect time machine for our particular requirements...'

'Shall we go then?' Joe asked eagerly.

Uncle Percy nodded. 'Absolutely.'

Becky and Joe hurried down the steps, each trying to beat the other to see Beryl up close for the first time. At the bottom, they met up with Will. Uncle Percy followed them down, before inserting the Gerathnium cube into a slot above the boot; with a *clack*, it snapped into place. 'Hop in, then ...' he said, opening the rear doors.

Becky and Joe leapt inside, the sweet, soothing smell of scots pine filling their nostrils. Then Uncle Percy climbed in, Will joining him up front.

Typing a destination code on to Beryl's keypad, Uncle Percy turned to Will. 'Are you ready, William?'

Will gave a knowing smile. 'For whatever arises...' he replied, patting his jacket pocket mysteriously.

'Excellent,' Uncle Percy said, sitting back. 'Then let's get going. After all, in the words of Mister Frank Sinatra, 'Chicago is my kind of town!''

'Who's Frank Sinatra?' Becky asked.

Shaking his head, Uncle Percy's disappointed tut was masked by a soft sputtering sound as streams of blue and white light encircled them. A moment later, Beryl had vanished.

13

TO REBECCA, WITH LOVE...

Becky looked ahead to see a wall of dull white light. Fearfully, she glanced around. It was everywhere. This couldn't be Chicago: had something gone wrong? Her concerns soon faded when she heard Uncle Percy say, 'Now, it won't look much at the moment, but you just wait...' It was then she realised she was staring at a muddy grey sky.

Uncle Percy climbed out, straightened his tuxedo and levelled his bowtie. Then he opened the rear door. Instantly, Becky felt an icy wind pummel her face. 'Wow!' She clamped her hat securely to her head as she got out. 'That is some wind.'

'They don't call it the Windy City for nothing.'

Joe looked around, confused. 'Where exactly in Chicago are we?'

'The Palmer House Hotel,' Uncle Percy replied.

Joe looked disappointed. 'Really? Then it's either very small or -'

Becky's gaze tilted downwards. 'I think we're standing

on it, Joe,' she said, suddenly noticing the muffled hum of traffic drifting up from below. She and Joe walked across the roof to a wide ledge.

Cars were everywhere, clattering along, horns tooting. Hundreds of people scurried along the broad, tree-lined streets like soldier ants, dashing in and out of gigantic, flat-roofed buildings. In the distance, she saw a vast stretch of water coated in a low-hanging mist, through which boats dipped up and down like ducks on a pond.

'Time Travel is wicked!' Joe said.

Uncle Percy walked over to them, Will at his side. 'That's Lake Michigan,' he said, pointing. 'She's impressive, isn't she?'

Becky could barely find the words.

'Now let's go and purchase a painting.' Uncle Percy pressed the Invisiblator button on his key fob and Beryl instantly vanished. Then he turned to Becky and Joe. 'Follow me...'

As they approached what looked like a trap door set into the roof, Becky caught sight of a rectangular piece of cherry-red card; flapping wildly, it appeared to be nailed to the door. Confused, she glanced over at Uncle Percy, and her blood turned to ice. He had stopped dead in his tracks, his entire body rigid.

'What's is it?' Joe asked.

'I'm not sure,' Uncle Percy replied. He marched over and ripped the card from its nail. Becky saw it was an envelope. Then her stomach reeled. Written on its face in elaborate handwriting were four words:

To Rebecca, with love...

. . .

'T-THAT'S MY NAME,' Becky said. 'Uncle Percy, that's my name!'

Enraged, Uncle Percy tore it open and pulled out a red card. The words *Happy Valentine's Day to a Special Girl* glinted silver in his eyes. 'How dare you,' he growled.

Becky's head was spinning. 'Uncle Percy, why has it got my name on it?'

Uncle Percy didn't reply.

'Should we depart?' Will asked Uncle Percy.

'Not yet.'

'What's going on?' Becky asked, her voice rising. 'Pass it to me!'

Uncle Percy gave a heavy sigh. Then he handed it over.

Her fingers trembling, Becky took it. And when she turned the page, it felt like time itself had stopped.

DEAREST REBECCA,

Roses are Red
Violets are Blue
Daddy is bleeding
And it's all down to you

Oh, and Percy, you continue to astound me. You are either supremely stupid or supremely brave. My money, as always, is on the former. In fact, I always thought you were a something of a Moran. Anyway, I know you're going to have fun. I have, after all, read tomorrow's newspaper.

Regards,

Emerson

BECKY SHIVERED WITH ANGER. She stared at the card again and again until anger blurred the words beyond recognition.

'This is just one of Drake's cruel little games,' Uncle Percy said softly to Becky. 'You mustn't take his words to heart.'

'Why not?' Becky replied quietly. 'He's right. Dad is suffering because of me.'

'He's not right.'

Becky's lip quivered as she held back the tears that once started would never stop. 'But if I had persuaded dad to give Drake the information he needs then –'

'Then neither of you would be alive now,' Uncle Percy said. 'Drake wouldn't let you go, and he would certainly know better than to release John. No, whatever it is your father knows, it's important enough to Drake to keep him alive. And as long as he is, there's hope. Never forget that.'

Joe looked baffled. 'Let's have a gander, Becks,' he said, reaching out for the card.

Before he could grab it, however, Becky had torn it into shreds and pitched them in the air.

Joe watched as the pieces soared like confetti towards Lake Michigan. 'What did it say?'

'It doesn't matter,' Becky replied. She looked at Uncle Percy. 'What did Drake mean: 'I've read tomorrow's newspaper?' Oh, and I know you say he's clever but he must be something of a moron himself if he can't spell 'moron.'

Uncle Percy opened his mouth as if to reply but closed it immediately. He sank into deep contemplation. Then his face drained of colour and he scooped up the suitcase. 'We're going back, come on…' He marched over to Beryl. 'Chop chop, everyone…'

'What?' Becky said. 'Why?'

'This was a big mistake. In the time machine, please.'

Becky didn't budge. 'We're not going anywhere. I'm not letting Emerson Drake's stupid card put me off.'

'Me neither,' Joe added.

'It's not the card,' Uncle Percy said. 'Well, it is, but that's not it. I mean, it's shocking, of course.' He appeared furious with himself. 'I just can't believe I didn't make the connection. I'm such a fool!'

'What're you harping on about?' Joe asked.

'It's just something happens today - February 14th 1929 - right here, in Chicago. Something monumental. And I forgot about it.' Uncle Percy shook his head, furious with himself. 'What a bloody idiot you are, Halifax!'

'What troubles you, old friend?' Will asked, as puzzled as Becky and Joe.

Uncle Percy exhaled heavily. 'Today is perhaps the most infamous day in the history of this great city, and I'm not saying we're involved, we're probably not. It's most likely just Emerson's idea of a joke. But I don't want to take that risk.'

'So what happens today?' Becky asked.

Uncle Percy hesitated. 'The Saint Valentine's Day Massacre!'

'Okay, I've heard of it,' Becky said. 'But I don't know anything about it. What happened?'

Uncle Percy sighed. 'It's not a pleasant story.'

Becky looked defiant. 'Nothing with the word 'massacre' in is gonna be cuddly wuddly. But I think we've got a right to know what happened before we make the decision whether to leave or not?'

'We're not making the decision. I am.'

'But we need that painting,' Joe said.

'We need to stay alive, Joe,' Uncle Percy replied, looking to Will for support. 'Don't you agree, Will?'

Will thought for a moment. 'I agree with Miss Becky.'

Becky gave a look of satisfaction as she turned to Uncle Percy. 'So what happened at this massacre?'

Uncle Percy fell silent. 'From what I remember, it is alleged that some of Al Capone's men –'

'Al Capone?' Joe repeated. 'He's like the number one gangster of all time, right?'

'He does have something of a reputation.'

'His nickname was Scarface, wasn't it?'

'I believe it was.'

'I wish I had a cool nickname like that.'

'What's wrong with the one you've got?' Becky asked, irritated. 'I think Wally Foo Foo suits you just fine. Now, shut up!'

'Eat me,' Joe barked back.

'Do you want to hear about this or not? Uncle Percy asked.

'Sorry,' Becky and Joe said at the same time.

Uncle Percy took a deep breath. 'As I was saying, it is alleged some of Al Capone's men captured seven members of a rival gang, lined them against a wall in a garage and shot them dead. The victims worked for the Irish mobster, *Bugs Moran*. You see, Becky, I'm guessing Emerson's spelling was just fine and dandy.'

Becky considered this for a moment. 'I mean obviously that's bad. I mean *really* bad. But at the end of the day there's nothing to suggest we're involved, is there? If we were, then surely we'd be in the history books and stuff.'

Uncle Percy looked unconvinced. 'Well, err, time travelling is complicated. Events can be changed, you know. The Omega Effect doesn't always happen.'

'I know,' Becky said, 'but we might only have one chance to get this painting. One chance. We have to get it, and then get out of here double quick - no gangsters, no garages, no hanging around.'

'That's right,' Joe said.

Uncle Percy's eyes met Will's, who nodded to indicate he agreed with Becky.

Uncle Percy looked defeated. 'Very well, I hope you're right.' He heaved open the trap door, to reveal a ladder that led below. 'Come on then...'

Eagerly, Joe followed Uncle Percy down, trailed by Will, leaving Becky to bring up the rear, feeling happy she had got her way, but racked with bitterness that her first Valentine's Day card had come from a murderous psychopath.

14

THE MAN WITH MANY NAMES ...

Becky climbed down the ladder to find herself in a cramped store room. Uncle Percy inched open the door, peered out, and upon seeing the coast was clear, ushered them into a long, dimly-lit corridor at the end of which was a lift. Reaching it quickly, they gathered inside as Uncle Percy pressed the button marked 'Lobby.'

As they descended, Becky found herself nervous, scared and angry. Emerson Drake knew they were here. How? Did he watch her read the card? And what did his message to Uncle Percy mean? Her mind spiralled, searching for answers, when her thoughts were cut short by the clang of a bell. The lift doors opened and they stepped out. The view took Becky's breath away.

Enormous golden chandeliers shed light over the vast lobby as hordes of elegantly dressed men and women sat on velvet seats, sipping champagne and talking in loud, snooty voices; dozens of bell-hops, sporting circular red hats, raced in all directions, heaving bulky suitcases. A banner that read 'Christie's Charity Auction - 'A Taste of the Caribbean' fluttered high above two bronze winged statues which surveyed the room like gleaming sentries.

'Very posh!' Joe said, impressed.

'Indeed, Joe,' Uncle Percy said, looking more relaxed now than he'd been in the last few minutes. 'I've never actually visited the Palmer House Hotel before ... she really is a treat, isn't she? If I can draw your attention upwards.'

Becky looked up to see the most spectacular ceiling. Hand-painted with rich, vibrant colours, there were twenty one giant frescoes, each one depicting a different mythological scene.

'Painted by French muralist, Louis Pierre Rigal, in 1900,' Uncle Percy said, 'each panel features a famous Greek myth. For example, if you look over there...' he gestured to their left, 'you may recognise that particular one. It does, after all, include a couple of our friends.'

Becky looked over to see that one of the frescoes contained the image of a ferocious-looking Minotaur engaged in a mighty battle with a muscular Greek warrior.

'Theseus and the Minotaur,' Joe laughed.

'Since when did the real Theseus look like Jason Statham?' Becky said.

Uncle Percy looked baffled. 'Who?'

This time, it was Becky who gave a disapproving tut.

'Much as I would appreciate investigating the lobby further,' Uncle Percy said, 'the Auction starts in ten minutes. And I think we should take a peek at the lots, don't you?'

Becky trailed Uncle Percy into another room where she saw row upon row of tables, buckling under the weight of thousands of pieces of pirate paraphernalia: cutlasses, muskets, cannons, boarding axes, jewelry, tattered black flags emblazoned with white skulls, and even a ship's figurehead in the shape of a mermaid.

'This-is-ace...' Joe said.

'It brings the schoolboy out in me, too, Joe.' Uncle Percy pulled out a booklet from his pocket.

'What's that?' Becky asked.

'It's the auction brochure,' Uncle Percy replied. 'I had Barbie acquire it for me in advance.' He flicked it open to a page Becky couldn't quite see.

'Yeah, but we know what we're buying,' Becky said. 'The painting that was in the optomediaphibic folio, aren't we?'

With a disinterested grunt, Uncle Percy continued to peruse the page, glancing up from time to time to look around the room.

Becky was about to scold him for his lack of interest in what would be their million dollar investment when she heard Joe say, 'And there it is ...'

Becky looked over to a collection of paintings being scrutinised by a crowd of engrossed onlookers. One painting, in particular, had captured their attention. It captured Becky's, too. Twice the size of the others, the portrait of Blackbeard looked positively fearsome. Sitting on a huge golden throne and wearing his finest regalia, Blackbeard could have been mistaken for royalty, except for the ferocity of his expression; his sunken eyes were so wild they appeared to pop out of the canvas, his gritted yellowing teeth barely visible behind the untamed mass of pitch-black whiskers. He held a cutlass in one hand and a gleaming silver compass in the other.

'Scary guy,' Joe whispered to Becky. 'So if it's a marker then how's it going to work?'

'I dunno,' Becky replied. 'Maybe there's a map on the back.'

Joe's eyes ignited. 'Or maybe it has something to do with the compass? Maybe there are clues all over the painting? We just have to know what to look for.'

Becky arched round to ask Uncle Percy's thoughts on the matter but to her surprise he wasn't even looking at the painting. He was talking in hushed tones to Will, the brochure wide open before them. His finger flicked between the brochure and a small painting to their left, depicting a pretty but sad-looking woman and a newborn baby wrapped tightly in a thick woolen blanket.

Becky looked confused. 'You do know the painting you're about to spend a million dollars on is this one, don't you?' She pointed at the portrait of Blackbeard.

'What?' Uncle Percy glanced over but appeared to lack any genuine interest. 'It is impressive, isn't it?' he said half-heartedly.

At that moment, they heard a voice from behind. 'Ah, the Halifax party has finally decided to show. Greetings. I was getting worried.'

Becky felt a stab of fear, until she saw a short, rotund gentleman with a shiny head shuffle towards them. He wore a tartan kilt which barely covered his bulbous knees, a horsehair sporran, and a snow-white tuxedo that struggled to contain his ample midriff. Becky recognised him at once as Keith Pickleton, Uncle Percy's friend and fellow time traveller.

'Keith,' Uncle Percy replied, extending his hand. 'I'm so glad you came.'

'A pleasure, old chap,' Pickleton replied, although Becky detected a hint of doubt in his voice. Then he whispered, 'Any sign of the bad guys?'

Uncle Percy shook his head. 'Not as yet.'

'Smashing,' Pickleton said, sounding relieved. 'Not that they worry me, you understand?'

'Of course not.'

'But we don't want any bother,' Pickleton added.

'Indeed, we don't,' Uncle Percy replied. 'Anyway, although the irony is not lost on me, time isn't on our side, so do you think you and I could have a quiet word?' He led Pickleton out of earshot and soon the two of them were deep in conversation; every now and again, they would glance up at the Blackbeard portrait before refocusing on the open brochure.

'What's he up to? Joe whispered to an equally confused Becky.

'No idea,' Becky replied. She watched intrigued as Uncle Percy slipped something into Pickleton's right hand, which the little man subsequently thrust into his sporran.

After a few seconds, a grave looking Pickleton gave a firm nod and disappeared through a door, above which was a sign that read, 'Charity Auction – this way!'

Uncle Percy walked over to Becky, Joe and Will.

'You didn't mention any other travellers being here?' Becky asked.

'I've invited Keith for a reason,' Uncle Percy said mysteriously. 'And now we're here, I'm rather glad that I did.'

'Why?'

'Well, before –' Uncle Percy stopped mid-sentence; his face turned deathly pale.

Becky knew immediately something was very wrong.

'What is it?' Uncle Percy didn't reply. She tracked his eyeline and a lump caught in her throat. A group of men had entered the viewing room, colossal men wearing heavy black coats and mirrored sunglasses. However, it was only when she saw the towering, flaxen-haired man at the rear of the group that she felt sick to her core.

Otto Kruger's eyes locked on Becky, and a heartless smile crossed his lips.

Becky sensed movement to her right. Will had spotted Kruger and was marching over to him, fists clenched.

Uncle Percy threw himself into Will's path. 'Will, please,' he begged. 'Not here. Not now.'

'No, Will!' Joe said,

Upon hearing Joe's voice, Will's anger faded.

The disorder, however, seemed to delight Otto Kruger all the more. He nudged his companions and they walked over.

Kruger moved promptly to Will, his smile widening. 'Please, groundsman ... carry out what I know you are keen to start. Nothing would give me more pleasure.'

For once, Will maintained his composure. 'Our day is coming, Kruger.'

'Make it today.' Kruger's huge hands fanned the collection of weapons lain on the tables. 'Pick one, and we shall do this now...'

Before Will could respond, a tall, willowy man with a gaunt face and a thick dark-brown moustache approached them. He was carrying a two-handled leather briefcase. 'Mister Kruger, this is not a place for brawling,' he said, a trace of a European accent in his voice. He turned to Uncle Percy. 'Could this be *the* Percy Halifax? The one I've heard so much about.' He glanced at Kruger who nodded.

Just then, Becky remembered Bruce's words: '*This was some gangly dude with a thick walrus moustache. Strange accent.*'

Scalpel Man!

Uncle Percy turned to face the man. 'And I can only assume you're another one of Emerson's little errand boys, eh?'

'I'm much more than that,' Scalpel Man replied icily. Then his sunken black eyes fixed on Becky. 'My, my ... what-a-pretty-thing!' His hand drifted to her cheek.

Before he made contact, however, Becky slapped the hand away. 'Don't touch me, freakoid!'

Uncle Percy swelled with rage. 'Don't you ever try and lay a finger on her again, do you understand me?'

'Is that a threat?'

'It's considerably more than that, I assure you,' Uncle Percy fired back.

Scalpel Man smiled coldly. 'How very exciting!' He glanced at Otto Kruger. 'Mister Kruger, entertaining though this affair has been, I think Mister Drake would prefer it if we focused our attentions on the auction.'

Kruger nodded.

Scalpel Man's gaze fell again on Uncle Percy. 'I shall look forward to seeing you again, Mister Halifax. I believe it'll be sooner than you think.'

Uncle Percy hesitated. 'Who are you?'

'I have many names...' And with that, Scalpel Man walked away.

Heart thumping, Becky watched him disappear into the bustling crowd like a snake in long grass, quickly followed by Otto Kruger and the Associates.

For what seemed like an age, no one said a word, as if

not one of them dared voice what they were actually thinking, that they had just been in the presence of something
inhuman, something monstrous.

Absolute evil.

15

SCARS, STARS AND CADILLAC CARS

'Who-was-that?' Joe said.

'No idea,' Uncle Percy said. 'Anyway, we haven't got time to worry about him now, the auction's about to start...'

If Becky hadn't felt so anxious, she knew the Grand Ballroom would have taken her breath away; eight chandeliers, glittering with thousands of hand-cut crystals, shed a warm flush over the tables below, sitting at which were stylishly dressed people talking very loudly, as if mere volume alone would secure their standing in the cream of Chicago society.

Uncle Percy escorted them to a front table where a satin-trimmed place card read 'The Halifax Party.'

As Becky sat down, she felt like she was being watched. Looking to the back of the room, she saw Scalpel Man studying her, an ugly glint in his eyes. A shiver shot down her spine. She nudged Uncle Percy and whispered, 'At the back.'

Uncle Percy didn't have to look. 'I know,' he replied.

'But don't worry, they won't start any trouble here. And between you and me, I have prepared for certain eventualities.'

'What d'you mean?'

Uncle Percy's response was lost amidst an excited round of applause, as a skinny, dark haired man with a head that narrowed to a point so he resembled a pencil, mounted a raised podium. He picked up a gavel and brought it down three times, bringing the room to a hush.

'Good morning, Ladies and Gentlemen, or should I say -' The auctioneer's voice turned into a snarl. '- AHOY, ME HEARTIES.' The room rang with laughter. 'I'm Timothy Cheeseman and on behalf of Christie's, I bid you welcome to the 'Taste of the Caribbean' Charity Auction. And what an honour it is to be here in such a salubrious setting as the Palmer House Hotel's Grand Ballroom. Anyway, without any more ado, I say we stop shivering our timbers and travel back two hundred years on a daring quest for hidden gems.' He paused for effect. 'Let the auction commence ...'

Although each lot drew loud, appreciative reactions from the room, Becky remained silent throughout. She couldn't relax. Uncle Percy, on the other hand, seemed to have forgotten any worries he may have had and was thoroughly enjoying himself. His eyes twinkled at the array of objects paraded before them. To Becky's surprise, he even bid on a few; these included an unopened keg of rum that supposedly belonged to Mo Baggely also known (to Joe's delight) as Gingerbeard; a stuffed blue parrot nailed crudely to a plinth, the beloved pet of Norwegian pirate, Magnus Magnerson; and a gigantic iron anchor from the pirate ship, The Bigby Hind.

It was twenty minutes in when two burly assistants

heaved the portrait of Blackbeard onto the platform. Applause filled the room.

Cheeseman seemed particularly happy with the impact it had made. 'Yes, you're quite right, ladies and gentleman. This is a wonderful item. It's the only known portrait of Edward Teach, otherwise known as the most famous buccaneer of them all, Blackbeard. This lot is one of a kind. The artist was Blackbeard's trusted lieutenant and sail master, Israel Hands. Now, it may not be Da-Vinci, but it is an impressive piece and certainly one for the collectors. So dig deep, and let's see where the bidding takes us. There's a guide price of four hundred dollars, so shall we start at - what … two hundred?'

Becky glanced behind. With a slight turn of his head, Scalpel Man acknowledged her and smiled cruelly. Then she looked at Uncle Percy, who winked back, before shouting at the top of his voice.

'FIVE HUNDRED THOUSAND DOLLARS!'

A loud gasp stunned the room.

Cheeseman looked bewildered. 'I'm sorry, sir,' he panted. 'C-can I confirm you said five hundred thousand dollars?'

'You can, and I did.'

'But…' Cheeseman's voice became little more than a squeak. 'Err, very well. I can only assume that will be the first and final bid on - '

'Six hundred thousand dollars!'

Even though she expected it, Becky's stomach churned. Scalpel Man's hand hovered high in the air.

The crowd went wild. Riotous applause and deafening cheers echoed on all sides.

'Seven hundred thousand dollars,' Uncle Percy pressed.

The crowd didn't have time to respond, when Scalpel Man bellowed, 'Eight hundred thousand!'

As the crowd went crazy again, Uncle Percy fell silent. For a moment, it looked like he'd given up. Then he turned, stared with disdain at Scalpel Man, and his mouth formed the words, 'Nine-hundred-thousand-dollars!'

'One million dollars!' Scalpel Man spat back.

The room exploded. Amid the uproar, Becky saw a wide, bull-like man to the left of Otto Kruger leave his seat and stride purposefully towards them, his features shrouded by a cloud of smoke that rose from the giant cigar in his right hand. Then Becky saw something that filled her with dread. Each person the man passed stopped clapping and gawped at him with a mixture of surprise and horror. Even Cheeseman noticed, his eyes widening.

The man reached their table, stared coolly at Uncle Percy and said, 'The bidding stops now.'

Uncle Percy looked up and his expression morphed into one of dismay.

And then Becky saw why. On the left hand side of the man's face, just visible beneath a fine layer of talcum powder were three deep scars of various lengths. She remembered Joe's earlier enthusiasm for a certain nick-name: *Scarface*.

Al Capone had joined them at the table.

'A-ANY ADVANCE ON A MILLION DOLLARS?' Cheeseman stuttered, his gaze never leaving Capone.

Uncle Percy stared at the painting and shook his head miserably.

Flustered, his hand trembling, Cheeseman slammed down his gavel. 'Sold for one million dollars,' he said quickly. 'Now I think we all deserve a break. The auction will recommence in thirty minutes.' And with that, he scrambled off the podium and disappeared from sight.

'It seems you and your friends over there got your wish, Mister Capone,' Uncle Percy said, nodding at Scalpel Man.

'I always get my wish, buddy,' Capone said.

'You have no idea what you're getting yourself into.'

Capone laughed. 'Limey, you've no idea what yer already in. Now, my boys are on every door and I've a nickel plated .38 Special that says you're all gonna come with me now.' He opened his jacket to reveal a gun. 'And in case you ain't noticed, I could plug you full of holes right now and not one person in this joint would see a thing, know what I mean? He gestured for them to follow. 'Get movin'...'

Petrified, Becky got to her feet, as the others did the same. She looked at Uncle Percy, fully expecting him to feel as concerned as she did. Instead, she saw him glance furtively across the room to give a small but distinct nod to Keith Pickleton, who nodded back, before burying his head in an auction brochure.

The group weaved through the tables and before Becky knew it, they were standing before Scalpel Man.

'Very good, Mister Capone,' Scalpel Man said. 'Mister Drake will be pleased.'

'You just make sure he delivers the cash as agreed, *Chapman*.'

'He is a man of his word, I assure you,' Scalpel Man replied. He turned to Uncle Percy. 'Well, that was exhilarating.'

But Uncle Percy hadn't heard him. 'Chapman?' he breathed. 'George Chapman?'

Becky looked at him and fear shot through her. She had never seen him so alarmed. Will and Joe had noticed, too.

'I see you've heard of me.'

'But that's impossible,' Uncle Percy said. 'You're dead. They hanged you in 1903.'

Delight spread across Chapman's face. 'I'm afraid not, Mister Halifax. Certainly the authorities declared as such, but I trust that was to save a measure of face, wouldn't you agree?'

Uncle Percy was stunned to silence.

'Anyway, Mister Capone, I believe it's time to leave.' Chapman leaned into Uncle Percy's ear and whispered, 'You see, I've arranged a little surprise for you. Mister Drake informs me that history can be changed. I want to test that theory…' He turned to the Associate on his left and handed over his briefcase. 'Pay for the portrait and take it to the rendezvous point. I shall see you there in one hour. Mister Capone, if you would lead the way …' Capone grunted and moved away, tracked by Chapman, Kruger and the remaining Associates.

Becky, Joe, Uncle Percy and Will were suddenly surrounded by five of Capone's men, a number of whom tapped their jackets to emphasise they, too, were armed. Uncle Percy sighed and moved towards the door.

Becky rushed to his left, keeping her voice down. 'What's going on? Who's George Chapman? What did he say to you?'

Uncle Percy said nothing. Instead, he glanced at Will and the two of them exchanged a curious look.

Becky didn't appreciate being ignored. 'Will you answer me?'

'We'll discuss it later, Becky,' Uncle Percy said. 'Just don't worry.'

'Don't worry?' Becky blustered. 'Al Capone! Scalpel Man! Otto Kruger! I think now's a great time to worry.'

Uncle Percy forced an unconvincing smile. 'Trust me. Everything is in hand.'

Becky didn't believe a word of it.

The group entered the lobby. With Capone leading the way, the crowds parted quickly and without protest, Becky soon found herself standing outside the hotel, shaking as much from fright as the bitter Chicagoan wind. Capone tramped right and soon they were heading down a side street, staring at four vehicles: a large olive green Cadillac, two maroon Chrysler Imperials and a gigantic coal-black van. It was the van that caused Becky to do a double take; etched onto its doors were two large white stars, each containing the words 'Chicago Police Department.'

'Where are you taking us?' Uncle Percy demanded, although Becky had a funny feeling he already knew the answer.

'An Irish buddy of mine owns a joint near here,' Capone replied.

'Let me guess,' Uncle Percy replied coolly. 'Is it a garage, by any chance?'

Capone appeared genuinely stunned. 'Go figure, limey. No one told me you read goddamn minds...'

16

STREET FIGHTING MAN

Becky, Joe, Uncle Percy and Will were bundled into the back of the police van. Two of Capone's men - one tall and lean with a long, slim neck, the other short and stubby with a wide, thick neck - trailed them inside, pistols drawn. A third gangster moved to the driver's seat. Capone, Chapman and Kruger climbed into the Cadillac, while the rest of Capone's men and Associates filled the Chryslers.

Inside the police van, Becky glanced round at the murky interior and saw two police uniforms folded neatly in the corner. Then she watched as the shorter gangster sat down opposite and trained his pistol on Will. She felt Joe tense beside her.

'I hear yer somethin' of a brawler, buddy,' the short gangster growled at Will. 'Believe me, one false move, and I gotta bullet here that's faster than your fist.'

Will cast him an indifferent look and turned away.

Becky heard the engine turn over and her stomach reeled. Within seconds, the police van tailed the Cadillac onto the main street. Passing a streetcar, full to bursting with people, they were soon hurtling along, every rut in the road sending shockwaves through them, before turning down a narrow side road, lined with parked cars.

'We're going to die, aren't we?' Becky said to Uncle Percy. 'I mean … this Valentine's Massacre thingy - that's us, isn't it? We're dead meat.'

'I do hope not,' Uncle Percy replied. 'That would be a dreadful end to our day trip to Chicago. I mean - '

The van squealed to a sudden halt.

Becky looked over at Uncle Percy, who appeared as confused as she was.

The short gangster struggled to keep hold of his gun. 'What the -?'

Dazed, Becky peered through the front window. She couldn't believe her eyes. 'Oh – my – God,' she said.

Some distance away, a large, gleaming motorcycle was blocking the road, making it impossible to pass. Bruce Westbrook was sitting astride Sweet Sue, his Stetson tipped back on his head, a long tubular object in his hand.

Capone climbed out the Cadillac, waving his pistol in the air. 'GET OUTTA THE WAY, YOU GODDAMN BUM!'

Bruce looked at him with contempt. 'Capone, I ain't no bum,' he muttered. 'I'm the cavalry!' He hoisted the tubular object on to his shoulder.

'T-that's a bazooka!' Joe stammered.

With a thunderous *whoosh*, a missile blazed towards them. *BOOM!* It slammed into a water hydrant, showering water everywhere. Confused and enraged, Capone gestured for his men to join him.

Bruce hurled the bazooka aside and pulled out a Winchester rifle. Then he kicked Sweet Sue into life. 'Yee

Haaww!' he yelled, and powered down the road as if in a medieval joust, firing repeatedly. The gangsters took cover as he sped past, brought the Harley to a halt at the road's mouth, and readied another assault.

Inside the police van, the short gangster, unnerved by the events outside, cocked his pistol and directed it at Will's head. 'Now don't go gettin' any crazy ideas.'

Will smiled. Then, in a flash, ploughed his fist into the gangster's face. The other gangster turned his gun on Will, but wasn't quick enough. With a terrible *crunch*, Will elbowed his nose and his eyes rolled white. The driver didn't even have time to react when Will smashed his head against the steering wheel. In a matter of seconds, all three gangsters were out cold.

'Whoa!' Joe gasped, his mind playing catch up.

'You really are very good at hitting stuff, William,' Uncle Percy said.

''Tis a poor talent,' Will replied, 'but can be of worth.' He pulled the pump-like object and pencil case from his pocket. A thin cord was attached to the case, which he looped across his shoulder.

Joe pointed at the two strange objects. 'What exactly are they?'

'Your uncle is an admirable craftsman,' Will replied. He squeezed the pump's casing and a giant bow unfurled before them.

'I call it the Joe-Bow,' Uncle Percy said.

Joe's eyes bulged. 'That is the most awesome thing I've ever seen.'

Then Will removed what looked like a pencil from the case. With a click, it extended into a two-foot long arrow.

Joe looked as though he was on the verge of tears. 'You

really are the coolest uncle ever....' Suddenly, they were all brought back to reality by the whip-like crack of gunfire outside.

'Bruce!' Becky uttered.

Will fixed the arrow to the bowstring. 'Stay!'

Uncle Percy shook his head. 'You're not doing this alone, Will, you can -' Before he could finish, however, Will had leapt out. Swiftly, Uncle Percy picked up the short gangster's pistol and turned to Becky and Joe. 'Do-not-move!' Then he raced after Will.

Becky's heart thundered in her chest. Uncle Percy and Will had run blindly into a gunfight, outnumbered and poorly armed. Frantic, she watched as Associates and gangsters fired at Bruce, who dodged and weaved out of the way. Then she heard an agonising scream. Becky looked over to see a gangster clutching his hand, an arrow firmly embedded in its palm. Will was racing between parked cars, firing arrow after arrow at gangsters and Associates alike. Suddenly, all guns were trained on him. BANG. BANG. BANG. BANG. Will hurled himself behind a car, bullets shattering the windows above, showering him in glass. Uncle Percy fired back and raced to his side.

Seeing this, Bruce gunned Sweet Sue in their direction, shooting, reloading, and shooting again. Then he ran out of ammo. Casting the rifle aside, he leapt off the motorbike, and rolled to Uncle Percy's left. 'Howdy, boys.' Then he pulled a colt pistol from his belt.

'Hello, Bruce,' Uncle Percy said. 'Lovely to see you.'

'The feelin's mutual, buddy.'

'Er, what exactly are you doing here?'

'Ol' Maria told me where you'd gone. Had a hunch y'all might need a hand. Turns out, I was on the money.'

'Well, thank you very much,' Uncle Percy replied. 'But I assure you we would've been fine.'

'Sure looks that way,' Bruce quipped. 'Besides, who could turn down the chance of an old school gunfight with Al Capone?'

A bullet whizzed past Uncle Percy's ear. 'All things being equal, I believe I could!'

BECKY WAS PANICKING NOW. Uncle Percy, Will and Bruce had disappeared from sight and she had no idea if they were injured or worse. Then she saw Joe scrambling about on the floor, his hands rummaging beneath the tall gangster's limp body. To her utter dismay, he was waving a gun.

'That'll do nicely,' Joe said admiringly.

Becky looked horrified. 'What the hell d'you think you're doing?'

'I'm gonna help.'

'No you're not,' Becky barked at him. 'What do you know about guns?'

'I've completed level ten of Zombie Assassin.'

'That's a computer game, idiot,' Becky snapped. 'This is _'

But Joe didn't listen; vaulting from his seat, he burst through the doors into the street.

'If Al Capone doesn't kill you, then I will,' Becky grumbled, before rushing after him.

FROM THE CADILLAC, Chapman spied Becky leap out of the

police van. His lips twitched into a smile. He leaned over to Otto Kruger, whispered something in his ear, then hoisted up his shirt sleeve to reveal what looked like an overly large wristwatch covered in numbers and symbols. Pressing six digits on the watch face, his hand was suddenly ablaze in fine streams of light, which then curled round his arm like a fiery snake, before enveloping his entire body.

THE GUNFIGHT WAS AT AN IMPASSE, when Uncle Percy glimpsed a light flare inside the Cadillac. At the same time, an identical blast erupted behind the police van, followed by an earsplitting *snap*. A few moments later, Chapman's sneering voice could be heard all around. 'This will cease now!'

Sick to his stomach, Uncle Percy watched as Joe moved into plain sight, head down, crestfallen and defeated. A second later, Becky followed him out, Chapman's arm wrapped powerfully around her neck.

He was holding a scalpel to her throat.

17

2122 NORTH CLARK STREET

'WE SURRENDER!' Uncle Percy shouted without hesitation. He stood up, threw his gun to the ground and held up his hands.

'No!' Becky yelled back. 'Don't you dare! Not on my account.'

Will looked over and sighed. Making sure he wasn't seen, he unlooped the quiver and squeezed the Joe-Bow, which promptly retracted into its smaller form. Then he slipped them both into his pocket, before standing, hands raised. A disgruntled Bruce completed the surrender.

'You didn't have to do that for me,' Becky said.

Uncle Percy ignored her. 'We've surrendered, Chapman,' he said. 'Lower the knife.'

Chapman smiled nastily and leaned into Becky's ear. 'You may not like me now, but one day your heart will be mine.' He let the scalpel fall to his side and weakened his grip on Becky's neck.

The sweet, sickly smell of his cologne filled her nostrils as she wrenched herself away. Racing into Uncle Percy's open arms, she felt contaminated, as if a thousand baths couldn't wash Chapman's stench from her.

Suddenly, the distant wail of police sirens cut the air. Moving quickly, Capone turned to one of his henchmen. 'Frankie, get the wounded to Milwaukee Avenue. Get Doc Juliani to patch 'em up. I'll meet you at the Lexington in one hour. Anyone asks where I am, I'm in Florida, you follow?'

'Right, boss,' the gangster replied.

Capone turned to Uncle Percy. 'Limey, I'm a reasonable guy, but one more stunt like that and I'll crack all your skulls open with a bat. You catch my drift?'

'Your drift is indeed caught,' Uncle Percy replied flatly.

A few moments later, Becky trailed the others back into the police van. This time, however, Capone and two armed Associates accompanied them inside. Becky watched as Capone scolded the driver and the other two gangsters who had now regained consciousness but were still groggy. Then he sat down and waved his pistol at Sweet Sue, who lay in a gleaming heap on the roadside. 'Hey, cowboy, where d'you get a motorcycle like that?'

'A shop in Frisco,' Bruce replied disdainfully. 'Just over-lookin' Alcatraz Island. Maybe you'll get to see it one day.'

Capone was about to respond when the sound of sirens swelled outside. '2122 North Clark Street. NOW!' he bellowed at the driver.

Before Becky could catch her breath, they were hurtling through the city at a breakneck speed. Snow was falling now like icing sugar, coating the landscape in a silvery haze as the tall, grand buildings of the city center were replaced by smaller residential properties.

Becky had no idea how long they'd been driving when the van pulled up in front of a large redbrick building, the

Cadillac trailing close behind. A thin, pointy-faced gangster wearing a gray fedora hat opened a set of heavy wooden doors. The van turned into the building and continued down a steep incline into a sprawling dimly lit warehouse.

Numb with fear, Becky looked around. Naked bulbs hung from the ceiling, illuminating a large truck, chained to which was a German Shepherd dog that barked noisily as it paced in a circle. Then she shivered with horror. Three of Capone's men were pointing machine guns at seven disheveled looking men sat on the floor, their hands bound with thick rope. She remembered Uncle Percy had mentioned seven victims during the Saint Valentine's Day Massacre. But where did it leave them? She glanced at Uncle Percy, looking for some semblance of hope. She didn't see any.

Capone threw open the van's doors and growled, 'What're you jerks waitin' for?'

Becky followed the others out. Looking over, she saw Chapman exit the Cadillac, glance at his wristwatch and whisper something to Otto Kruger, who nodded his agreement. Then Chapman marched over, his scalpel glinting in the half-light and grabbed Uncle Percy's arm, dragging him out of earshot.

'I shall make this perfectly simple, Mister Halifax,' Chapman said when he was certain he couldn't be heard. 'You know only too well who I am and what I'm capable of doing. What I enjoy doing. The simple truth is, you will die here this very morning, in this warehouse, beside your archer friend and the cowboy. The children, however, will be leaving with me.'

To Chapman's frustration, Uncle Percy looked calm, serene even. 'That's not going to happen, I'm afraid.'

Chapman's temple twitched. 'Oh, but it is.' His eyes flitted over to Becky. 'And whether I introduce the girl to my blade or not depends on the answer you give to this question: What do you know of the Box of Eternity?'

'The Box of Eternity, eh? Is that what we're calling it? Anyway, I know very little. I know you're looking for it. I also know that I'll find it before you do, and Emerson Drake will be denied another one of his little relics.'

'Your self-assurance surprises me, Mister Halifax,' Chapman sneered. 'Surely it's somewhat unfounded considering your death is but seconds away.'

'Heard it all before, George,' Uncle Percy replied. Then his voice lowered to a whisper. 'And if you remember, I'm a time traveller. A second is an age…'

Chapman laughed coldly before turning to Capone. 'Mister Capone, shall we execute Mister Drake's plan.'

Snatching a rifle from one of his men, Capone aimed it at Uncle Percy, Will and Bruce. 'Against the wall, boys. Fraid you've made yourself some pretty powerful enemies. Ones that pay well, too…'

On Chapman's signal, an Associate advanced on Becky. Before she knew it, powerful arms had enfolded her. 'Get off me!' she screamed, kicking and punching wildly as she was carried away from the wall.

A second Associate moved towards Joe, but Joe anticipated it and threw a punch. With a sneer, the Associate caught Joe's fist and twisted it behind his back.

'Arghh,' Joe shrieked in pain.

Will made to leap at Joe's attacker when Uncle Percy's firm hand held him back. 'No, Will,' he pressed in a low voice. 'Remember what I showed you last week!' Then he shouted over to Becky and Joe. 'Don't struggle, Becky, Joe. Everything's just fine. It's all in hand… No biggie!'

Capone began to laugh. 'Just fine, he says.' He looked over at one of his men. 'Hey, Mikey. Looks like we got ourselves a comedian.'

'Sure looks that way, boss,' the gangster replied.

Instantly the smile fell from Capone's face. 'Sadly for you, limey, I ain't in a jokin' mood.' He cocked the gun.

Becky's mouth went dry

Uncle Percy, however, looked unflustered. 'Now if we're going to do this properly, I believe it's courtesy to allow the condemned man a few last words.'

Chapman's eyes narrowed. 'Shoot him, Capone. Do it now!'

Capone ignored him. 'Last words?'

'Well –*word*, really …' Uncle Percy cleared his throat and held up his hand as if ushering someone over. 'Taxi!'

Just then, Becky saw something gleam silver in his hand: *his car keys.*

All of a sudden, a *snap* echoed outside, followed by the roar of an engine and a piercing squeal. BOOOOM! The garage doors exploded and Beryl emerged through a cloud of splinters and dust. She thundered down the slope to be met by a mass of incredulous faces, screeching to a halt between Uncle Percy and Capone. A single beep of her horn blasted out and her front and rear doors shot open.

Uncle Percy turned to Will. 'Now, would you care to do your thing, William?'

'As you wish,' Will replied, pulling the Joe-Bow from his pocket. It extended in his grip.

Bewildered and disorientated, Capone saw Will fix an arrow to his bowstring. Promptly, he raised the gun and took aim, but it was too late. As his finger found the trigger, Will unleashed an arrow. Slicing the air, it shot up the gun's barrel. Capone pulled the trigger. *Click.* Nothing happened.

Joe panted with astonishment.

It was the single best shot he had ever seen.

Gangsters and Associates alike began to grasp just what was happening.

'Becky, Joe ... jump in,' Uncle Percy yelled.

Becky dived on to Beryl's back seat, followed by Joe, who slammed the door shut behind him. PEOWW. A bullet cracked against Beryl's side window. To Becky's amazement, it didn't shatter. A split second later, a storm of bullets thumped into Beryl. The noise was deafening. However, not a single bullet penetrated the bodywork. *Beryl was bulletproof!*

'In you go, Bruce!' Uncle Percy shouted, pushing a disorientated Bruce onto the backseat. Then he jumped onto the driver's seat and looked back at Will, who had just loaded another arrow. 'Will...We're leaving. Get in!'

Will didn't hear him. His eyes had found Otto Kruger. As if in slow motion, both men stared at each other. Then Kruger raised his pistol quickly, cocking the hammer. Not having time to ready his aim, Will let an arrow fly. BANG! The bullet missed. Kruger was about to take a second shot when - *whizz* – the arrow sliced his right cheek. Blood splashed his face.

'Get in, Will. Now!' Uncle Percy yelled again.

This time, Will heard him and, grinning at the bloodied Kruger, threw himself into the time machine.

Relieved they were all safe, Becky's gaze fell on the seven prisoners. 'We must save them.'

Uncle Percy shook his head as he typed on to Barbie's

timepad. 'I'm sorry, Becky, I really am,' he said sadly. 'But they're history....'

Becky didn't have time to protest, when streams of light filled the taxi. From the corner of her eye, she saw Chapman, his teeth bared with rage, let out a wild, guttural scream.

Then, with a *crack*, Beryl vanished, leaving nothing but an empty space.

———

WHAT NONE of them could possibly have known was what happened next: a crazed Chapman heaved the prisoners to their feet and lined them up against the garage wall. Snatching a Tommy gun from one of Capone's men, he fired mercilessly at them, again and again, until each one of them slumped to the ground.

The dog was the only survivor.

18

ISRAEL'S MESSAGE

Becky stared at the Time Room walls, her pulse racing as she grasped for breath. Glancing round, she saw disbelief on everyone's faces as they struggled to grasp their safe return to Bowen Hall. The sudden silence seemed as disturbing as the thunder of gunshots from which they had just escaped. Slowly, dazed, they exited the time machine.

'Well, that was hair-raising stuff, wasn't it?' Uncle Percy said, blood returning to his cheeks. 'Still, we're home, safe and sound. No harm, no foul.'

Everyone stared blankly at him. Then Joe spoke up. 'But what about the painting? In case you hadn't noticed, Chapman's got it.'

'I wouldn't worry about that. As a matter of fact, I would say everything worked out as planned.'

'So you planned on a shootout with Al Capone?' Becky replied flatly. 'Coulda done with knowing about that one.'

'No ... granted, that was unforeseen,' Uncle Percy

admitted. 'But let's just say I did anticipate certain events that may come as something of a surprise to you.'

Joe was getting exasperated now. 'What are you jabbering on about?'

'All in good time, Joe. All in good time.'

Normally, Becky would have been annoyed by Uncle Percy's evasiveness, but at that moment there was only one thing on her mind. 'Who's George Chapman?'

Uncle Percy shrugged indifferently. 'Let's worry about him later.'

Becky wasn't nearly satisfied. 'I think we should worry about him now!'

'Really?' Uncle Percy replied. 'I don't.'

Feeling her temper rise, Becky was about to give him a piece of her mind when Joe interjected. 'And how did Beryl just appear like that?'

'Ah, I'm glad you asked,' Uncle Percy replied, seemingly relieved he didn't have to answer to Becky. 'I've only just installed the system, actually. Embedded within Beryl's circuitry, is a voice remodulation device, a temporally autorated Intronicater, and a biogene locator. All of which is a very long-winded way of saying that this -' He held up his key fob, '- is a very sophisticated dog whistle. I shout *Taxi* and Beryl comes running.'

'Wicked,' Joe said, nodding his appreciation.

'You really are a total egghead, Perce,' Bruce said. 'I gotta get me one of those fixed to Sweet Sue.'

'I'd be delighted to install it for you, Bruce.'

'Thank you kindly,' Bruce said. 'Which reminds me … any chance I can use a Portravella to go and get her?'

'Of course.'

'Excuse me,' Becky interrupted, rather irritably. 'But will you answer my question. Who is George - '

Just then, Barbie's head popped up from behind a work-station. 'Nice to have you back, sir.'

Becky growled with frustration.

'It's nice to be back, Barbie,' Uncle Percy replied.

'I judge from your rapidly decreasing heart-rates, you've been engaged in some incident of note.'

'You could say that, Barbie.'

Barbie seemed confused. 'I believe I just did, sir.'

'It's just an expression, Barbie. It means 'to agree.''

'Very well, sir. I shall update my linguistic databank.'

'It was pretty ace, Barbie,' Joe said, beginning to feel his normal self. 'We fought Al Capone, battled this scalpel-wielding nutter with a moustache like a dead hamster, and sliced off half of Otto Kruger's face.'

Barbie bowed. 'Then Barbie is delighted Master Joseph survived the extreme violence.' Just then, the workstation gave three shrill rings and the words, 'Incoming Call' flashed across the screen.

Uncle Percy looked rather surprised. 'Would you get that, please, Barbie?'

'Certainly, sir.' Barbie's blue eyes gleamed amber. 'Keith Pickleton is requesting a landing pass for the Time Room. Shall I input the grounding code into his precognator?'

'If you would, my dear.'

A second later, a milk float materialised to Beryl's left.

Keith Pickleton was sat in the driver's seat, a look of deep concern on his round, fleshy face. Looking over at the group, his expression changed. 'Oh, thank goodness,' he said with relief. 'You're safe. I was getting worried. I'd heard there was a gun fight on Eighth Street -'

'Everyone's fine, Keith,' Uncle Percy replied.

'Good.' Pickleton scrambled out of the milk float, a rectangular brown paper package tucked securely beneath his arm. 'Anyway, I believe this is what you asked for, old boy.' He passed the bundle over to Uncle Percy, who returned a triumphant smile.

'Oh, smashing, Keith. Well done.'

'Not a problem,' Pickleton replied. 'As a matter of fact, I was the only bidder. The gavel went down on fifty dollars, a bargain, I'd say. And if your theory is correct I believe Emerson Drake will be as sick as the proverbial pig.'

Becky and Joe swapped intrigued glances.

'What's that?' Joe asked.

Uncle Percy raised the package into the light. 'This, Joe, unless I've made an error of gargantuan proportions, is the marker!'

Joe gasped. 'What?'

'This is the Israel Hands' painting we're looking for.'

Joe looked baffled. 'So why did we nearly spend a million dollars on that massive one of Blackbeard?'

Uncle Percy gave a wry smile. 'That's precisely the point, Joe. We *nearly* spent a million dollars on the Blackbeard portrait. They *did* spend a million dollars. I bid so enthusiastically because I wanted them to believe that painting was the one I was after, thereby deflecting all attention from this little one by a supposedly anonymous artist.'

'You mean Chapman's just spent a million dollars on nowt?'

Uncle Percy chuckled. 'I wouldn't say *nowt*. In my opinion, he's got a splendid piece of maritime history, but yes, one could argue he has overpaid for it, somewhat.'

Joe's face cracked into a smile, which soon became a full-blown laugh. Soon, everyone was laughing. Everyone, that was, except Becky.

'But how did you know about *that* painting?' she asked, pointing at the package.

'That, Becky, is a long story,' Uncle Percy replied. 'Shall we get changed out of these uncomfortable clothes and I'll tell it to you?'

BECKY FORGOT all about George Chapman as she dashed back to the Hall, threw on a pair of jeans, a sweater and a raggedy pair of trainers, before rushing to Bowen library, where she saw Uncle Percy clutching the unopened package. A moment later, Joe appeared, panting, behind her.

Becky's gaze fell on the painting. 'Go on then, tell us why you think this painting is the marker?'

Uncle Percy took a deep breath. 'Well, after seeing Israel Hands' optomediaphibic folio, it seemed clear we needed to know more about his life ... *and* death, and not just the kind of information that can be gleaned from the secondary sources we saw in the folio, but firsthand knowledge. Actual events. With that in mind, I activated Barbie's Invisi-blator and programmed her to travel back in time on a reconnaissance mission.'

'Good idea,' Joe said, sounding impressed. 'Let's see the painting then?'

'In a mo, Joe.' Uncle Percy said. 'Anyway, Barbie did manage to obtain some crucial information. In short, most of what Reg said was correct. Israel did indeed supposedly create some markers that led to Blackbeard's Treasure. She couldn't find out what they were, but she does believe one of them to be this very painting.' He raised the package up. 'You see, Israel survived the Ocracoke incident and was captured by the Royal Navy, amazingly negotiating a pardon for his crimes. However, at the same time he found out he was dying with only months to live. The treasure was of no use to him anymore, and believing Blackbeard to be dead, he thought he was the only one who knew where it was. Subsequently, he devised the markers so his child-hood friend, Edward Mallory, a priest, could find it at some point in the future. He entrusted his fellow pirate, Richard Young, to deliver the painting to Mallory in England. Anyway, neither the painting or Richard Young made it back to England.'

'What happened to them?' Joe asked.

'No idea. All we know is that the painting somehow vanished into the haze of history, and only resurfaced at the auction in Chicago.'

Becky's voice fell to a whisper. 'May we see it?'

'Of course,' Uncle Percy replied. He pulled a small penknife from his coat pocket and cut the string. The paper fell away to reveal an oil painting set in a gilded frame. A misty ray of sunshine caught it like a spotlight, illuminating the image of the sad looking woman and baby Becky recalled from the auction.

'Do you think that's his wife and child?' Becky asked.

'I'm certain of it,' Uncle Percy replied.

'She looks so sad,' Becky said.

'Yes, she does,' Uncle Percy agreed. 'I wonder, however, how much of that was Israel's state of mind when he painted it? After all, men like him often wouldn't see their families for years at a time, and if caught would probably never see them again. Anyway, shall we take a more comprehensive look?' He inserted the knife into the corner segment. With a soft crack, the wood split and the rear panel came away, revealing a brittle yellowing paper inside.

Becky's heart slammed in her chest. In the top left hand corner, scribbled in elegant handwriting, were the following words:

DEAR EDWARD,

By the time ye read this, I shall be dead. I have no fear of it and, for my countless sins, surely warrant it. However, although I do not regret my conduct in life, I can only pray my spoils be used for goodliness in my death. I leave to you the trail to a world of riches. A dangerous path, it surely is, but one I urge ye take. For the rewards would put Solomon's haul to shame. Do this for my wife and son, for your parish, and for God.

I wonder if you remember the deception Mister Icabod Ferbeezle, our schoolmaster, revealed to us as children. If not, this should aid your recall. 'A lemon shall write a wrong.'

I know I ask of much of you, dear friend, but look inside yourself as you must me, and you will see clearly the path to take.

Israel

SILENCE CLOAKED THE ROOM. Seconds bled into minutes. Becky read and reread the note, before looking up at Uncle Percy. 'I don't get it,' she said finally. '*A lemon shall write a wrong*? That's just nonsense.'

'And it's spelt wrong, too,' Joe stated, pointing. 'He's put 'write' instead of 'right'.'

Becky huffed. 'And if we've got to go back in time to try and discover this deception we're stuffed? We wouldn't even know when to go back to.'

'True,' Uncle Percy said, nodding absent-mindedly. 'Very true.'

For an age, Becky watched him span the length of the room, muttering, drumming his chin and muttering some more. Then, all at once, his expression changed, and he hopped up and down on the spot like an excited child, chuckling loudly. 'Oh, wonderful, he gushed. 'How simply wonderful.'

'What is it? Becky asked impatiently.

Uncle Percy pulled out his car keys and spoke into the fob. 'Barbie, if you could join us in the library, please.'

'What is it?' Becky repeated.

'You just wait,' Uncle Percy replied. 'I don't want to spoil Israel's big reveal.'

At that moment, an orb of white light appeared to the left of Uncle Percy. Swelling in size, the light vanished with a *crack* to show Barbie standing there. 'You called, sir.'

Breathlessly, Uncle Percy picked up the painting. 'Barbie, would you be so kind as to use your *Radiax instillor* and heat the paper up for me?'

'To what temperature, sir?'

'I'm not sure. Just take it slowly and we'll see how we do.'

A mystified Becky watched as the robot raised her tiny hand. With a soft hum, a blurred haze surrounded Barbie's fingers. Then she allowed her hand to move steadily across the paper. At once, letters appeared from nowhere.

Words were forming before their very eyes.

W-what? Becky spluttered. How?'

A satisfied expression crossed Uncle Percy's face. 'It's the oldest Steganographic technique in the world.'

Becky and Joe looked at him blankly.

'Steganographic technique: the art of composing secret messages. And this one is the all-time classic. He's used invisible ink.'

Joe laughed. 'Wow.'

'W-where would a pirate get invisible ink?' Becky stammered.

'Lemons,' Uncle Percy replied simply. 'Hence Israel's phrase 'Lemons can write'. There was no spelling error. He wrote this with lemon juice. You see … lemon juice is an organic substance that appears invisible, but oxidizes and turns brown when heated. Gosh, I do feel young again. You know, I did my first experiments with invisible ink when I was about three.'

'You've always been the uber-geek, haven't you?' Becky grinned madly.

'I do believe I have,' Uncle Percy replied. 'Anyway, let's see what he's got to say for himself.' He began to read.

From faithful Peggy, ye should glean
The map, few souls hath ever seen
And see the chart doth plainly show
The cursed archipelago
Find a Godly crew, and a worthy ship
And bade farewells, before yer trip
Then off to Nassau ye shall go
To find the Surgeon, Stinky Mo

For with good Mo, I've left the light
That will guide you in your plight
Then bear the voyage long and cruel
Where winds and swells and tempests rule
Just listen closely to my friend
And ye shall find the journey's end
Where Mary's treasures, gained from strife
Can give your flock a finer life

Israel

BECKY FELT DIZZY WITH EXCITEMENT. She glanced at Joe, whose eyes were so wide they threatened to cover his entire face. 'What does it mean?'

'I think it means many things,' Uncle Percy replied. 'I think it tells us everything we need to know to find Blackbeard's Treasure.'

'Who's Peggy?' Becky asked. 'It looks like she's a got a map.'

Uncle Percy shrugged. 'No idea. A friend? A mistress? A fellow pirate?'

'What's an archipelago?' Joe asked.

'It's a chain of islands.'

Joe exhaled. 'So the first map, the one we get from someone called Peggy, is one that shows a group of islands.'

'That's right.'

'And Mary Island is one of them?'

'That's my guess.'

'What's Nassau?'

'It was an infamous pirate port in the Bahamas.'

Joe considered this for a moment. 'And that's where we find this surgeon, Stinky Mo?'

'So it seems.'

'But we start by finding Peggy!' Becky said.

'I think so,' Uncle Percy replied.

'Great ... then let's get to it then,' Joe said determinedly.

Uncle Percy shook his head. 'Tremendously exciting though this most certainly is, I suggest we give ourselves a much needed break. Need I remind you we have had a hectic morning. Let's rest now, eat, spend some time as a family, and maybe even take our minds of all of this. And then, tomorrow, we'll do some research and take it from there. What do you think?'

Just then, Becky realised just how shattered she was. 'Okay,' she nodded.

'Fair enough,' Joe agreed reluctantly. 'But we start again first thing tomorrow?'

'Indeed.'

Joe looked at Becky. 'I'm going on the net to see if I can find anything out. You coming?' He hurried towards the door.

Becky was about to follow when she remembered something. 'I'll meet you in your bedroom in ten minutes.'

'Suit yourself,' Joe said, exiting the room.

Becky hesitated for a moment, before turning to Uncle Percy. 'Will you give me that answer now?' Her voice was calm but firm. 'Who's George Chapman?'

Uncle Percy knew at once he had to tell Becky the truth. His expression hardened. 'George Chapman or Severin Klosowski, to give him his real name, was a convicted murderer and, as far as I was aware, was put to death at Wandsworth Prison in 1903 for the poisoning of three women. However, although that is in itself a monstrous crime, it doesn't stop there. When Chapman was arrested, a prominent Scotland Yard detective, Frederick Aberline, was convinced they had finally caught the man guilty of a series of other murders ... murders that occurred in the Whitechapel district of London in 1888 ... murders that have since gained a certain amount of notoriety across the world.' He took a moment to study Becky's reaction. 'And judging by the look on your face, you know precisely who I'm talking about?'

Becky couldn't respond. The moment Uncle Percy had mentioned Whitechapel she had felt sick to her stomach. 'You're talking about Jack the Ripper, aren't you? You're saying that George Chapman is Jack the Ripper!'

Uncle Percy paused. 'It's a distinct possibility ...'

19

PEGGY'S SECRET

'Jack the Ripper?' Joe blustered, ten minutes later. 'Jack the bloody Ripper! You've gotta be kidding me?'

Becky sighed. 'I wish I was.' Her fingers traced their way to her neck. 'I can't believe he was holding a scalpel to my throat.' She shuddered. 'I'm gonna throw up.'

Joe flopped onto his bed, head in hands. 'And Uncle Percy's a hundred per cent sure?'

'He said it's a *distinct possibility* but we both know what that means.'

'Yeah, it means Chapman's Jack the bloody Ripper...'

Becky nodded. 'And he's asked us to not research the details of the Ripper case. In fact, he made me promise we wouldn't.'

Joe looked up. 'We don't really need to. The clue is sort of in the name. That along with the fact that he's the most famous serial killer of all time.'

For the next few minutes, Becky and Joe said nothing.

'Maybe we shouldn't worry about Chapman anyway,' Becky said finally.

'Why not?'

'Well, a baddie's a baddie. What's the difference between him and any one of the thousand baddies Drake could've plucked from history?'

'He's Jack the Ripper, Becks,' Joe replied. 'He's number one in the historical nutter stakes. I mean, if it was just Colin the Crabby it wouldn't be so bad, but –'

Becky giggled. 'Colin the Crabby? With that daft moustache it should be Reginald Ratface.'

Joe found himself smiling, too. 'Or Stoat Nosed Stan?'

'Or Vince Volemouth?'

'Or Bertie Badgerchin.'

Soon, they were rolling around in fits of laughter. Finally, struggling to catch her breath, Becky changed the subject. 'We should work on this poem?'

'Okay. Where do we start?'

'What about this name: Peggy. We can scour the net for something. Maybe we'll get lucky.'

'There's nowt there,' Joe replied. 'I checked my laptop before. There's nothing online about a connection between someone called Peggy and Blackbeard or Israel Hands.'

Becky frowned. 'I suppose it was a long shot.' Then something else occurred to her. 'And Peggy might not be a woman at all…'

'What else could it be?'

Becky moved over to the window and looked outside. High above the distant forest, she saw Will's golden eagle, Marian, circling the trees, her eyes searching out her next meal. 'I dunno. A ship, maybe?'

Joe thought hard for a moment. 'It had to be something obvious enough for Edward Mallory to find.'

Becky began to pace the room. 'Ask yourself this, if you had a treasure map where would you hide it?'

Joe's brow furrowed. 'Well, I wouldn't give it to someone else, that's for sure. No, I'd keep it somewhere close, somewhere personal. But this is different ... Israel Hands wanted it found. He wanted Mallory to find it based on the information in that poem, so it has to be pretty simple to work out, I reckon.'

But they didn't find it simple. They didn't find it simple at all. The late afternoon sun gave way to an early dusk and a spray of stars dappled the murky sky. At five o' clock, Becky returned to her room feeling despondent and down-cast. She had desperately wanted to solve the poem, to unlock its secrets, but they weren't getting anywhere. She showered, threw on leggings and had just put on a sweat-shirt when she recalled a sequence from the optome-diaphibic folio. And then it hit her like a thunderbolt.

Faithful Peggy.

Heart pounding, she dashed from her bedroom. Moments later, she was slamming her fist against Joe's door. It opened with a creak. 'I've figured it out. I know what Peggy is.'

'What?'

'Not telling you.' And with that, Becky hurtled off down the corridor, leaving Joe to growl to no one. She flew down the stairs into the Entrance Hall and saw the morning room door ajar. Rushing over, she pushed it open and saw Uncle Percy sat at his window seat, an open book resting on his lap. At seeing Becky's cherry-red face, a look of concern crossed his face. 'Is everything all right, Becky?' he asked, as Joe appeared at her shoulder.

'Yes,' Becky panted. 'I've done it. I've cracked the poem. Well, the first bit anyway. I know where the map is.'

Uncle Percy looked bemused. 'Really?'

'I think so. I mean, I might be wrong, but it does make sense.'

'Go on then,' Joe pressed. 'Tell us.'

Becky inhaled deeply. 'It's in his leg.'

Joe looked at her as though she had gone mad. 'What are you talking about?'

Becky ignored him. 'In that note on the back of the painting it said something weird, something about looking inside him. And that optomediaphibic folio said he lost a leg in a raid or something.'

A smile arched on Uncle Percy's face. 'Ah, of course. Very good, Becky. Very good, indeed.'

'What's very good?' Joe asked, baffled.

Becky shot him a superior look. 'Faithful Peggy is his peg-leg!'

Uncle Percy clapped heartily. 'Well-done, young lady. Bravo.'

'All we've got to find out is where Israel Hands died,' Becky said. 'And then go and get his leg.'

'And I happen to know precisely where that was,' Uncle Percy replied.

'Where?' Becky asked. 'How?'

'Barbie mentioned it after you'd both left the library. He died and was buried on Devil's Spear Island. It's a small island not far from New Providence, the capital of which is Nassau.'

'Which is where we're we'll find Stinky Mo,' Joe said.

'Indeed.'

'So when are we going?' Joe asked. 'Tonight?'

Uncle Percy chuckled. 'Well, I'd like to do some more research.'

'Ah, what's the point?' Joe said. 'We know what we've got to do. We know where we've got to do it. Let's just go and get it done.'

'You know it's not that simple, Joe,' Uncle Percy replied. 'We may be gone for some time. We need provisions and clothes and Gerathnium and I need to make you a Joe-Bow and - '

Joe looked as though all his Christmases had come at once. 'I get a Joe-bow?'

Uncle Percy gave a joyless smile. 'I think we know by now we're dealing with some very nasty people. And although I hate to admit it, I am putting you in harm's way. It seems only fair that you're armed.' He looked proudly at Joe. 'And from what William tells me you've become quite the archer. I hope I can trust you to use it responsibly.'

'You can,' Joe replied sincerely. 'I promise.'

Uncle Percy smiled back at him. 'I know.'

Becky looked at Uncle Percy. 'And what weapon do I get?'

'What do you believe you can handle?'

As Becky took a moment to consider this, George Chapman's sinister face crept into her head and provided an answer.

'How about Bruce's bazooka?'

20

DEVIL'S SPEAR ISLAND

L ater that evening, Bowen Hall was as still as a churchyard. Uncle Percy had disappeared into the Time Room with a request not to be disturbed. Joe had gone to visit Will in the tree house to explain precisely why Manchester City were the best football team in the world. Jacob and Maria had left for Addlebury to watch a Brahms recital at the village hall.

Becky, on the other hand, had no plans whatsoever. She wandered the grounds with Pegasus and Gump for an hour or so and then, when it was so dark she couldn't see her hand in front of her face, she returned to the Hall and opted for an early night.

It was nearly seven in the morning when her eyes inched open. She gave a bleary yawn, padded down her pillow and was about to turn over for a further doze when she glimpsed something hanging from her wardrobe door. Her eyes shot fully open. Flicking on her beside lamp, she threw off the duvet and hurried over to the new set of clothes that had appeared: a pair of tanned leather trousers, a white baggy cotton shirt, a knitted woolen cap and a pair of shin high leather boots adorned with a burnished brass buckle. There was also a note.

DEAR BECKY,

I thought this would make a nice change for you. No frilly dresses. No lace bonnets. No satin. Women in the eighteenth century Caribbean often pretended to be men to be afforded the same rights as their male counterparts. Subsequently, you may wish to do the same. I was thinking we could even call you Bucky! As you youngsters say 'LOL.'

U P

PS. We're leaving at 8.00am.

BECKY GLANCED at the clock on her bedside table: 7.01am. An excited shiver tickled her spine. In less than an hour, they were leaving for the Caribbean. In no time at all, she had showered and put on the clothes. Looking in the mirror, she gave a satisfied nod. With a *bang*, the door crashed open and Joe raced in, dressed in a similar outfit to Becky, his face split by an enormous grin.

When Becky saw the object in his hand, she understood why. 'So you got one then?'

Joe waved the Joe-Bow excitedly. 'How cool is this?' Squeezing the grip, it extended into a long, curved bow.

'It's very cool.'

'I'm going to the archery field to practice with it. You wanna come?'

'Nah.'

'Suit yourself. Did you get your bazooka?'

'No. Go figure ...'

As ever, Maria was furious that Uncle Percy had agreed to take them on the trip. She hurled great dollops of scrambled egg onto his breakfast plate with no consideration for whether they met their target or not (indeed, a flap of egg ended up dangling from his eyebrow) and fired various German words at him like a stray dog barking. It was no surprise to anyone that Uncle Percy was the first to leave the table and asked Becky and Joe to meet him in the Time Room in thirty minutes.

Although chilly, the sky was cobalt blue and the sun high and bright as Becky trailed Joe over the lawns to the Time Room. Uncle Percy stood beside the open door. Dressed immaculately in a vibrant purple velvet jacket, silk breeches, white stockings, a wide-brimmed tricorne hat and a walking cane with a silver balled handle, he looked every bit the eighteenth century gentleman. He also looked quite ridiculous. 'What a wonderful morning for a trip...' he said brightly.

Joe stifled a giggle.

'You look really, err –' Becky couldn't find the words, '- authentic.'

Uncle Percy gave an appreciative bow. 'I thank you.'

Will surfaced from the trees. He was wearing a long black leather coat, white shirt, tanned trousers and a leather tricorne hat; a gleaming bronze cutlass and two daggers hung from a loose fitting belt around his waist.

'It's Captain Jack Ostrich,' Joe said, nudging Becky, who choked back a laugh.

'And who may that be?' Will replied.

'Doesn't matter,' Joe said. 'Have you got your Joe-Bow?'

'Indeed,' Will replied, patting his coat pocket.

'Me too,' Joe replied. 'It's great.'

Will smiled. 'As I stated, your uncle is an admirable craftsman.'

Becky was about to ask which time machine they were taking when, trailing Uncle Percy into the Time Room, she had something of a shock. Beryl was standing there, gleaming black and looking as good as new, her bodywork and windows free from any sign of bullet damage. 'How did you fix Beryl up so quickly?'

'Barbie's been busy,' Uncle Percy replied. 'She's been working all night. That's the good thing about a robot assistant. She never needs a break, never tires, never moans, never goes on strike. She really is a blessing.'

'Are we registering the trip with GITT?' Joe asked eagerly.

'I already have,' Uncle Percy said. 'And Annabel's informed Charlie Millport in the Tracker Division in case we get into any serious bother. We have plenty of Gerathnium, a Portravella of my own devising, and a few other bits and bobs.'

Within minutes, they had taken their seats and Uncle Percy was inputting the coordinates on to the time pad.

Becky could feel adrenaline surge through her. Once again, they were heading into the unknown, embarking on the ultimate treasure hunt, on a quest for the ultimate treasure. And for a second, she considered what her mum would say if she knew what really went on when she and Joe visited Bowen Hall. And as Beryl shuddered, she felt deeply thankful she didn't have a clue.

A FEW SECONDS LATER, Becky found herself staring at the bluest ocean she had ever seen. A giant turtle lolled around in the shallows.

'Here we are - May 4th 1719,' Uncle Percy said. 'Devil's Spear Island.'

Climbing out, Becky saw a hummingbird weave a line of palm trees that sprung from the sand like lampposts. 'Why is it called Devil's Spear Island?'

Uncle Percy pointed over her shoulder. 'I believe that may have something to do with it.'

Becky turned and gave an involuntary gasp. The island was only very small but at its midpoint, dwarfing the skyline, was a gigantic rock formation in the unmistakable shape of a trident. Just then, her eyes were drawn back to the sea.

On the horizon, a three-mast sloop sailed away from the island; a black flag fluttered from its tallest mast. She stumbled over her words. 'T-that's a p-pirate ship!'

Uncle Percy tracked her gaze. 'Ah, yes, it most certainly is. That's 'The Winchester Man' - Richard Young's flagship, the pirate that buried Israel Hands on this very island. He's just set sail for England to deliver the painting to Edward Mallory. Of course, he never gets there.'

'So Israel Hands has only recently died?' Joe asked.

'About six hours ago.'

'So he won't be, like, green with half his face eaten off by worms?'

'What a charming image, Joe,' Uncle Percy said. 'But I doubt there will be any noticeable decomposition just yet.'

Joe looked disappointed. 'So where's he buried?'

'Barbie informs me he's at the base of the rock. Apparently, it's a very tranquil spot.' He opened Beryl's boot, pulled out two spades and threw one to Will, who caught it. 'Anyway, digging up dead pirates isn't my idea of fun, so shall we do this as quickly as we can and get out of here?'

DESPITE A WELCOMING BREEZE, the air was moist and the heat stifling as they padded over hot sand to the rock formation. Throughout, Becky felt undeniably queasy. She'd never seen a dead body before and the fact they intended to tear its leg off albeit a wooden one did not sit particularly well with her. They reached the rock in a matter of minutes to find a copse of pine trees encircling a raised mound, on top of which sat a crude wooden cross. The following words were carved into it.

Here sleeps a fine sailor, a brutal buccaneer, and a
moral man

Becky's heart skipped a beat. They were standing at Israel Hands' grave.

'Good morning, Israel,' Uncle Percy said, turning to Becky and Joe. 'Now, if the two of you would rather not see this you can go for a walk. In fact, I'd prefer it if you did.'

'We'll stay,' Becky said without hesitation.

'Course we will,' Joe agreed. 'We don't wanna miss all the fun.'

Will shot Joe a disapproving look. 'Death is never a slight matter, and should not be treated as such.'

'I'm sorry. But we do want to stay.'

Uncle Percy gave a heavy sigh. 'Very well.' He began to

dig. With Will's assistance, it was only a short while before they heard the solid *clump* of metal striking wood.

Uncle Percy brushed a thin layer of earth aside to reveal a makeshift coffin. He looked up at Becky and Joe. 'Now are you sure you're both okay with this?'

Becky gave a hesitant nod.

Joe didn't appear quite as confident as before. 'Yes.'

With the crack of splintering wood, Uncle Percy wrenched the lid open.

Becky prepared herself for the worst. However, when the lid was removed, she had something of a surprise. Israel Hands wasn't the fierce-looking ogre she'd expected as Blackbeard's second in command. In fact, he had an agreeable face, handsome even, and appeared very much at peace; his braided black hair was contained within a scarlet bandana, his eyes closed serenely as if taking an afternoon nap. She lowered her gaze. Attached to his right leg at the knee was a wooden peg.

'He's not that old, is he?' Joe said.

'Most men in his line of work died at a very early age, Joe,' Uncle Percy replied. 'Anyway, let's get this over with.' He crouched down, cupped Israel Hands' knee in his hands and carefully detached the peg leg from its harness. He examined it closely for a few seconds until realisation struck. 'Ah, I see...' He sounded impressed. Then he twisted its base, which unscrewed like a cap to reveal a hollowed out compartment lined with velvet. Gently, he inserted a finger inside and inched out a lip of paper. Removing it with great care, he pulled free a large piece of yellowing parchment. Becky felt her body quiver with anticipation.

The map existed.

Uncle Percy flattened the map onto the dusty ground so everyone could see. Ten islands of all shapes and sizes were clearly visible, skillfully drawn in black ink.

'The archipelago,' Joe whispered.

Uncle Percy nodded. 'Indeed.'

'And Mary Island is one of them?' Becky asked quietly.

'Yes ...'

'Which one?' Becky asked.

'I have no idea,' Uncle Percy replied honestly.

At once, Joe recalled Israel Hand's poem. 'So now we go to Nassau?' he said, 'to find Stinky Mo and hopefully the next marker.'

'That's the plan,' Uncle Percy replied, his face growing serious. 'But I do feel I should warn you that although I've never been, what I've heard about Nassau is all bad. All of the major pirate chieftains and their crews lived there at some point: Calico Jack Rackham, Charles Vane, Black Sam Bellamy and even Blackbeard himself. And there was a reason for that. Apparently, it's just about the most appalling human cesspit of corruption, villainy and all-round wickedness to have ever existed.'

'Oh, goody,' Becky replied flatly.

Joe didn't seem bothered at all. 'You should see our school...'

21

STINKY MO'S SHARK SHACK

Becky and Joe walked back, feeling excited if nervous about the trip to Nassau. Joe reminded Becky he was armed with his Joe-bow and would protect her at all times. In turn, she reminded him he was the last person she'd ever turn to for protection and would crack his head open like an egg if he ever suggested it again.

Returning to Beryl, Becky watched as Uncle Percy did a rather curious thing. Pressing the map face down on the Alto-radar, he flicked on a switch and a purple light traversed the map, covering every inch of paper. Then a low bleep sounded and a mystified look crossed his face.

Becky walked over, followed by Joe. 'What is it?' she asked.

'This is strange,' Uncle Percy said. 'Very strange indeed.'

'What is?' Becky asked.

'The Alto-Radar has an inbuilt Photo-atlas converter. It's a very straightforward device, rather like a conventional desktop scanner. Essentially, it transfers the diagrammatic representation, hand-drawn or printed, of tracts of land and identifies their whereabouts on a twenty first century world map. It's very useful for travellers. I was hoping to use it to pinpoint precisely where in the Caribbean the archipelago is.'

'Fair enough,' Joe said. 'So why do you look so freaked out?'

Uncle Percy frowned. 'According to the Alto-Radar, the islands don't exist. Not one of them. At least they don't exist in our time.'

Joe looked confused. 'What do you mean?'

'I mean precisely that,' Uncle Percy said. 'The converter can't match these images with any islands that exist in the twenty first century.'

'Maybe they're rubbish drawings,' Becky suggested. 'Maybe that's why it can't find a match.'

Uncle Percy shook his head. 'The converter makes allowances for things like that, it's really quite sophisticated. No, this is very odd. I mean, islands do sink, but still -' He was about to say something else but stopped himself.

Becky noticed. 'What's the matter?'

'Maybe there is one explanation, albeit a rather woolly and unscientific one.'

'What do you mean?' Becky asked.

'We are presently standing in an area known as The Bermuda Triangle.'

A flash of recognition spread across Joe's face. 'I've heard of that. Don't ships and planes and people just, like, disappear there?'

'All kinds of mysterious events have happened in this part of the world, Joe. Most of which, I am certain, have a perfectly rational explanation for being. However, there are some that certainly do seem to defy any scientific logic.'

'But an entire archipelago disappearing?' Joe said.

'And how does this affect us?' Becky asked.

'Hopefully it doesn't.' Uncle Percy gave a half-hearted smile. 'Anyway, we've got enough to worry about without thinking about the existence of The Bermuda Triangle. Let's get to Nassau and see what Stinky Mo's got to say for himself.'

'Do you know where he'll be?'

'As a matter of fact, I do,' Uncle Percy said, injecting enthusiasm into his voice. 'Barbie's handiwork again. Apparently, he lives on the outskirts of town on the edge of a swamp.'

'Sounds perfect for a bloke called Stinky,' Joe muttered.

'That's precisely what I thought ...'

———

BERYL MATERIALISED on the edge of a shallow stretch of brackish water. Shards of blue sky were just visible through giant ferns. Towering Red Mangrove trees surrounded them on all sides, their knotted roots submerged in water. It was dark and gloomy and the air was as thick as soup.

Becky climbed out of the time machine, trailed by Joe. She glanced around and saw a narrow rope bridge which led to a sloping rickety wooden house, painted black and gray; above the front door hung a crude timber sign which read *Stinky Mo's Shark Shack.*'

'Shark Shack?' Joe said with surprise. 'What's that all about?'

'Dunno,' Becky replied.

'Isn't Mo supposed to be a doctor?'

'Apparently.'

'Remind me not to get sick round here then.'

Uncle Percy and Will caught them up.

'Isn't this charming, eh?' Uncle Percy said, swatting an enormous insect that threatened to perch on his nose. 'Now, if you remember, Stinky Mo is expecting Edward Mallory, so I'll pretend to be him.'

'You're a bit old, aren't you?' Becky said.

Uncle Percy looked quite affronted. 'It's a hard life being a man of the cloth.' He pulled out the Invisiblator remote, pressed it and Beryl vanished.

Becky followed Uncle Percy on to the rope bridge, which creaked under their weight. They took each step with care, not wishing to fall into the murky water below. Becky glanced right. A pair of green eyes stared unblinkingly at her before sinking slowly beneath the surface. She shivered and quickened her pace. Will remained at the back, his hand firmly gripping the hilt of his cutlass.

As she approached the shack, the most horrendous, stomach-curdling stench filled Becky's nostrils. 'It smells like your bedroom,' she whispered to Joe.

'It seems his home is as delightful as his name,' Uncle Percy said.

'What is this place?' Joe asked, looking up at the sign.

'I hope it's not a restaurant,' Becky replied.

Uncle Percy approached the front door and took a deep breath. 'Well, here goes...' He rapped twice. Nothing. He was about to knock again when the door burst open.

Becky's knees turned to jelly.

Filling the doorway was the largest man she'd ever seen. His tangled head of carroty-red hair brushed the ceiling.

Nearly as wide as he was tall, his massive belly was pressing against an off-white apron stained with blood. In his right hand he held a set of rusted iron tongs, which contained an enormous shark's jaw, devoid of flesh.

But it was when the man leaned into the light that Becky had to choke back a scream. There was a wide, hollow crater in his bearded face where his nose should have been.

Uncle Percy appeared lost for words. Then something quite unexpected happened. The man chuckled. 'Swab me poop deck and call me a cuttlefish, Ol' Stinky Mo's got himself some visitors.'

'Er, indeed you have, sir,' Uncle Percy said, bowing. 'Can I assume you are Stinky Mo... the doctor?'

Stinky Mo's grin widened. 'I ain't no medical man, sir. Known as *The Surgeon*, but it's just because I be well known round these parts fer hackin' off limbs. See ...' He held up his left arm to reveal a gleaming iron hook instead of a hand. 'I even done me own.'

Uncle Percy masked his surprise. 'Oh, well done, very impressive.'

Stinky Mo nodded proudly. 'Had no choice. Had 'alf of it bitten off by a Tiger shark just off Melee Island. It had my nose, too.' He pointed the hook's tip to the hole in his face. 'Can ye believe it? Still, it took some years but I got my revenge on that shark. No one messes with Ol' Mo Baggely. Anyway, where's me manners? Come on in.' He turned and disappeared into the shack.

Uncle Percy raised his eyebrows. 'What a friendly chap.'

Once inside, Becky was stunned to see dozens and dozens of shark jaws mounted on three of the four walls. On the fourth wall, just below a black flag with a silvery shark stitched into its midpoint, was a gigantic dead shark;

perfectly preserved, it was perhaps sixteen feet in length, with an off-white underbelly, striped markings on its back and a distinctive ruby-red fin.

Becky's eyes were glued to it.

Stinky Mo noticed. 'I see yer admirin' me prize possession, girlie. Some people like paintin's, 'specially well-heeled folk, like you, sir.' He gestured at Uncle Percy. 'Me, I like to decorate me home with the beast that took my conk.'

'That's the shark that ate your nose?' Joe said.

'That it be. It took me six years ter find him ... Ol' Blood Fin - that's what I named him. Six years, and I never once stopped searchin'. Gave up a perfectly good career as a pirate, I did ... *Gingerbeard,* they called me - scourge of these seas in my day. But I gave up piracy ter become a sharker.'

'You're Gingerbeard?' Joe asked, recalling the keg of rum at the auction in Chicago.

'Aye, boy. That I was,' Stinky Mo said, pointing at the shark. 'Then, when I finds him, I hung up my compass and charts, gave up my name, and retired to this 'ere swamp. Anyway, who are ye all and wha' yer want with Ol' Mo?'

'Where are my manners?' Uncle Percy said. 'My name's Edward Mallory.' He nodded at each of them in turn. 'May I introduce William Shakelock, and Becky and Joe Mellor. We've travelled some distance to find you.'

But Stinky Mo's face had lost its colour. For an instant, Becky thought he didn't believe Uncle Percy, but then his expression turned to one of grief.

'Yer the priest, eh?' Stinky Mo said. 'Then that must mean young Israel has passed on.' He exhaled heavily. 'I am sorry. Israel was a good man. A tough sea-wolf, no doubt, but a bucko of fine character... You know, I was the one who taught 'im the ways of the ocean ... I was his first proper captain. Before he sailed with that bilge-sucking Blackbeard.' He spat on the floor. 'Thank the Lord that rapscallion's gone.'

'Blackbeard's dead?' Uncle Percy asked.

'I reckon so, aye. Disappeared from these waters some time ago. And scum like Edward Teach don't just vanish. Aye, he's with Davy Jones, I be certain of it... Anyway, I s'pose yer come fer Israel's effects. He said yer would. Ter be honest, I never held no store in it. I never thought you'd make the trip.'

Uncle Percy looked perplexed. 'Why not?'

'Yer've journeyed from England, 'ave yer not?'

'Yes ... we have.'

'Then that's a long way ter sail for some wax and a good fer nothin' bag of feathers.'

Becky shot Joe a puzzled look.

'What do you mean?' Uncle Percy asked.

Stinky Mo disappeared through a side door on the left hand wall. When he returned, he was carrying a large candle in the form of the Madonna and child. 'Bein' a man of the cloth I suppose you may appreciate it. But, I'll tell yer this ... it ain't Blackbeard's Treasure.'

Becky's heart thundered. She remembered the poem: *For with good Mo, I've left a light, that will guide you in your plight.*

The light was a candle!

She glanced at Joe, whose eyes had doubled in size.

'Thank you, Mo.' Uncle Percy said quietly. 'It means a lot.'

Stinky Mo didn't look convinced. 'Arr, if that's what ye think, then so be it. You just make sure yer be takin' the other thing, too. If *he* stays here any longer I swear I'll feed the beggar to the crocs.'

Uncle Percy seemed confused. 'He?'

'Israel didn't tell ya?'

'About what?'

Stinky Mo gave such a vigorous laugh that a number of the shark jaws rattled noisily on the walls. 'Sounds like Israel, that does. He didn't mention Mister Flint?'

'No.'

'Come with me.' Sniggering, Stinky Mo shuffled through the right hand door.

They emerged on to the rear porch overlooking the swamp. The deafening chatter of a thousand insects filled their ears.

Becky watched as Stinky Mo approached a tall iron cage cloaked in a long, ragged piece of green cloth.

'Hello, Flinty.' Stinky Mo's eyes gleamed wildly. 'Looks like our voyage is at an end. Yer new owners be 'ere for ya.'

A piercing, high-pitched screech bellowed from the cage.

'Faaaaatso! Faaaaatso!'

Stinky Mo growled as he whipped the cloth off the cage to reveal a blue and white parrot. 'Yer shut yer beak, yer lily-livered, hog-squigglin', rum guzzlin' bilge rat... I've told you, I'm heavy boned ... I ain't fat.' He looked at Uncle Percy. 'Anyhows, that's what Israel left ya - a candle and a bird that can't fly. Now considerin' he was Blackbeard's second, it ain't much, but that's all yer get.' He nodded at the cage. 'And it be only fair I warn ya - you bein' a man of God – the feathered rat only drinks rum ... and plenty of it!'

TEN MINUTES later they were standing beside Beryl. Stinky

Mo had invited them to share his lunch, but as he was serving Salamander Surprise everyone seemed rather keen to leave as soon as possible.

Joe poked his fingers through the cage bars at a decidedly bored looking Mister Flint, while Uncle Percy rolled the candle between his fingers, studying it closely.

'He really was an excellent artist, wasn't he?' Uncle Percy said. 'A painter and a sculptor!'

'What do you mean?' Becky asked.

'Israel carved this piece himself.'

'And how will it help us find Mary Island?' Joe asked.

'The answer to both questions, I believe, will soon be revealed.'

'And what about this parrot?' Joe asked. 'Should we just let it go?'

'That doesn't seem fair, really. He can't fly. He'd be the victim of a predator in no time at all. Besides, he's a very pretty parrot, aren't you, Mister Flint?'

Mister Flint puffed out his chest. 'Prettyyy as a pppicttuuree...BWARRKK... Pretty as a Pictttuuurreeeee.'

'Can we just forget about the parrot for a moment,' Becky said. 'What do you mean the answer will soon be revealed?'

Uncle Percy rooted in his pocket and withdrew his keys. 'Again, as with the painting, which incidentally also depicted a mother and child scene, this is another childhood amusement that perhaps Israel enjoyed with his friend. It's certainly another stenographic device for hiding secret messages. Do you know what I'm referring to, Will?'

Realisation dawned on Will's face. 'Indeed. It was a practice used by both sides during the crusades.'

'I imagine it would have been,' Uncle Percy replied.

'What are you two talking about?' Becky asked.

'Observe.' Uncle Percy positioned the candle on the floor then directed a key at its tip. 'Stand back.' He squeezed the key and a thin jet of flame shot out. The wick ignited. Turning a tiny dial on the key, the flame intensified until it spurted out like a flame-thrower. The wax melted quickly, leaking to the floor in gooey clumps.

Becky looked on, transfixed. More wax fell away. Slowly, bit-by-bit, something was being revealed beneath: a strangely shaped block of wood.

Uncle Percy extinguished the flame and scraped the remaining wax from the wood. Then he jumped into Beryl, only to emerge seconds later with Israel's map. Smoothing it out on the ground, his eyes examined each island. Then a look of satisfaction crossed his face, as he set the wood on to the island in the top right hand corner. A perfect fit. 'I think we've found Mary Island, don't you?'

22

THE SOGGY FLANNEL

Becky stared at the map with amazement. They had solved another part of Israel Hands' poem. Of course, she knew they still didn't know how to find the archipelago, but it was certainly a step in the right direction. 'What do we do now?'

Uncle Percy pondered for a moment. 'I think we need some advice.' He pressed something in his pocket. Almost immediately, the temperature dropped. A stale wind blew back Becky's hair. She glanced happily at Joe who looked back at her, his lips forming a name, as a ball of light swelled before them. Becky shielded her eyes as she heard a whip-like *snap*.

'Howdy all ...' Bruce Westbrook's smile covered his entire face, his huge legs straddling a shinier than ever Sweet Sue. He was wearing a red velvet coat and trousers with knee-length boots and a wide-brimmed leather Tricorne hat; four flintlock pistols and a heavy cutlass were tucked securely into a wide leather belt.

'Bruce!' Becky raced over and hugged him.

Bruce seemed overwhelmed, 'Well, missy. Ain't that just the finest welcome any man could have.'

'You look great,' Joe said.

'Thanks, buddy.' Bruce dismounted Sweet Sue and straightened the lapels on his coat. 'I've won many a doubloon in this get up. Lost plenty, too.'

'Thank you for coming, Bruce,' Uncle Percy said sincerely.

'My pleasure, Perce,' Bruce replied as Will walked over and shook his hand. 'Good to see you've arrived in Nassau.' He scanned the swamp and his brow crumpled. 'You've not picked the prettiest part of town, have you?'

'Not exactly,' Uncle Percy replied.

Uncle Percy spent the next few minutes explaining to Bruce what had happened since they had last seen him, about Devil's Spear Island, the procurement of the map, the meeting with Stinky Mo and the wooden block in the form of Mary Island. Bruce listened intently, offering murmurs of approval every now and again.

'So although we've a map of this archipelago,' Bruce clarified. 'And we know which one of these islands is Mary Island ... we still don't know how to get there?'

'That's about the size of it,' Uncle Percy replied.

'So what we need's a sailor that knows these islands and a ship to take us there.'

'Yes.'

Bruce thought hard for a moment. 'I ain't as familiar with Nassau as your old mate Reg Muckle, Perce, but I'd bet a dime to a donut that someone at The Soggy Flannel would be willin' to help if the price was right.'

'The Soggy Flannel?' Becky giggled.

Bruce smirked. 'The Soggy Flannel is a real pirate bar. And it's run by an old friend of mine, Battle-axe Beattie.'

'Battle-axe Beattie?' Joe snorted.

'That's right, kid. A whole lotta woman is our Beattie, tough as a sandstorm and used to be a buccaneer herself. She knows everythin' and everyone in this town.'

'Is she single because Will's available?' Joe said.

'Will's a tough hombre, but she'd eat him up faster than grass through a goose.'

'Tis a shame,' Will replied with a smile. 'She sounds as fair a maiden as Venus herself.'

Everyone laughed.

'And where is The Soggy Flannel?' Uncle Percy asked.

'It's right on the docks. First bar a sailor sets eyes upon when he arrives in port. Many don't get much further. They'll just squander any money they've earned right there.'

'Then that sounds just like the place for us,' Uncle Percy said. 'Care to come along for the ride?'

'I ain't dressed like a Hog's feast for nothin', Perce,' Bruce replied. 'Besides, The Soggy Flannel sells the most disgusting grog this side of Port Royal. And I love the stuff …'

Bruce entered the coordinates for The Soggy Flannel into Beryl's chronalometer. Then he programmed Sweet Sue to return to his ranch in Arizona and joined the others in the taxi. Moments later, Beryl materialised behind a large timber building. Although the sun was dazzling, long shadows cloaked them in a cooling darkness. Leaving Mister Flint in the taxi, Uncle Percy ushered them out quickly and flicked on the Invisiblator button. Beryl disappeared without a trace.

Becky felt worried and thrilled in equal measure as she heard Bruce say 'Welcome to debauchery central,' and followed him on to the quayside. At once, she felt like she'd walked onto a film set. Dozens of ships were docked in the wide harbour; flags of every colour caught the slight wind from towering masts. Drunken pirates were everywhere, swearing, shouting, stumbling around and waving half-full bottles of rum, their contents slopping messily on to the dusty ground.

Joe looked taken aback. 'What time of day is it?'

'Two in the afternoon,' Uncle Percy replied with a frown.

Becky watched as a fistfight broke out.

Joe looked shocked. 'Pirates were like Chavs but with bigger earrings!'

Uncle Percy made a disapproving murmur as they reached a sign that read: *The Soggy Flannel*. Then he turned to Becky and Joe. 'Actually, I think it's best if the two of you return to the time machine. I'm not at all sure it's wise for you to come in here.'

'Why not?' Joe replied indignantly.

'It's good for our education,' Becky said at once.

Uncle Percy scowled. 'You tell me how observing a hundred inebriated criminals is good for your education?'

Becky thought for a moment. 'I think it's important for Joe and me to be aware of the dangers of alcohol, don't you?'

Uncle Percy couldn't find a response. 'Er, well, you're right, of course, but '

'- And you can't just show us a rose-tinted vision of history all the time, can you?'

Again, Uncle Percy was lost for words. Eventually, he

gave a reluctant sigh and said, 'Very well, you can come in.' He was about to open the door when - *SMASSHHH* - the window shattered. With a dull thump, a pirate landed at his feet, groaning. He looked down, horrified.

'Make certain ya can afford t' pay fer yer Grog before ya go in,' the pirate mumbled, 'that landlady ain't ter be trifled with.' Then he lost consciousness.

'Thanks for the advice,' Uncle Percy said weakly. He looked back at Becky and Joe. 'Promise me you'll stay close.'

Becky couldn't take her eyes off the unconscious pirate. 'Yeah,' she squeaked.

Clasping his walking cane tightly, Uncle Percy pushed open the door, which unleashed a thick cloud of tobacco smoke and the booming yells, raucous laughter, and tuneless singing of the pirates inside. Becky watched as Uncle Percy led them to a long, crowded bar where a huge woman with an eye patch over her right eye and a neck as thick as a barrel was serving drinks. The moment she spied Bruce, the woman's visible eye widened with delight.

'Bruce Westbrook,' she said with a wide smile that exposed her six remaining teeth. 'It be grand to see you, deary.'

Bruce smiled. 'Howdy, Beattie. How're ya darlin'?'

A stocky pirate with no neck stared down at his empty tankard. 'Oi, Luv!' he barked at Beattie. 'Any chance o' another grog!'

Beattie ignored him, her eye trained on Bruce. 'Oh, I be doin' fine.'

The no-necked pirate looked increasingly irritated. 'Luv! Any chance a buccaneer can actually get himself a drink in this hell-hole?'

Beattie looked over at Bruce. 'Hang on a tick, deary.' She turned to the no-necked pirate. 'I be beggin' your pardon, sir, but –' BAM! She slammed her massive fist into his jaw, before turning back to Bruce. 'Sorry 'bout that…'

Even Bruce didn't know where to look. 'It's rowdy today, Beattie.'

'Aye,' Beattie replied. 'Calico Jack's ship has just got back and his boy's be throwin' pieces of eight all over Nassau. I'm more than happy ter take my share. Anyway, you come for a game?'

'No game, Beattie,' Bruce replied. 'I'm here on business.' He gestured at Uncle Percy. 'My friend here is lookin' to charter a ship.'

'And who is your friend?'

Uncle Percy stepped forward. 'Percy Halifax, at your service.'

'I doubt yer could handle bein' at my service, handsome,' Beattie said with a wink. 'But any friend o' Bruce's is a friend o' mine.'

Uncle Percy smiled back. 'Thank you.'

'So yer lookin' to charter a ship? Well, I reckon there's plenty round 'ere that'll willingly take that contract. Most are just rogues, mind. To get a loyal and dependable crew will cost.'

'We can pay,' Uncle Percy replied. 'We can pay very well.'

Beattie looked him over. 'Judgin' from the cut of your jib, I'm sure ya can, deary. So where are heading fer?'

'Mary Island.'

Beattie turned a dull grey. In an instant, she barged from behind the bar, seized Uncle Percy's lapel and dragged him forcibly to the side, making sure no one could hear what she had to say. 'Don't be spoutin' that name round 'ere! These walls talk.'

Uncle Percy didn't waver. 'Do you know a crew that can take us there?'

'Even if I did, I wouldna tell yer. Yer after something that should jus' be left alone.'

'We're not after Blackbeard's treasure,' Uncle Percy replied. 'Not as such. We're after a single item from it, but the crew that delivers us to Mary Island can have the rest.'

'And yer think yer know the whereabouts of his haul, do ya?'

'No. But we'll find it.'

Beattie shook her head in despair. 'If I'd a guinea for every time I'd heard that I'd own Nassau. Many have gone lookin'… few have returned. And none have been any the richer.' She glanced kindly at Becky and Joe. 'And yer got young ones with ya. It's not a trip ye should be taking.'

'Believe me when I say that we have no choice …'

Staring into Uncle Percy's remorseful eyes, Beattie's expression softened. She glanced at Bruce. 'Yer trust him, Bruce?'

'With my life, Beattie,' Bruce replied. 'He's a good man. And he speaks the truth. We need to find Mary Island. And I swear on my momma, it ain't outta no greed.'

Beattie hesitated. 'Come with me. I may know of someone that can help ye.' With a heavy sigh, she stomped over to a door at the far end of the room. Knocking twice, Beattie opened it and disappeared into blackness.

Moments later, they all filed into a large, airless room. Sunlight bled through a crack in the ceiling, exposing an old man sat at a crooked wooden table. Wearing a long ragged cloak, he had long, lank, grey hair and a pale, gnarled face.

He was staring impassively at the wall and drinking rum from a pewter tankard. 'Who goes there?' he roared gruffly.

'All's well, Hugh. It's me, Beattie.'

'Who's with ya, girl?'

'Strangers … But I'm promised they're fine, honest folk. They want to talk business with ya.'

The old man paused for a second. 'Very well.'

To Becky's surprise, she saw the old man's eyes were as white as snow. He was blind.

'They're lookin fer a crew,' Beattie said. 'A crew willin' ter go places others won't. And they'll pay, Hugh. They'll pay handsomely.'

'Oh, aye,' the old man said, suddenly interested. 'Then, all of ya, come over 'ere and take the burden from your feet.'

'I'll leave ya to yer business,' Beattie said, and she left the room. Everyone walked over and joined him at the table.

'Thank you, sir,' Uncle Percy said, sitting down. 'I'm Percy Halifax. These are my friends Bruce Westbrook and Will Shakelock. And this is my niece and nephew, Becky and Joe Mellor.'

'And they call me Hugh Livsey … but ter most it's just Blind Hugh. Anyways, what's this 'bout you needin' a charter? Where d'you 'ave a mind to go?'

'We don't exactly know,' Uncle Percy replied. 'Do you speak for a ship and crew?'

'Best ship and crew in these waters,' Blind Hugh said. 'And what ya mean ya don't know?'

'We need to get to Mary Island. But we don't know where it is.'

Blind Hugh fell silent. Slowly, he raised his tankard and

drained it. 'Ah, another fool hopin' to find Teach's gains, eh?'

'Not exactly.'

'Then what ya want with Mary Island?'

'That's our business. Do you know where it is?'

Blind Hugh chuckled sourly. 'No. Mary Island is one of the ten Macaco Islands. Only Teach himself knows which one it is. And Israel Hands, maybe. Both of them are dead or dying, from what I hear.'

'We know which one it is. If we can get to these Macaco Islands, we can identify the island.'

Blind Hugh scowled. 'And how you be knowin' that?'

'Let's just say a voice from the grave told us.'

Blind Hugh laughed coldly. 'And a grave is exactly where yer'll be if ya try ter get there. A watery grave.' His face grew stern. 'Them waters are cursed, so it's told. And protected, too.'

'Protected?' Uncle Percy asked.

'Aye. A serpent guards those waters, so they say. A serpent as long as the Thames.'

'A sea-serpent?' Joe said quietly.

'Aye, lad,' Blind Hugh replied. 'A beast that'd scare Poseidon himself. At least, that's the way the story goes...'

Uncle Percy noticed the look of dismay on Becky's face. 'Have you seen this sea-serpent?'

'Nope,' Hugh replied.

Uncle Percy shrugged. 'Then it could be just that ... a story!'

'Could be,' Blind Hugh replied with a sneer. 'Except the story came from an old salt, Billy Benson ... and Billy never told me no lies in all the years we sailed together, not until scurvy took him fer dead. You see, Billy was a boatswain in the King's Navy, and as he told it, in the summer of 1708 were part of a fleet of six gun ships sailin' through them Macaco Islands. Anyway, accordin' to Billy, a serpent rose from below and took five out of the six ships to Davy's locker. Billy's ship was the only one ter stay afloat. Years later, he gave me the bearings fer those waters. But I ain't never used them.'

'And will you use them now?' Uncle Percy asked.

Blind Hugh turned away as if something else, something important was playing on his mind. 'What be your deal?' he asked faintly.

'If you can take us safely to Mary Island, then I guarantee all of Blackbeard's treasure is yours to share between you and your crew. You can have everything with our thanks. All we ask is to keep but one item: his treasure chest, or at least one of them. We'll tell you which one.'

Blind Hugh looked confused. 'A box?' he said with disbelief. 'All yer want is a box?'

'Yes,' Uncle Percy replied simply. 'And as a sign of good faith, you can have this now.' He pulled something from his pocket.

Becky saw his fingers were curled round something that resembled a small apple. Then she gasped. He was holding the largest emerald she had ever seen.

Uncle Percy placed the emerald in Blind Hugh's hand, whose fingers promptly traced its jagged contours. A smile curved on his face.

'Well, I may not be able ter see it, but I knows me a remarkable stone when I feels one. An emerald, right?'

'That's right,' Uncle Percy replied.

Blind Hugh tucked it swiftly into his cloak pocket. 'Now

tell me, what manner o' man pays their passage with a jewel like that?'

'I'm just a simple traveller.'

'Well, traveller, it looks like yer've acquired the services of The Black Head.'

'The blackhead?' Joe spluttered, about to laugh, until Uncle Percy looked at him reproachfully.

Blind Hugh didn't notice. 'Aye, lad,' he said proudly. 'She may not be the sprightliest on the Spanish Main but she ain't ready ter swallow the anchor just yet.'

Uncle Percy looked confused. 'Don't you need to talk this through with your Captain?'

Blind Hugh laughed. 'The Black Head don't have no captain. The crew works as equals. We're all old salts and sailed under captains fer too long.' His expression mellowed as he said, 'Well, excepting one and he's too young ter 'ave a say in the matter. Anyhow, when is it ya want ter set sail?'

'When can you be ready?'

'Within the hour,' Blind Hugh replied. 'And if yer'll pardon my leave I'll go inform me buckos and make preparations.' And with that Blind Hugh stood, lifted up a thin cane that rested on his chair and tapped his way to the door.

Becky waited until Blind Hugh had left and giggled, 'The Black Head? Is he serious?'

Joe grinned. 'Should've called it The Red Zit.'

'Or The Blue Boil.'

'Or The Purple Pimple.'

Uncle Percy laughed with them. 'As long as it's seaworthy, I don't care if it's called the - 'His sentence was cut short by a voice from the doorway.

'How very charming...'

Uncle Percy whirled round. Will's hand shot to his cutlass.

George Chapman moved snake-like from the shadows. He wore an English naval officers uniform and held a gleaming sword. Dressed identically, Otto Kruger trailed him in, a thick scar down his right cheek that seemed to glow against his cold features. Just behind him, stood a colossal pirate with a shaven scalp and tattoos that covered every inch of his chest and face. Two Associates brought up their rear.

Chapman approached them, glaring at Uncle Percy. 'Let me make the following matters simple, Mister Halifax. I am here for the map and whatever else you possess in relation to The Box of Eternity. You will give me that which I ask now. In exchange, I offer nothing bar your lives.' He struggled to contain his rising anger. 'You have already made a fool of me and I assure you it will not happen again. Mister Kruger, if you would care to show Halifax how serious we are then please do so.'

Smirking wildly, Kruger pulled a Luger pistol from his coat, turned it on Will ... and fired.

Becky didn't have time to scream when Will's blood showered her face.

23

FIREARMS AND FOREARMS

Time stood still. Trembling, Becky's eyes watered as she waited for Will's body to slump to the table. Instead, relief swept through her as she saw him tilt his head coolly to the side, revealing a deep bloody channel in his cheek. Then, veiling any pain he might have felt, his eyes met Kruger's and he smiled.

Unable to process what had just happened, Uncle Percy opened his mouth to say something but closed it at once.

Chapman, on the other hand, appeared more than willing to talk. 'Now the map, please, Mister Halifax, or the next bullet will meet his brain.'

'It's in the time machine,' Uncle Percy said without hesitation.

Chapman pointed the sword at Becky. 'Give the child the keys to your vehicle.' He glanced at the bald pirate. 'Mister Doublehook …accompany her, and if she proves troublesome, show her why Mister Drake was keen to recruit you.'

The tattooed pirate nodded and raised his arms into the

light. To Becky's horror, she saw two razor-sharp iron hooks instead of hands.

Chapman turned back to Uncle Percy. 'And if you attempt to repeat the trick you employed in Chicago she will be punctured like meat on a skewer. Now pass her your keys.'

Uncle Percy pulled the keys from his pocket and threw them to Becky, who caught them. 'The map is in the glove compartment.'

Chapman gave a pitiless laugh. 'Mister Drake was correct about you. These children are your weakness.'

'I'm afraid you couldn't be more wrong about that.' Uncle Percy glanced at Will and the two of them exchanged a curious look. 'What do you think, Will?'

'I believe they give me strength,' Will replied. Then, in a blur, he pulled free a dagger and pitched it at Otto Kruger. Before Kruger could react, the blade struck the pistol, sending it rattling across the floor. In the same movement, Will drew his cutlass and glowered at Kruger. 'Perhaps we should finish this now?'

Kruger's eyes burned with wild delight. 'I agree.' Slowly, he unsheathed his sword, then, with lightning speed, he attacked. Blades collided. Kruger broke off and swiped high. Will ducked, the blade whistling above him. Kruger attacked again, stabbing at Will's stomach. This time, Will parried.

Becky could barely look.

Time and time again, Kruger threw everything into his assault. But Will was faster, more agile. He dodged every assault. Seeing this, an Associate charged into the fray, sword held high. Like a dervish, Will fought them both off, blocking and attacking, twirling and slashing.

Becky's heart was in her throat. Then she saw something that sent shockwaves through her.

Uncle Percy had unscrewed the handle of his cane and pulled free a sword. 'Chapman,' he said. 'En garde...'

Chapman smiled as he raised his sword and lunged at Uncle Percy.

At the same time, Bruce stepped toward Doublehook. 'Well, buddy, I don't know 'bout you, but I feel kinda left out.' He withdrew his cutlass. 'You wanna dance?' With a wild grin, Doublehook sprang, arms outstretched, hooks glinting in the half-light.

Horror-struck, Becky surveyed the bedlam. The clatter of metal on metal shattered the air. Then her eyes widened. Joe had extended his Joe-Bow. 'What are you doing?'

Joe ignored her. He set an arrow on the bowstring and aimed at Kruger. The remaining Associate saw this and charged at him like a bull, nearly bowling him over, before seizing him in a headlock and squeezing hard.

Desperate to help, Becky looked round. Spying Blind Hugh's empty rum bottle, she grabbed its neck and, with one almighty swing, smashed it across the Associate's head; the glass shattered on impact, sending the Associate crashing to the floor.

Joe gulped a lungful of air. 'Thanks, sis.'

'My pleasure,' Becky replied. Looking round, she saw the fighting had intensified. It was surely only a matter of time before Uncle Percy, Will or Bruce was hurt or killed. She had to do something. Suddenly, she spied a flash of metal: Kruger's pistol. Sprinting over, she fell to her knees, skidded a few feet and scraped it up. Then she aimed at the ceiling and fired. The sound ricocheted off the walls.

'STOOPPPP!' she yelled. Then she pointed the gun at Chapman.

Slowly, one by one, each duel stopped. Everyone turned to face her.

Chapman began to laugh.

'SHUT UP!' Becky shouted at him, her hand tightening around the grip. 'I know who and what you are and have no problem pulling this trigger.'

'You know nothing,' Chapman sneered.

'I know you'll drop that sword or I'll shoot you in the leg.' Becky had never sounded more serious. Chapman appeared to recognize this and, grudgingly, released his sword. She turned the pistol on Kruger. 'And you, goob!'

Kruger hesitated for a second, and then shrugged coolly as if he, too, was about to comply. But, with a piercing yell, he swung the sword at Will's head. Becky didn't have time to scream a warning. It didn't matter. With lightning reflexes, Will pivoted on his back foot and leaned back. The blade missed by an inch. As the sword's momentum continued, Will brought his cutlass upwards. It sank into flesh, severing Kruger's arm at the elbow. Kruger gave a horrific, inhuman scream and dropped to his knees, agony lacing his face. Instinctively, Will whirled round for the kill. But then a quivering voice filled his ears.

'No, Will!' Joe pleaded. 'Don't kill him. He's finished.'

Will's rage dissolved. He let the cutlass drop to his side. Slowly, darkly, he leaned into Kruger's ear. 'That was for my friends, Maria and Jacob. Should our paths cross again, it will be for their kinfolk and you will not be left with a single breath in your unholy body.'

Uncle Percy walked slowly over to Becky and tendered

his open palm. 'Please, Becky,' he said. 'May I have the gun?'

Unable to tear her eyes from Kruger's severed arm, Becky felt close to fainting.

'Please, Becky, the gun …' Uncle Percy repeated.

Shaking uncontrollably, Becky passed the gun over.

Uncle Percy turned it on Chapman. 'I'm going to give you a courtesy you would never give us…' He exhaled deeply. 'I'm allowing you to leave with your life.' He nodded at Kruger. 'Now go … get out of here, and take his arm with you! I wouldn't want Beattie to have to clean that up.'

Chapman glared back. 'This affair isn't over.'

'Perhaps. But it is for now …'

Within minutes, Chapman, Kruger, Doublehook and the two Associates had left, leaving Becky feeling sickened, confused, and fearful of what was to come. Somehow, George Chapman had discovered precisely where and when in time they were. She didn't know how. She didn't know what he had in store for them. But she was under no doubt his parting words were no idle threat.

Nothing was over.

24

THE BLACK HEAD

B ecky couldn't leave the backroom quick enough. Still shaky, she trailed an ashen-faced Joe to the bar where Uncle Percy had pulled Beattie to one side, apologised profusely for the bloody state of the backroom and thrust a bag of gold into her hand for any inconvenience caused. To his surprise, Beattie laughed the whole thing off, saying she'd once found a pair of severed legs in the same room after a particularly grisly bar fight.

'And the owner never came back ter reclaim 'em, either!' she cackled, pointing at the far wall where the legs had been proudly mounted as a trophy.

Becky looked over and retched.

Looking somewhat peaky himself, Uncle Percy quickly ordered two bottles of rum for Mister Flint and made a beeline for the door.

'Tis a shame yer didn't keep the arm, me dearies,' Beattie shouted as they walked off. 'It would've looked lovely on me limb wall...'

Outside, Uncle Percy spent the next ten minutes

patching up Will's cheek with various implements from Beryl's medi-box. Even with his skilled work, Uncle Percy told Will he would probably be scarred for life, which Will immediately dismissed with a shrug of his shoulders and the words, 'I have more scars upon my person than a tree has leaves.'

Just as they were about to leave for the Black Head, Uncle Percy filled Mister Flint's water bowl with rum and everyone sat back to watch what happened next.

'Through the mouth ...' Mister Flint screeched excitedly, his head dipping left and right. He drained the rum in one gulp, gave a satisfied burp and squawked, 'Into the bowels ...' Then he extended his wing, buried his face into his back feathers, and closed his eyes. Soon, he was fast asleep and snoring loudly.

'Why exactly are we taking an alcoholic bird with us?' Joe asked, picking up Mister Flint's cage.

'I'm not exactly sure, Joe,' Uncle Percy replied weakly.

'Faatttsooo!' Mister Flint whimpered in his sleep.

Joe nudged Becky. 'He must be talking to you.'

Becky kicked Joe's shin with such venom his howl resembled one of Mister Flint's squawks.

———

A SHORT WHILE LATER, they were weaving their way along the bustling quayside, passing enormous gunships with names like The Ranger, The Orca and The Adventurer. Gulls laced the air, swooping down and plucking bits of fish off the jetties before returning to the silken blue sky.

But Becky couldn't enjoy any of it. They were about to board a pirate ship, after all, and her experience of pirates thus far didn't indicate they were anything other than drunken, violent thugs. However, her thoughts were interrupted when she saw Uncle Percy remove something from his pocket, show it to a stunned looking Will and Bruce, before promptly returning it. Her curiosity stirred, she was about to question him when she heard Joe's voice.

'I hope The Zit isn't going to be like The Argo.'

Becky recalled the crushing sense of disappointment when they first spotted Jason and the Argonaut's legendary ship, The Argo, on Ancient Crete. 'If it is, I'm swimming to Mary Island...'

'And there she is,' Uncle Percy said, pointing ahead.

Forgetting all about Uncle Percy for a moment, Becky saw a two mast Schooner with the name 'The Black Head' painted crimson on its bow. It had a narrow, chestnut brown hull, and a bowsprit that made it look considerably longer than it actually was. Relief swept through her. Although by far the smallest and oldest ship in the harbour, it appeared to be robust and seaworthy. It did, however, look deserted.

Uncle Percy approached the ship's stern. 'Er ... Ahoy!' he shouted at the top of his voice. 'Anybody there?'

Blind Hugh's head peeked over the side. 'Welcome, me hearties.' Then he turned and shouted. 'Avast me bucko's ... straighten yer baldrics and scrub up yer manners ... our well-to-do guests be here!'

A dozen figures emerged from below deck and shuffled into line, their arms (those that had them) clamped to their sides, their chests puffed out proudly as if on parade. Scanning each of their faces, Becky had quite a shock. They were old. They were very old. More than that, each appeared to have suffered a major disfigurement; most had lost an eye, a hand, or a leg at the very least; some had lost all three. Then Becky had a further surprise. Standing at the end of the line, head down, was a young boy. He wore oil-stained breeches, a torn, collarless white shirt and a raggedy Monmouth cap.

'Climb aboard, maties,' Blind Hugh said, his arms open wide. 'Welcome to The Black Head.'

'Thank you very much, Hugh,' Uncle Percy smiled, carefully navigating a wooden plank onto the deck.

As Becky followed, she sensed a dozen wary eyes fall upon her. Feeling suddenly on edge, she was about to say something when a one legged pirate with an orange nose like a kumquat spoke up, "'Ere, Hugh, ya never said nuthin 'bout bringin' no woman on board. Ye should know they bring the worst of luck.'

Blind Hugh laughed heartily. 'Jedidiah Quint, what you be thinkin'? As yer well know, where we be goin' the last thing ter worry about is some lass. Besides, none of you seadogs have had any blasted good luck in yer lives, so what does one girlie sharin' yer deck matter?'

Jedidiah Quint appeared to mull this over, then smiled. 'You ain't wrong there, Hugh.' He tugged his bandana from his forehead and turned to Becky. 'I be beggin' yer pardon, miss. I fink me manners got flung out with the bilge water.' He glanced at Uncle Percy. 'Our ship is your ship, sir. Ain't that right, lads?' One by one, each man nodded and shouted their welcome.

'Now that be more fittin',' Blind Hugh said. 'Anyhow, Percy Halifax and company, this shoddy lot be the heart and soul of The Black Head. There's Short Jack Copper, Windy Pete McGuiness …'

As each name was read out, the corresponding pirate shouted, 'Aye.'

'Elbert Fridge,' Blind Hugh continued. 'Jedidiah Quint, Burly Bill Brundle Skinny John Prinny, William Turnip, Hunchback Henry Brody, Alf 'Lockjaw' Morgan, Hairy Harry Hooper, One Toe Tom, and last but ne'er least, Jim Dorkins …'

A silence hung in the air after the last name was read out.

'Jim?' Blind Hugh said at once. 'Where are ya, lad?'

Timidly, the young boy stepped forward. 'Here, Mister Livsey, sir.'

'Don't yer be shy, Jim lad. He's the real treasure of The Black Head,' Blind Hugh declared. 'Ain't he, boys?'

Every single man bellowed their agreement, many of them patting Jim's back with such force he was nearly knocked off his feet.

Blind Hugh beamed with pride. 'Jim's also the finest powder monkey on the seven seas.'

Jim blushed. 'Thank you, Mister Livsey, sir.'

Uncle Percy bowed. 'Then hello, Jim. And hello to you the rest of you. My name is Percy Halifax, this is Will Shakelock, Bruce Westbrook and Becky and Joe Mellor.'

'Old Man's Beeeeeeeard!' Mister Flint screeched. 'Through the mouth …'

'Oh, yes,' Uncle Percy smiled. 'And of course, we mustn't forget Mister Flint.'

A pirate stepped forward, every inch of his head, face and body coated in shaggy grey hair so he resembled a shagpile carpet. 'I knows that creature,' Hairy Harry Hooper said. 'That be Israel Hands' parrot! Never seen him without the creature…' He paused for a moment. 'So Israel is dead, eh?'

Uncle Percy nodded. 'Yes.'

'So tis true yer be goin' after Blackbeard's treasure?'

There was an awkward silence. The pirates exchanged hesitant looks.

'Yes.' Uncle Percy replied simply.

'And ye know where it lies?' One Toe Tom asked.

Uncle Percy gave a sharp shake of his head. 'Not at the moment. What I do have is this…' He withdrew the map from his jacket pocket and unfolded it before the crew. 'This map was drawn by Hands, himself.' Then he pulled out the block and positioned it over the island in the far corner. 'And this, I believe, was carved by him. That is Mary Island…' A collective gasp rang out. 'And if you can get us to the island I believe we can find the treasure.'

Hairy Harry Hooper didn't look convinced. 'And how can ye be sure o' that? I'm doubtin' Blackbeard would leave it on the beach 'neath a coconut tree fer all ter find!'

'I have my reasons,' Uncle Percy said mysteriously.

Joe glanced at Becky, who threw him a puzzled look. What did Uncle Percy mean? As far as either of them knew, he hadn't a clue where to look for the treasure.

Hairy Harry Hooper looked bewildered, too. 'I ain't a clever man, but my head ain't so full of seaweed that I canna see the strange in this. Hugh tells us yer don't even want Teach's treasure. Yer only want his treasure chest! Now are ya tellin' me that be the truth?'

'That's right.'

'And we can have all the booty 'cept this box.'

'Indeed.'

'And yer do know that if yer tries ter hornswaggle us

we'd hang you from the Mizzen then feed yer corpse ter the Blacktips?'

'I would expect nothing less.'

Hairy Harry Hooper took a few moments to digest this. Then he turned to the others. 'Let's be settin' sail, boys, it's a twenty hour passage, so may Saint Elmo be lookin' over all of us.'

The crew cheered loudly.

Blind Hugh clapped his hands. 'Short Jack Copper, if ye would do the honours...'

'Aye, Hugh,' Short Jack Copper bellowed. 'Let's way anchor, me brothers ...'

Despite their age, the crew sprang to life with the vigor of men considerably younger than their years; climbing, pulling, scaling and lifting. Everyone had a job to do and performed it with such effortlessness and precision that in no time at all, the main sail swelled in a stiff breeze and The Black Head inched away from the docks.

As they worked, the crew broke into song.

Fer we're the crew of the grand Black Head
And a finer throng, there ne'er was said,
Could tame the squalls with such delight
That we rule the seas by day and night
Fer we may be old and creased from sun
But we fight like devils on a belly o' rum
And the wenches still do not forget
Fer there still be life in the seadog yet
Our limbs be gone but we ne'er get stuck
Fer who needs a hand when ya got a hook
Aye we're the crew of the grand Black Head
And proud ter be 'til we be dead

Within twenty minutes, Nassau had faded to a speck on the horizon. Becky stood beside the others on the bow as the Black Head clawed speed, the taste of salt on her lips, the wind licking her hair.

'Jim, lad, if yeh'd show our guests to their quarters,' One Toe Tom said in a thick Irish brogue. 'There be spare hammocks in the hold which should suit 'em fine.'

'Yes, sir,' Jim replied quietly.

One Toe Tom threw Becky a sympathetic look. 'I hope ya don't mind, you bein' a lady an' all, but the quarters are mighty cramped and the smell o' thirteen sleepin' pirates has been known to stun a baboon.'

Becky's stomach turned. *Whoopee!*

Jim ushered the group to a door, which opened to reveal a set of wooden steps below. Climbing down, they passed through the gun deck, lined with six demi-cannons, buckets filled with cannonballs and barrels of gunpowder, before stopping at the berthing deck. Looking round, Becky saw thirteen hammocks hung from low timber rafters. There was an overpowering smell of feet. Trying to put this from her mind, she followed Jim as he made his way across the cluttered floor.

'How old are you, Jim?'

Jim looked like he'd never seen a girl before. 'I – I don't know.'

'What do you mean you don't know? When's your birthday?'

'I don't know, miss. Never had a birthday. Mister Livsey thinks I may be seven or eight.'

Becky had never heard of anyone not knowing how old they were before. 'Isn't one of the crew your dad or grandad?'

Jim shook his head. 'No, miss. I have no kin. Mister Livsey found me four years ago wanderin' by myself on Port Royal. No one knows what happened to any kin I might've had, and I was too young to be rememberin'. But the good crew of The Black Head gave me shelter, fed and watered me and gave me such kindness I don't deserve.'

'You don't know what happened to your mum or dad?' Becky asked, aghast.

Jim shrugged. 'No, miss. Mustn't have wanted me, I'm guessin'. Anyways the crew are my family now. I couldn't ask for more ...'

Jim spoke so matter-of-factly about his tragic situation it made Becky feel terrible. Her life hadn't always been easy, but she'd never once doubted how much her mum and dad loved her; she'd certainly never been abandoned by a parent unable or unwilling to cope with raising her. Quickly, she turned away, careful not to let Jim see the tears that were filling her eyes.

THE BLACK HEAD sliced effortlessly through the ocean as an orange dusk melted into the blackest of nights. For what seemed like hours, Becky stood on the prow, watching a pair of dolphins take it in turns to dip in and out of the oily water. Joe, on the other hand, spent his time on the gun deck trying to teach Mister Flint a few swear words. He felt like he was really making progress until Uncle Percy caught him and gave him a firm (if not entirely convincing) ticking off.

The Black Head's crew turned out to be great fun. Just after the evening meal (spiced chicken, salted beef, turtle eggs, hard tack biscuits and a variety of fruits) the pirates gathered on deck around an empty barrel for a game of 'hookling'; a game that followed the rules of traditional arm wrestling but with hooks replacing hands. As most of the crew sported at least one hook it proved to be quite a competitive if utterly corrupt contest. Elbert Fridge cheated his way to victory and celebrated by sinking an entire bottle of rum in one gulp and collapsed on the deck with a wide smile on his face.

Although it was way past midnight when Becky climbed into her hammock, she knew there was no chance of sleep. Surrounded by thunderous snores, along with the creaks and groans from the ship's frame, she lay there wide-awake for ages before curling her blanket around her shoulders, leaping out of the hammock, and climbing the steps onto the deck. It was then she noticed she wasn't the only member of their group who wasn't asleep. Uncle Percy was crouched at the front of the boat. Deep in thought, he appeared to be studying something on the floor.

'Uncle Percy?' Becky said, walking over.

He didn't reply.

'Uncle Percy?' Becky repeated, louder this time.

With a jolt, Uncle Percy snapped out of his trance. 'Oh, I do beg your pardon, Becky. I didn't hear you.'

'What're you doing?' Becky asked curiously. 'Is this something to do with what you showed Will and Bruce earlier?'

'Yes,' Uncle Percy said. 'As a matter of fact, it is.'

Looking over his shoulder, Becky saw the two gold coins Bruce had won from Gilbert Threepwood in Tortuga. They were piled one on top of the other and pressed tightly against the wooden balustrade. 'Are the coins sending you nuts again?'

'Not exactly,' Uncle Percy replied. 'Watch this ...' Ensuring his hand was fully wrapped in his handkerchief, he scooped up the coins and placed them a few inches apart and an arms length away from the balustrade. Becky watched closely. For a moment, nothing happened. Then, as if stirred by an invisible force, the left hand coin rattled violently, quickly followed by the other. Then they inched to precisely the position they were in before.

'H - how are they doing that?' Becky asked. 'How are they moving?'

'It started when we arrived in Nassau,' Uncle Percy replied. 'But it was hardly noticeable then. Since we've been on the boat it's become considerably more apparent, as you can see.'

'What does it mean?'

Uncle Percy looked at her solemnly. 'I think they know we're getting closer to Mary Island, to Pandora's Box. And I think they're trying to make their own way home.'

25

THE TEMPEST

A t that moment, Becky heard a tapping sound from behind. Looking back, she saw Blind Hugh hobbling over, cane in hand.

'Is that you I be hearin', Mister Halifax, sir?'

'Yes, Hugh.' Careful not to touch them directly, Uncle Percy slipped the coins back in the pouch and stood up.

'And Miss Becky?'

'Hi, Hugh,' Becky said.

'I was wonderin' if I may have a word with ye?'

'Of course,' Uncle Percy replied. 'Is everything all right?'

'Aye,' Blind Hugh replied hesitantly. 'Well ...' He fell silent. 'The crew wish ter amend our deal.'

Uncle Percy's eyes narrowed. 'Continue...'

'We wants yer ter have this back.' He pulled out the emerald and offered it over. Becky glanced at Uncle Percy, who appeared as bewildered as her.

'No, it's yours,' Uncle Percy said. 'I want you to keep it.'

'That's most kind, sir. But we can't. Don't be misunderstanding me, we're still askin' fer payment. But it's got nothin' ter do with jewels or coinage. We need yer ter do us a deed.'

'What kind of deed?'

Blind Hugh sighed heavily. It was then Becky noticed his bottom lip was quivering.

'It's quite simple,' Blind Hugh said. 'You seem like a fine gentleman, Mister Halifax. A rare kind of gentleman in these parts. Yer nephew and niece are fine, too. And so be your friends. Well, and I be speakin' for every bucko on this ship, the payment for yer passage is that you take the boy, Jim, with you when ye go. Take him back to England. Give him a life he can live long and good. An honest life. Take him and set him up nice...'

'But you're his family,' Becky said, appalled. 'I talked to him earlier and you're all he's got.'

'I know, lassie,' Blind Hugh said. 'And that isn't right. He's a good boy. And he deserves more than a band of old seadogs fer company.'

'But you can't do that to him!' Becky shouted, ignoring the disapproving scowl from Uncle Percy. 'You can't just abandon him.'

'Lassie, this ain't no desertion. We be doin this because every salt on this ship loves that boy as if he were their own. Thing is, there isn't a man 'ere that will see another five winters, never mind ten. Many of us are already starin' down ol' Nick's musket and waitin' fer him to fire that fatal shot. And what happens to Jim when we go? He's all alone. And in this neck of the woods he'll be dead himself in no time at all. We've all lived a long life. Much longer than most in our game. Jim should be given the chance to live a long life, too, but brought up right, not havin' to survive by eatin' hard tack crawling with weevils or livin' at the will of the tides.' He turned to Uncle Percy. 'I can see yer've got a good heart, sir. I may be blind but this I see as if lookin' through a younger man's good eyes. Ye can do this fer us. Ye must do this. If Jim stays piratin' he won't see manhood.' A tear trickled down Blind Hugh's cheek.

Tenderly, Becky reached over and placed her hand on his.

The old pirate blushed as he squeezed her hand tightly. 'Arr, look at me… cryin' like a Frenchie. You must forgive an old seadog, Miss Becky. I thought fifty years at sea had toughened me up a bit. Perchance I was wrong.'

'There's nothing to forgive,' Becky replied softly. 'I'm sorry I shouted.'

'Pay no mind to it,' Blind Hugh replied. 'So what do you say, Mister Halifax? Do we have a deal? Because that be the true price fer The Black Head.'

Uncle Percy looked grave. 'Are you sure it's what the crew wants?'

'Every man would give his life fer it. The boy's got a dozen fathers and each one of them be wantin' what I ask.'

'And what about Jim? What does he say about it?'

'I'll be talkin' to him at first light,' Blind Hugh said gravely. 'He'll be sad, fer sure, but that's only because he don't know different from this life. In time, he'll understand we done it out of carin'.'

Uncle Percy said nothing. When he did speak, there was a trace of uncertainty in his voice. 'Very well. Jim can come with us.'

'And I can 'ave yer word as a gentleman?' Blind Hugh pressed.

'I give you my word.'

'Thank the good lord,' Blind Hugh breathed.

Becky didn't know what to think. She looked at Blind Hugh and his body wilted as though he'd used every bit of strength to make the request and had nothing left to give. Sadness ripped through her. 'Jim will be well looked after.'

'Aye, I believe that, lassie.' Blind Hugh forced a half-smile. 'Anyway, I shall retire now and bid you a restful night. But I thank ye, Mister Halifax. And you, Miss Becky. A thousand times I thank ye.' Then he turned, set his cane against the deck and rapped his way into darkness.

After Blind Hugh had gone, Becky turned to Uncle Percy and said, 'What are you going to do? Will Jim come and live at Bowen Hall?'

'I don't know,' Uncle Percy replied. 'But Hugh is right. This is no time or place for a young boy like him. And I would never forgive myself if something happened to him, knowing I could have helped. Of course, if I take him out of time I am breaking section three, paragraph two of the GITT regulatory code for time travelling which is punishable by the revoking of my TT license, but ...'

'– But you live with a dinosaur, two sabre-tooth tigers, a flying horse, a dodo and Will Scarlet. Since when have rules stopped you?'

Uncle Percy chuckled. 'Believe it or not, I'm normally a very rule abiding person.' He curled his arm round Becky's shoulder and together they stared out at the velvety ocean. 'But I suppose some rules were made to be broken ...'

BECKY SOON FOUND herself feeling exhausted and returned to her hammock, falling asleep straight away. When she awoke she was surprised to find she and Mister Flint were the only ones left on the berthing deck.

'Good morning, Mister Flint,' she yawned, slipping on her shoes and coiling her hair into a ponytail. She made her way over to the ladder.

'BWARRKK ...' Mister Flint screeched loudly. 'Intoooo the bowels.'

'Lovely!' Becky muttered, climbing the steps to the decks above.

Entering the gun deck, Becky heard a loud sniff and saw a pair of feet sticking out from behind a gunpowder barrel. Straight away, she knew who it was and what had happened. Stepping off the ladder, she walked over to Jim, her heart sinking when she saw his eyes were swollen, his cheeks red raw. 'Hi, Jim.'

'M-mornin', miss.' Jim wiped his eyes and got to his feet.

'Are you okay?'

'Got brine in me eyes,' Jim mumbled. 'Stings a bit. I'll be right in a while.'

Becky knew it was a lie - that Blind Hugh had talked to him about leaving with Uncle Percy. She wanted to offer words of comfort, but what could she possibly say to make him feel better? Instead, she smiled sympathetically and said, 'D'you want to come up on deck or are you staying down here?'

'No, miss,' Jim replied. 'I shall join you ...'

Moments later, Becky opened the hatch door and was surprised to find the deck deserted. Then her eyes were drawn to the ship's bow and everything became clear. Standing in line, frozen like statues and strangely silent, Uncle Percy, Joe, Will, Bruce and the crew were staring out at the horizon. She trailed their eye line and fear flooded her.

In the distance loomed the most terrifying dark green sky, lit by recurrent bursts of scarlet lightning. Dozens of small tornados spiralled above giant waves, and rain hammered the sea like cannon balls.

Becky gulped. Scarlet lightning? She'd never even heard of such a thing. Unable to tear her eyes from the maelstrom, she walked over and sidled in between Will and Joe. 'Please tell me we're not going to have to go through that?'

Will's face grew somber. 'Yes.'

Joe looked at him. 'You must have been on plenty of ships, have you ever seen anything like it before?'

Will looked grave. 'I have not.'

All of a sudden, One Toe Tom yelled, 'Buckos ... Man yer stations! We got ourselves a battle with a squall from Hell itself.' He glanced at Uncle Percy. 'Mister Halifax, I need ya ter take yer folk and our Hugh below and if ye have a God then now would be the time ter do some prayin'.'

'I shall stay!' Will said resolutely. 'You will need the hands.'

'Me, too,' Bruce said.

Uncle Percy stared determinedly at One Toe Tom. 'The three of us are staying here.' He turned to Becky and Joe. 'Take Jim and Hugh to the berthing deck and hold on to anything that's nailed down.'

'I'm not going anywhere!' Becky replied.

'Please, Becky,' Uncle Percy implored her. 'There's nothing you can do here...'

Becky was about to object when the temperature tumbled. The blue sky above turned a sickening green.

Uncle Percy couldn't believe it. 'Crikey.'

In that moment thunder roared, rain pelted down, and the sky flashed scarlet as sheets of blood red lightning splintered the air. Then - *CRASH* - a gigantic wave smashed into them, knocking the ship sidewards. Joe was thrown off his feet, landing hard against the deck.

'Joe!' Becky cried.

A second wave struck. This time, Becky was pitched against the balustrade –her skull smashing into wood. Blood leaked down her face, into her mouth. Through blurry eyes, she saw Uncle Percy secure Blind Hugh to a bollard. Her eyes flicked to Will, who struggled to remain upright as he fought his way across the deck to help Short Jack Copper at the ship's wheel.

With a *crack*, a lightning bolt struck the tip of the mizzen mast. Uncle Percy saw it. 'BECKY! OUT OF THE WAY!'

Hearing his urgency, Becky barreled left as the mast's tip shattered at the spot she'd just been. Crawling to an iron capstan, she flung her arms around it and her fingers locked tightly. Looking up, struggling to feed her lungs with air, she watched the chaos. The crew valiantly fought to regain control, but she knew it didn't matter. The ship would overturn. They were dead. Her eyes sought out Joe, only to find he was already staring back at her. She knew immediately he felt the same way. And at that moment she wanted to hold him, to kiss him, to say goodbye.

Then, as quickly as it started, the storm passed. The sky became blue again, the sea calmed.

Stunned, Becky's gaze swept the deck. Each face she saw was etched with astonishment. She stood up only to be nearly bowled over by Uncle Percy, who had raced over to her, his arms wide open.

'Thank God,' Uncle Percy breathed, squeezing her tightly. He pulled Joe into the embrace. 'I thought I'd lost you both.'

Becky had never really seen Uncle Percy display such raw emotion, but neither she nor Joe minded one bit, and sank happily into his arms. Suddenly, Joe looked flush with panic and pulled away. 'Mister Flint!' He rushed off in the direction of the hatch. A few anxious minutes later, he returned, Mister Flint bobbing up and down merrily on his shoulder. 'He's fine,' he said, sounding relieved.

'FLINTYYYY FINE!!!' Mister Flint squawked.

Becky began to laugh when she heard Will Turnip's voice. 'LAND HO!' Looking over, she saw his extended finger pointing at a stretch of custard-coloured sand.

Then another voice rang out. 'AND O'ER YONDER, LADS!' Burly Bill Brundle was looking in the opposite direction. Becky whipped round to see another island, this time populated by a dense wall of trees. As The Black Head ploughed further on, more islands appeared on the horizon.

'We're there,' Joe breathed. 'The Archipelago. The Macaco Islands.'

A relieved smile formed on Uncle Percy's face. 'I believe so.'

The pirates were all celebrating, slapping each other on the back and belting out a hearty chorus of 'The grand Black Head' when a high-pitched voice cut through the singing.

'Leviathan!' Jim yelled, his voice rising. 'LEVIATHAN!'

The singing stopped at once.

'LEVIATHAN!' Jim repeated, pointing at a spot about a hundred meters away.

Becky glanced at the ocean and her blood turned to ice.

An enormous jet-black head, the size of a large car, with smooth, oily skin had broken the water's surface, its wide, cavernous jaws framed on either side by two tentacle-like whiskers. Gradually, the head rose higher and higher until it threatened to touch the sky.

Becky froze to the spot, unable to breathe.

The sea serpent's mouth opened slightly as if in a mocking grin, and then with an almighty splash, it plunged into the depths below.

26

SNAKE, RATTLE AND ROLL

'TAKE ARMS, ME BUCKOS ...' One Toe Tom yelled. 'THERE'S A BEAST THE SIZE O' OLD NICK HIMSELF LOOKIN' FER A BRAWL.'

At this, Windy Pete, Skinny John Prinny, Hunchback Henry, Lockjaw Morgan and Hairy Harry Hooper raced to the decks below.

'Arm yourself, boy,' Will told Joe. Reaching into his coat, he grabbed his Joe-bow and ran over to the side of the boat.

'Look after Mister Flint.' Joe passed Mister Flint to Becky, who squawked irritably as if he found it all a major inconvenience.

Bruce drew a flintlock pistol from his belt and thrust it into Uncle Percy's hand. 'Here, Perce, I can design fancy stuff, too.' He pulled out two more flintlocks and cocked them. 'I think you'll find it's got more kick than your average eighteenth century shooter. For one thing, it's got a ten-bullet mag in the grip.'

Uncle Percy looked at the gun with surprise. The single

shot pistol had been converted into a twenty first century semi-automatic weapon. 'I'm not a usually an advocate of firearms, Bruce … but nice job.' The two men joined Will and Joe, each of them aiming at the water.

Short Jack Copper had opened a wooden chest and was distributing cutlasses, boarding axes and spears to those who had remained on deck. Windy Pete and the others then returned clutching an array of muskets and blunderbusses, and together they lined all sides of the deck, ready to protect their ship.

Time passed.

But still no attack came.

Everything fell still, quiet, tranquil.

Becky allowed a tinge of relief to seep through her. Had the Leviathan gone? She exhaled loudly, but then - *BAAAAAM* - the Black Head shuddered violently as if struck by a torpedo. Becky lost her footing and crashed to the floor, just managing to keep hold of Mister Flint. Clambering to her feet, she dashed to the starboard side and saw the serpent slice the water. She wheezed with horror. It was colossal, easily a hundred feet from head to tail.

Bruce and Uncle Percy fired repeatedly. Time after time, the bullets hit their mark but were merely pinpricks in the serpent's hide.

From some distance away, the serpent's head surfaced, its jaws inching open and a thin, crimped two-pronged tongue flicked out. It dived again.

'Ready yourselves, Boys!' One Toe Tom shouted.

Becky saw the serpent charge at them like a train.

Uncle Percy tore open his shirt to reveal the black lining of a Tracker Pack. He unhooked a squid grenade and pitched it with all his might. BOOM! It exploded on the water's surface, just above the beast, but to no effect. He threw three more. BOOM. BOOM. BOOM. Nothing.

The air rang with gunfire, thick with arrows, but nothing could stop the inevitable collision. The Black Head nearly upturned, sending Skinny John Prinny and Hairy Harry Hooper hurtling into one other.

Then all went still again.

Lockjaw Morgan frantically reloaded his musket when the serpent's tail appeared behind him, tree-trunk thick and glistening with slime. Becky saw it. 'Lockjaw,' she yelled, but it was too late. The tail encircled his waist, squeezing the life out of him.

'Arrgghhh!' Lockjaw screamed.

Heart pounding, Becky looked around. An abandoned cutlass lay on the deck. Releasing Mister Flint, she grasped it and raced over to Lockjaw. Raising the sword high, she sank it into the serpent's flesh. Tar-like blood gushed over her hands. The tail twitched, releasing Lockjaw, who fell heavily, clasping his ribcage.

Then, on the opposite side of the ship, the serpent's head rose slowly from the water. Everyone froze. Climbing the air, it stopped parallel to the damaged mizzen mast, its whiskers wriggling like giant worms. Then its dull black eyes locked on Joe ... and it lunged.

'JOE!' Becky screamed.

Joe dived right. The serpent's jaws missed him by inches, smashing into the deck like a sledgehammer, misting the air in a fog of dust and splinters, before returning to the air.

Will turned to Uncle Percy, fury in his eyes. 'Hand me an explosive device.'

Uncle Percy didn't question the request, swiftly

thrusting the last squid grenade into Will's hand, who sprinted over to the main mast. Scaling it in seconds, Will leapt into the crow's nest. 'YAHHHHH!' he shouted, waving his arms. The serpent's head twisted slowly, its eyes finding him. Then its jaws stretched open and it pounced.

A half-smile formed on Will's lips. Then he launched himself into the open mouth; jaws clamped shut around him. The serpent pulled back, satisfied with its first kill.

For a few moments, time stopped.

Becky wanted to scream but no sound came out. She glanced at Joe, whose mouth had fallen open.

'Will?' he said in a whisper.

Becky felt numb, crushed. She glanced at Uncle Percy, his face fixed with disbelief. More time passed. Then, from beneath them, a muffled *boom* shook the boat. At once, waves bubbled all around; the water turned a sickening red. She looked up at the serpent, its features frozen with shock, as it fell lifelessly with a thunderous *crash*, sinking to the ocean bottom in seconds.

And then Becky understood. Will had sacrificed himself and taken the serpent with him. She scoured the ocean, desperate for a sign he was still alive, but as the swells subsided and the blood-red water turned blue, she realized it wasn't going to happen. Minutes crept by, and still no one said a word.

Tears leaked down Joe's face now. Becky moved over and wordlessly took him in her arms, tears forming in her own eyes, her insides screaming. She looked to Uncle Percy, hoping for some sign this was all some kind of grand plan, but he was white as stone, crushed, his expression solemn and downcast.

It was then that she spied movement from the ship's portside.

A pair of hands clasped the side. Pulling himself over, Will jumped onto the deck, bruised, bloodied, but alive.

Becky gasped. Joe tore himself away and ran into Will's arms. Soon, Will was besieged with handshakes, pats on the back, and words of congratulations.

'You are one crazy dude,' Bruce said to Will, pulling him into a bear hug.

However, before the celebrations had finished, Windy Pete emerged from the lower decks and shouted. 'Abandon ship! The Black Head is no more. Abandon ship. Our lady be gone…'

'N - not she?' Will Turnip stammered.

'Aye, Mister Turnip,' Windy Pete replied sadly. 'There be a hole the size o' Jupiter in her hull. She'll be at the bottom o' the briny in a catfish's whisker.'

Loud groans of dismay came from the crew.

Uncle Percy, however, became suddenly alert. 'Listen everyone, I am so sorry about your ship, but I don't think there's much I can do about that. I do, however, take full responsibility for our situation and fully intend to uphold my part of the bargain on all counts.' He flashed Blind Hugh a smile. 'Perhaps being wealthy men will ease your loss.'

Lockjaw spoke up. 'Wealthy? With respect, we'll be marooned on these cursed islands with no ships that'll stop ter give us passage. Ain't no point in wealth round 'ere.'

'Ah, well, of course you're right but I've not been completely honest with you. And as I'm running out of time, it's probably best to show rather than tell.' He reached into his shirt and pressed something on the Tracker Pack. A second later, a thin shard of dazzling white light crossed the vest straps, before encircling him in electrical charge. Then, with a *snap*, he vanished.

Becky knew at once the Tracker Pack was a Portravella. The crew, on the other hand, hadn't a clue what was going on, when Uncle Percy reappeared in precisely the same spot, clutching a pile of freshly laundered clothes.

'Miss me?' Uncle Percy grinned. 'These are for you, Will.' He passed over the dry clothes to Will, who began to change.

Will Turnip fainted; Jedidiah Quint and Hunchback Henry backed into each other and clashed heads; and Windy Pete showed everyone how and why he deserved his nickname. The rest of the crew just stood there, open-mouthed and dumbstruck.

'What is it?' Blind Hugh said, gauging from the dazed silence something significant had just happened.

'H - Halifax is a sorcerer,' One Toe Tom puffed.

'Hardly,' Uncle Percy replied. 'I'm an inventor and a time traveller, which I'd appreciate if you didn't mention to anyone, I could get in terrible trouble ...'

'W - what's a t-time traveller?' Short Jack Copper stammered, as a stunned Burly Bill Brundle helped Will Turnip to his feet.

'I really don't think we have time to go into that. For now, you just need to know I've just travelled back in time and sorted out the issue of anyone being marooned. Now, if you'd care to look over there....' He pointed to their rear.

Whirling round, Becky was amazed to see a pirate ship heading towards them, a large jet-black flag fluttering from its mast. Then she gasped. Emblazoned on the flag, in glittering silver, was a shark. Straight away, she remembered seeing the flag before. 'Is that Stinky Mo?'

'Apparently he prefers to be called Gingerbeard on the water,' Uncle Percy said with a smile.

'*The* Gingerbeard?' Hunchback Henry gasped. 'Mo Baggely?'

'The very same,' Uncle Percy replied. 'He's joined by Battle-Axe Beattie, and a small but reliable crew from The Soggy Flannel. It wasn't hard to persuade them to make the trip, to be honest … they all seemed rather taken with the prospect of a share in Blackbeard's treasure.' His smile broadened. 'Anyway, I'm afraid we're going to have to leave.' He scanned the crew's dumbstruck faces, before his gaze finally settled on Blind Hugh. 'I promise we'll return with your treasure and, should it still be your wish, I'll take Jim with me and set him up with a new life. You have my word.'

Blind Hugh nodded glumly 'And I believe it to be a fine word, sir. I don't know what kind of magic man you are, Mister Halifax, but I knows deep down yer can give our Jim the kinda life he deserves.'

'But Mister Livsey –' Jim pleaded.

'Please … that be my final word on the matter, Jim,' Blind Hugh replied firmly. 'The boys and me be right on this. If ye were us, yeh'd do the same.'

'Talk it through once more,' Uncle Percy said. 'If I take Jim, there really is no going back.'

'Agreed,' Blind Hugh said.

'Very well,' Uncle Percy replied. 'Anyway, could I ask you all to take three steps back?'

Everyone did, creating a wide circle in the middle of the deck. Then he raised his key fob to his mouth and said, 'Taxi!'

Just then, Beryl materialized to a chorus of disbelieving gasps. Will Turnip fainted again. Uncle Percy opened her doors.

With Mister Flint chattering merrily in his ear, Joe clambered into the taxi, followed by Becky, Will, Bruce and finally Uncle Percy.

As Becky settled into her seat, something occurred to her. 'Uncle Percy, we don't know which one of these islands is Mary Island. We don't know where to materialise?'

Uncle Percy grinned mischievously. 'Oh, didn't I mention it? We're not time travelling there. We're taking the scenic route.'

Confused, Becky looked out at the surrounding ocean. 'What do you mean?'

'Watch!' Uncle Percy turned the key and Beryl roared into life.

'What are you doing?' Becky asked in a panic.

'I'd *really* prefer you didn't mention this to your mother!' Uncle Percy said. Then he placed his foot on the accelerator.

Becky didn't have time to respond as Beryl powered across the deck, Joe's whoops ringing in her ears, before crashing through the balustrade and plunging headlong into the sea, hitting the water like a battering ram.

Terrified, Becky glanced around, fully expecting seawater to gush in through any gaps. It didn't happen.

Uncle Percy pressed a purple button on the dashboard and, immediately, dials flipped about, knobs flashed various colours and a device that resembled a pair of binoculars lowered from the roof. He began to hum merrily as he steered Beryl parallel. Soon, they were gliding through the crystal clear water like a bird in flight. It was then Becky knew Beryl wasn't just a time machine ... she was also a submarine.

27

HAMMER TIME

'A submarine?' Joe spluttered. 'Beryl's a submarine!'

'She certainly is, Joe,' Uncle Percy replied with a chuckle. 'Do you remember I mentioned she may come in useful given the right circumstances. This is one of those instances, don't you think?'

'You are such a legend!' Joe replied.

'You're not wrong, kid,' Bruce said. 'Perce, you've more surprises up your sleeve than Bat Masterson's got bristles.'

Becky smiled. Now the shock of travelling underwater in a taxi had subsided, she allowed the aquatic spectacle to unfold before her. Huge shoals of angelfish swam in formation, stone crabs scuttled along fat slabs of coral, and a giant manta ray soared above them like a flying carpet. However, what surprised her most were the dozens of shipwrecks lying twisted and broken on the ocean bed, their detritus strewing as far as the eye could see.

For ten minutes they pushed gently on, absorbing every last detail of the strange, colorful world. But then, all of a sudden, the crystal clear waters turned muddy grey.

'What the –' Uncle Percy said, perplexed.

Then Becky's blood turned cold. A fish torso drifted past, its head missing. Then, all at once, fish corpses were everywhere - some large, some small - all of them headless. Her stomach lurched. Through the gloom, she saw a gigantic whale carcass, stripped of flesh, propped against the seabed.

'What the hell's happened here?' Joe asked.

'I'm not sure,' Uncle Percy said, 'but judging by our luck one can only surmise we're approaching Mary Island.'

Then - *BAM* - something struck the time machine from behind.

'What's that?' Becky spluttered, her head twisting round.

No one answered. Just as Uncle Percy regained control of the car, it happened again.

This time, Joe was thrown headfirst into Bruce, nearly squashing Mister Flint, whose wings flapped as he screeched in panic. Joe didn't have time to pick himself up when two more collisions came from beneath.

'What going on?' Becky cried. Then she stiffened with horror. From nowhere, the outline of a huge creature hurtled towards them.

The shark's conical head smashed into Beryl's windscreen, its jaws snapping wildly, before snaking left, revealing a wide, ragged hole in its underbelly where its abdomen should have been.

'Impossible!' Uncle Percy mouthed.

Then Joe remembered Bruce's story. 'ZOMBIE SHARKS!' he yelled.

And, from nowhere, zombie sharks surged from the shadows - bloodstained teeth bared, their black, frenzied eyes fixed on the taxi with deadly intent. Great Whites, Tigers, Hammerheads, some barely more than skeletons, slammed into the time machine again and again, in a relentless maelstrom of fury.

Becky was petrified. Just one crack in the window and they were dead: the sharks would strip their bones in seconds flat. Distraught, she looked to Will, but even he looked helpless.

'Can you zap us out of here?' Joe shouted above the noise of the assault.

'The Capicium Inflexor doesn't work underwater, Joe,' Uncle Percy yelled back, struggling to keep control of the wheel.

'Does Beryl have any weapons?' Becky yelled.

''Fraid not. But next time I promise I'll make sure we're armed like a tank.'

Joe snorted. 'Next time make a time machine *out* of a tank!'

'Suggestion noted, Joe,' Uncle Percy muttered.

Then, through the onslaught, Becky spied something that made her heart leap. 'Over there,' she yelled, pointing. 'Land!'

'Oh, thank goodness.' Uncle Percy forced the steering wheel left. 'C'mon Beryl, my dear. You can do it!'

Pushed to her limits and shuddering violently, Beryl battled the weight of a dozen or so sharks and inched into the shallows. Thick beams of sunlight sliced the water, making it considerably brighter, as a land mass blurred before them. And then a few seconds later, a miracle happened.

'The sharks,' Becky said. 'They're leaving.'

And she was right. One by one, the sharks were reacting

to the sunlight, turning away and slinking back into the depths. Then Beryl's tyres touched soft sand, and they were suddenly travelling at speed. Within moments, they powered out of the water onto a wide, sandy beach, coming to a halt beneath a palm tree.

The taxi fell silent.

With a relieved sigh, Uncle Percy turned to the others and said, 'What with a storm, a sea-serpent and zombie sharks, I think it's rather nice to be back on terra firma, don't you?'

Everyone was too dazed to respond. Everyone, that was, except Mister Flint. 'FLINTY RUM ...BWAAWKK ... FLINTY RUM,' he squawked, nudging Joe's leg.

'I think someone's thirsty,' Uncle Percy said.

'THROUGH THE MOUTH!' Mister Flint screeched.

Joe pulled a bottle of rum and a cup from beneath his seat. Filling the cup, he watched as Mister Flint drained it. 'INTO THE BOWELS ...'

Swaying slightly, Mister Flint stared out of the window, head bobbing. 'FLINTY HOME... FLINTY HOME...' he squawked.

And then it struck them. They had arrived at Mary Island.

An excited shiver shot up Becky's spine. She opened the door and watched Mister Flint hop onto the cool sand, clicking his beak joyfully. Slowly, she followed him out and looked around. Mary Island seemed larger than the other Macaco Islands, with thick jungle on all sides and a mountain range that dominated the eastern side of the island, the peaks of which glowed like rubies in the low sun.

Uncle Percy spent the next few minutes ensuring Beryl was still in working order. 'She may not look quite as pretty as she did, but other than that she's fine,' he said to a visibly relieved Becky and Joe. Then he bent down and kissed Beryl's roof. 'Thank you, my dear. You really saved our bacon...'

'When you've finished snogging the car,' Joe said. 'Can you tell us what we do now?'

Uncle Percy looked at Joe. 'I'm hoping the coins will lead the way.'

Joe shot him a puzzled look.

'Oh, yes, I haven't mentioned those to you, have I? Anyway, let's just say the coins have been rather active of late...' Uncle Percy reached into his jacket pocket. At once, his face creased. 'Oh, no!' He dashed over to Beryl, exploring every inch of her interior, before emerging minutes later looking downhearted and miserable.

'You've lost them, haven't you?' Becky said. 'You've lost the coins.'

Uncle Percy gave a feeble smile. 'I'm afraid at some point I must've torn my coat.' He poked two fingers through a hole in his pocket. 'The coins have, indeed, err, well... yes, they've gone.' He forced a chuckle. 'They've probably already made it back to Pandora's Box!'

'What are you gabbing on about?' Joe asked. 'What's this about the coins?'

'I'll tell you later,' Becky replied, before turning back to Uncle Percy. 'So how are we going to find Blackbeard's treasure now?'

Uncle Percy went silent. 'I have no idea.' He looked at Will and Bruce. 'Any thoughts, gentlemen?' But before either could respond, Mister Flint made a strange grumbling sound and bit Joe's ankle.

'Oww,' Joe cried. 'Flinty, what did you do that for?'

Mister Flint swiveled round and toddled into the jungle, shrieking, 'BWARKK ... FLINTY GO HOME ... FLINTY GO HOME.'

Uncle Percy's face ignited. 'That's it,' he said. 'Maybe we don't need the coins.' He looked at Becky, who stared back at him blankly. 'Who's the only living creature to have seen where Blackbeard and Israel Hands stored their treasure?' His smile broadened. 'I never thought I'd ever say this, but ... *follow that parrot!*'

28

MISTER FLINT'S REVELATION

Fortunately, tailing a tipsy parrot was just about the easiest thing Becky could imagine. Not only did Mister Flint make a great deal of noise trampling the undergrowth but, every now and again, he would stumble into a tree trunk, give a cantankerous squawk, before carrying on, only to do it again a few minutes later. Recognising it would probably take some time to reach their destination, she decided to hang at the back of the group and study the island. It was then she heard Bruce's voice.

'So, missy, is all of this the norm when you visit Uncle P?'

Becky thought for a moment. 'Well, it's not always zombie sharks and sea-monsters, but it can be pretty eventful.'

Bruce chortled. 'Jeez, and here's me thinkin' I had a crazy childhood.'

'What was yours like?'

'Ah, to be truthful with you, it was as perfect as a smile,' Bruce replied. 'How old are you – thirteen? Fourteen?'

'Thirteen. I'll be fourteen in March.'

'Then I was just about your age when I started travelling.'

Becky looked shocked. 'Time travelling?'

'Is there any other kind?'

Becky wasn't sure why, but she'd always assumed she and Joe were the first young people to be time travellers. 'But how?'

A wistful look crossed Bruce's face. 'My pappy introduced me to it. Great man, my pappy …great scientist, too. He died a few years back. Heart attack. Very sudden. Very sad.'

'I'm sorry,' Becky said.

'No matter,' Bruce replied. 'He's gone, but he's with me every single day if you know what I mean. The thing is, all of us are here by the grace of the big fella upstairs.' He pointed upward. 'So you just have to ride this bronco called Life and hold on for as long as you can. That's what those Black Head boys have done. And that's how I know *your* pappy is gonna be just fine.'

'Why do you say that?'

'Because I knew him pretty well - the two of us had some pretty wild trips in that pink ice-cream truck of his.'

Becky's heart flipped. 'I didn't know you knew him.'

'Oh, yeah,' Bruce replied. 'And I know he will not let go of this bronco easily, not while he's got you, your bro and your momma in his head and heart. You'll be with him every night when he closes his eyes, no matter where he is, no matter what Drake does to him. Your pappy will hold on because of you and yours. I am certain of that, missy…'

Becky went quiet. Her bottom lip trembled.

'Ah, look at me,' Bruce said guiltily. 'I've made you as sad as a sinner on Sunday.'

'No,' Becky replied at once. 'You haven't at all. I appreciate what you said, I do. I just hope you're right.'

'I am, missy,' Bruce said sincerely. 'I am.'

'Thank you. I'll be honest with you, Bruce, you don't sound like a scientist at all.'

'A scientist? Me?' Bruce chortled. 'Sweet Mary, no ... my pappy had all the brains, I just got the looks.' He smiled sadly. 'Nah, you'd think he'd be disappointed havin' a dunderhead like me for a son, but if he was, he never once showed it.'

'I thought all time travellers were scientists.'

'Nope. They used to be in the forties and fifties but we're all second or third generation travellers now.'

'But you converted that flintlock into an automatic weapon?'

'Ah, I just had the idea for it,' Bruce replied. 'I got someone else to put it together.'

'So what do you do then?'

'I own a few shops in Tucson. I ain't ever gonna be Donald Trump, but they keep the coyotes from my door.'

'Really?' Becky said, surprised. 'What kind of shops?'

'Flower shops.'

Becky nearly choked. 'You're a florist?'

'I certainly am,' Bruce replied proudly. 'Best job in the world.' He took a long, satisfying breath as if inhaling the most beautiful fragrance. 'I love the smell of Saguaro Blossom in the morning...'

'That's great,' Becky said sincerely. 'I thought you'd be – well, I don't really know what I thought.'

'Yeah, I know I don't seem the florist type, but isn't it true that the most interestin' people are the ones that surprise you? Take your uncle ... he might come across all Professor Nerdwhup, but when it comes to fightin' for his loved ones he's got more spunk than a skunk's got stink...'

Becky smiled. She knew Bruce was right.

The two of them continued talking as the group hiked deeper into the island. The sounds of the forest had reached deafening levels. Brightly coloured birds sang above, insects whirred below, and dozens of monkeys leapt gracefully from tree to tree, tracking their every move and chattering wildly to each other.

The longer the journey continued, however, the more Becky began to doubt Mister Flint had any idea where he was actually going. She was about to raise this with Uncle Percy when she heard Mister Flint screech, 'FLINTY SHACK ... FLINTY SHACK!'

The group emerged onto a rocky outcrop overlooking a wide valley. In the distance, Becky could see a waterfall that tumbled from a sheer rock face, feeding a river below. Then she turned and gasped. To her left was a large pine house with a decked veranda, furnished with two throne-like chairs. She watched as Mister Flint hopped eagerly through the front door, which stood slightly ajar, and disappeared from sight.

'So this is where Blackbeard lived?' Joe said, looking around. 'It doesn't look like somewhere he'd leave a massive pile of treasure.'

'It certainly doesn't,' Uncle Percy replied. 'But there's no harm in taking a look.' He followed Mister Flint through the front door, trailed by everyone else.

Inside, Becky was surprised to find it surprisingly cozy

and not at all the kind of place to be inhabited by pirates, particularly not one as allegedly ferocious as Blackbeard. Silks in every colour hung from the walls, huge red and gold velvet cushions covered the floor. She moved slowly through the living room, before turning into what she assumed was the kitchen. It was then she noticed something quite curious. Two long, thick leather straps, ragged at both ends as if cut by something sharp, lay on the floor beside a giant wooden table. Simultaneously, an odd, sickly-sweet smell she found vaguely familiar filled her nostrils. For some reason, she had an overwhelming urge to flee, to get out of there as quickly as she could. Telling herself she was being stupid, she noticed the panelling on the far wall had been damaged beyond repair; smashed glass and broken pottery spattered the floor.

'I wonder what's happened here?' Uncle Percy said curiously.

'Dunno,' Joe replied. 'Maybe some monkeys broke in and had a party.'

Uncle Percy chuckled, until he noticed Becky's expression. 'Are you all right, Becky?'

Becky opened her mouth as if to say something, then closed it at once. 'I'm fine,' she replied unconvincingly. 'I need some air.' And with that she paced from the room, her head reeling. By the time she had made it outside, she was panting heavily, her shirt damp with sweat. Taking deep breaths, she began to relax when Joe appeared, followed by Uncle Percy, Will and Bruce.

'Becks, what's up?' Joe asked.

'Nowt.'

'But you jellied out in there?'

'I didn't'

'Yes, you did. Didn't she Uncle Percy?'

'You did seem rather peaky, my dear.'

'I'm alright,' Becky replied with a wave of her hand. 'I just ... well, it's hot. Anyway,' she said, eager to change the subject, 'what are we going to do about finding Pandora's Box?'

Uncle Percy shook his head. 'At the moment, I'm not sure, but I'm certain something will arise. We'll take a short break, maybe have something to eat, and then interrogate a parrot...'

For the next few minutes, they said very little to one another. Mister Flint joined them outside, and together, they all stood there in silence, taking in the majestic views.

'Prettier than Moss Side, isn't it?' Joe said to Becky.

'Just a bit,' Becky replied.

Joe pointed at the mountain opposite and his smile grew. 'Hey, that cliff looks like Mister Taylor, our science teacher.'

To Becky's amusement, she found Joe was right. The cliffside did indeed resemble a human face, with a forehead, eyes, nose, and a long shimmering silver beard in the form of the waterfall. 'That is actually uncanny,' she laughed. And then goose pimples stood up on her neck. 'Oh – my – God,' she exhaled.

'What?' Joe replied.

'That's it,' Becky said, lifting Mister Flint and kissing him firmly on the beak. 'Mister Flint, you really are the best.'

'What are you doing?' Joe asked, bewildered.

Becky ignored him, returned Mister Flint to the ground, turned to the others and announced in a loud, steady voice, 'I know where Blackbeard's treasure is!'

Uncle Percy looked at her. 'What's that, Becky?'

'Remember Israel Hands' poem,' Becky said. 'It said *'Listen closely to my friend.'* Well, we all thought he was addressing his English friend, ermm -'

'Mallory,' Uncle Percy prompted her. 'Edward Mallory.'

'Yeah, him. Anyway, we thought the 'my friend' meant Edward Mallory and he'd just missed out the comma. But it doesn't. He wanted Mallory to actually listen closely to his other friend: Mister Flint.'

Joe looked confused.

Becky continued. 'Think about what Mister Flint's been saying to us: Old man's beard ... Through the mouth ... Into the bowels.' She pointed at the mountain. 'The cliffside looks like an old man's face, the waterfall looks like his beard. We just have to get behind it, into his mouth and head downwards. Don't you see, Mister Flint's been telling us all along where the treasure is...'

TEACH'S TREASURE TROVE

U ncle Percy beamed at her with pride. 'Clever girl.' Immediately, he withdrew what Becky recognised as a pair of amnoculars and trained them on the mountainside. 'Israel Hands, you really were far too intelligent to be a pirate.' He gave a satisfied nod. 'Yes, there appears to be a narrow path in the rock that leads up behind the waterfall. Oh, how exciting...'

Leaving Mister Flint at the hut with a promise to get him later, the group left with renewed vigor, reaching the mountain in no time at all.

Becky looked up at the waterfall in awe, a cool, welcoming spray speckling her face, when, through the corner of her eye, she saw Uncle Percy turn towards her and Joe.

'Now I'm aware there might be some opposition to this,' he said. 'But I'm going to ask you both to stay here and - '

Becky had been expecting it. 'Nope. We're coming this time.'

'Absolutely,' Joe agreed. 'Don't even try and stop us.'

' I thought you might say that.' Uncle Percy sighed. 'Very well. Now we don't know what we're going to find in there, but I think we should all prepare for the worst. Bruce, would you be so kind as to let Becky have one your flintlocks?'

Becky gasped. *She was getting a gun.*

'If you're sure, boss.' Bruce passed over a flintlock.

Uncle Percy looked heartbroken as Becky turned the pistol in her fingers.

Joe, on the other hand, turned green with envy. 'You are so lucky, Becks. Maybe I should have one?'

'Absolutely not,' Uncle Percy said firmly. Then he turned to Becky. 'Please, please be careful with it.'

'I will,' Becky replied. 'It's just … I've never fired a gun before.'

'It's pretty much just aim and pull the trigger, missy,' Bruce said. 'You've got ten bullets.'

Uncle Percy looked miserable. 'Frankly, if we do come across any trouble I would prefer you drop the gun and hightail it out of there as quick as you possibly can. And that goes for you, too, Joe.' With that, he unscrewed the sword from his cane and approached the path.

Taking each stride with care, mindful of the dampness underfoot, Becky trailed Uncle Percy to an altitude of about seventy feet when he disappeared from view. Following close behind, Becky soon found herself in a large, dank cave with oily black walls; shivering from the sudden drop in temperature, she spied a wide hole opposite that fanned into a long, dark tunnel.

Uncle Percy waited long enough for Joe, Bruce and Will to catch up, before entering the tunnel. Hesitantly, Becky did the same. She wasn't sure which was louder, the aeroplane-like roar of the waterfall or the pounding of her own heart. Glancing ahead, illuminated by swirls of light from tiny cracks in the walls, she saw the tunnel slope downwards before tapering into blackness.

'The last time we were anywhere like this we met a vegetarian Minotaur,' Uncle Percy said to Becky, trying to break the tension.

'No,' Becky replied sharply. 'I think *you* met a Hydra with nine heads!'

Uncle Percy's body deflated. 'Ah, yes,' he replied. 'I forgot about that one.'

From then on no one said a word.

All of a sudden, Becky spied a strange, misty, multi-colored light in the distance. 'Is that sunlight?'

'I'm not sure,' Uncle Percy replied, squinting.

The group pressed on, weapons raised, their footsteps echoing against the dull walls. Closer and closer, they advanced, watching intently as the curious light swelled before them. It appeared to be radiating from not one, but three caves.

Her pulse racing, Becky approached the first cave. As she did, her eyes widened with astonishment. The cave was crammed to the ceiling with gold: caskets, figurines, boxes, tiaras, bracelets, masks, statues and countless more pieces she couldn't see.

'Oh my word!' Uncle Percy whispered.

'Smother me in butter and call me a bagel,' Bruce said.

'We are sooooo rich!' Joe gasped.

'It's not ours, Joe,' Uncle Percy replied.

Then, one by one, they moved on to the next cave. This time, they found it bursting with silver: candlesticks, jugs, urns, strongboxes, bowls, cutlery and armour. In a daze, they moved to the final cave, which was jam-packed with jewelry; precious gems of all shapes and sizes cast kaleido-scopic colours on the dark walls.

'Blow my chaps off,' Bruce breathed. 'Forget floristry... I'm takin' up piracy.'

For what seemed like an age, they all stood there, stock-still, captivated by the immeasurable riches on display. Then they heard a deep, distant moan.

Becky jumped, startled.

'What was that?' Joe uttered.

'It's probably just the wind, Joe,' Uncle Percy replied, although Becky wasn't convinced by his tone.

'That didn't sound like wind,' Joe replied.

Becky had to agree. She faced front, her hand curling round the flintlock's grip. She saw the tunnel curve slightly, hiding the path ahead. His sword raised, Uncle Percy moved forward, trailed by Will who had set an arrow on his bowstring.

Heart pounding, Becky turned the corner and her eyes nearly popped from her head. They were standing at the edge of a vast sea-cave with walls as black as tar. A wide stretch of grey sand merged into seawater, which flowed out through a giant archway to the ocean beyond. A strange silvery mist floated above the water like a shimmering carpet. But the most surprising thing was the three-mast pirate ship anchored in the shallows. She recognized it at once. 'That's the ship that was at Devil's Spear Island, isn't it?'

'The Winchester Man,' Uncle Percy said, bewildered. 'Richard Young's flagship.'

As the group moved into the middle of the cave, Becky's

eyes scanned the ship's deck. It appeared deserted. 'So where is everyone?'

Before Uncle Percy had a chance to respond, however, the most terrifying sound penetrated the cave like a deadly gas. It was laughter. Low, foul, humorless laughter. The laughter quickly formed into very slurred, indistinct words. 'Welcome ter me abode....'

Terror flooded Becky. Looking over at the far end of the cave, barely visible through the velvety black shadows, she saw an enormous man sat on a golden throne, his disfigured, pale, bearded face illuminated for the briefest of moments. Then her heart plummeted further. Beside him, an enormous golden chest was tipped open on its side, a trail of gold coins leading into the water. The same silvery mist that filled the cave poured out of it like exhaust fumes.

'Pandora's Box!' Becky whispered out loud.

'Blackbeard!' Joe said at the same time.

Blackbeard leaned forwards, his face touched by a thick shaft of sunlight. Becky's hand shot to her mouth. The right side of his face had been completely torn off, exposing bone and sinews and blackened teeth. A large chunk of his neck was missing. Dried blood caked his mouth and whiskers. 'It be agreeable ter have y'all here ...' he rasped chillingly.

'Z - zombie Blackbeard,' Joe squeaked.

Becky felt paralysed with fear. But then it occurred to her: Blackbeard was alone. If he were a zombie, at least the kind of normal zombie she'd seen in films, he would be easy to kill.

Lazily, Blackbeard raised his hand. 'And ye have nothin' ter fear from me ... I've fed on many a brain fer a day now, and me belly is full ... It's made me strong. It's made me fast. It's made me clever ... but as fer my newborn ... well, yer blood will smell most temptin' ter them, I be sure ... And yer brains will taste sweet ...' His hollow eyes flicked to the shadows. 'So arise my army of the damned... Protect yer master ... and feast fer your first time...'

Suddenly, the walls came alive. Dozens of pirates emerged from the blackness; twisted, mutilated and misshapen, their long, skeletal arms stretched out before them, groaning so loudly it made the cave walls shudder.

Uncle Percy turned off-white. 'Oh, crikey,' he said, looking round to see they were approaching from all directions. 'The Winchester Man had a crew of about seventy five ...'

'Sweet mother of Bethesda,' Bruce muttered.

Becky turned hastily to Joe. 'Okay then, Zombie Assassin,' she said shakily. 'You're up. What do you suggest we do next?'

Joe gulped. 'Shoot brains ...' He raised his Joe-bow. 'Shoot a lot of brains...'

30

ONE FOR SORROW

A line of zombie pirates, their grey faces blurred and ghostlike in the mist, formed a thick, impene-trable barrier, three deep, hiding Blackbeard and Pandora's Box from sight. More zombies lumbered in from the sides, snarling, drooling, teeth bared.

Will didn't hesitate. An instant later, an arrow cut the air, striking a zombie through its eye. Without even seeing it slump to the ground, Will had reloaded and fired again. Another direct hit.

With Will's success spurring him on, Joe's eyes locked firmly on their target. He fired. Another zombie down. Within seconds, both he and Will were sending arrows one after the other, neither of them missing a shot.

Bruce spun round to face the zombies approaching at their rear. 'Here, good buddy.' He threw a flintlock to Uncle Percy, who caught it comfortably. 'Guns first, swords later...' He drew his remaining two flintlocks.

'Smashing!' Uncle Percy said flatly, taking aim. A

moment later, a volley of deafening *booms* rang out as he and Bruce fired at the same time.

Becky stared at the flintlock in her hand. Hands trembling, she lined a zombie in her sights. Ordinarily, she could never kill a living thing, but this felt different. These things were already dead. Definitely, absolutely, irrefutably dead. Steadying her hand, she pulled the trigger. *BANG.* The zombie crumpled to the ground.

Soon, zombies were dropping like flies, as arrow and bullet hit their mark, but the onslaught was far from over. 'There are too many of them,' Joe cried. "We'll be out of ammo soon.'

Becky glanced ahead, then behind. Joe was right. There were dozens left. In a matter of minutes, they would be torn apart. They needed to act and act fast. 'What should we do, Uncle Percy?'

'We must close Pandora's Box,' Uncle Percy shouted back. 'I'm sure it's the mist that's causing this.'

Out of arrows, Will cast aside his Joe-bow. 'Then it shall be done!' He drew his cutlass, and charged single-handedly at the oncoming horde.

'IS HE INSANE?' Becky screamed.

Uncle Percy glanced over at Will, who was slashing, slicing and carving up anything without a pulse. 'Almost certainly...' Then, with a *click*, he ran out of bullets. He glanced at Bruce, who had also just fired his last shot. Together, they drew their swords.

'Time to decapitate zombies, Perce,' Bruce hollered.

'Terrific!' Uncle Percy mumbled. He scanned the cave entrance. Bar a spattering of zombies, there was a clear path to the tunnel. 'Becky, Joe, you must leave. Dodge the remaining zombies and get outside. We'll meet you back at the hut shortly!' He gestured to Bruce and together they raced off to join Will.

Becky and Joe glanced at each other. It was clear neither had any intention of going anywhere.

Suddenly, through the thinning line of zombies, Becky spied Pandora's Box, the silvery mist pouring out thicker and faster and angrier than before. To her dismay she saw Blackbeard had gone, too. She turned to Joe. 'Cover me!'

Joe looked flustered. 'I've only got two arrows, Becks.'

'Here.' Becky thrust the flintlock into his hand. 'There are six shots left. Let's see you play Zombie Assassin for real.' And with that she sprinted off.

Becky powered across the sand, blood pumping in her ears. A zombie turned to her, its eyeball hanging sickeningly from an empty socket; snarling, it lunged at her when a bullet pierced its forehead.

Joe sighed with relief as he lined up his next shot.

Struggling for breath, Becky pressed on. Another zombie attacked. This time, she barrelled into it, sending it crashing to the ground.

Uncle Percy saw Becky race past. 'NO, BECKY!' he yelled, when suddenly he found his head clamped in a pair of powerful hands. A vile, putrid stench filled his mouth.

Blackbeard smirked, his discoloured fingers digging deep into Uncle Percy's face. 'Yer brains are mine ...' he jeered. Opening his mouth wide, he dragged Uncle Percy closer, his bloodstained teeth edging towards Uncle Percy's throat.

BECKY DIDN'T SEE any of it. She was running at full pelt now, swerving past one zombie, then another. Looking up, she saw a single zombie remained between her and Pandora's Box. Desperately trying to stay on her feet, she mistimed her run and stumbled slightly. The zombie sensed its opportunity. Arms stretched, its hands curled around her throat, choking the life out of her. She tried desperately to wrench the hands away, but it was too strong. Then – *BANG* – the fingers went limp and the zombie sank to the ground, a smoking bullet hole in its skull.

Becky inhaled deeply and, using the last of her strength, leapt on to Pandora's Box, slamming it shut, before rolling off and landing heavily on the ground, red faced and clawing for air.

In that instant, everything changed. The mist dissolved; zombies crumbled to dust before their very eyes; the cave brightened as if an endless night had finally blossomed into day.

The last thing to change was Blackbeard, who had frozen with disbelief an inch from Uncle Percy's neck. Then, like charred paper, he dissolved to nothingness, until there wasn't a trace left of him.

Uncle Percy looked around, relieved, speechless, struggling to comprehend all that had happened.

As Becky got to her feet, she saw Joe speeding towards her.

'Becky!' Joe seized her in a powerful hug. 'Are you all right?'

'You said we didn't do hugs,' Becky replied with a grin.

'Shut your gob,' Joe said. 'That was unbelievable.'

'I couldn't have done it without the Zombie Assassin.'

Uncle Percy's face was still fixed with shock as he

approached the two of them. 'Didn't I tell you both to go back to the hut?' he said, before taking Becky and Joe in his arms and squeezing them with all of his might.

Will walked over, waited a few moments for Uncle Percy to release them, then leaned down and kissed Becky's forehead. 'Young miss, we are all forever in your debt.'

Becky flushed tomato-red. 'Well, err, cheers, err, thanks, it was, err nothing.'

Bruce joined them, shaking his head. 'It was somethin' all righty. Your pappy would be proud. In fact, it was just the kinda crazy-ass thing he woulda done ...'

Becky was about to tell Bruce how much that meant to her, when she heard a deep, kindly voice. 'You're such a brave girl, lassie. Bruce is right. Your old man would be proud.'

Becky looked over. To her amazement, Reg Muckle appeared from a second tunnel behind Blackbeard's throne. Dressed in a threadbare shirt and frayed trousers, he looked as if he'd just come straight from serving drinks at The Magpie Inn. She glanced at Uncle Percy, fully expecting him to be delighted, but he wasn't. In fact, he looked quite the opposite.

'Cat got your tongue, Percy?' Reg said glumly. 'Now that's summat you don't see every day.'

'I - I don't understand, Reg.'

'I think you do, Percy. And I am very sorry ... more sorry than I can say, but I've got no choice.' Reg looked like every word caused him pain. 'I'm sorry to all of you. But that's life ... and death, too, as a matter of fact.'

Then a second voice filled the cave. 'You are undeniably correct, Mister Muckle.' George Chapman appeared at Reg's side, trailed by Doublehook and twelve Associates, each carrying sub-machine guns. They directed the rifles at Uncle Percy, Will, Joe and Bruce, who dropped their weapons and raised their hands.

Chapman smiled cruelly. 'It *really* is all a matter of life and death...'

31

THE EDEN RELICS

U ncle Percy closed his eyes, blocking out the scene that was unfolding before him. When he spoke, his words were laced with hurt and sadness. 'Do you know who you're working with Reg?'

Reg hung his head in shame. 'I don't care, Percy. I could be working with the devil himself and I'd accept that.'

'You are working with the devil.' Uncle Percy pointed at Chapman. 'Do you know who, *what*, he is?'

Reg flinched, but kept his voice steady. 'I do. I can't afford to think about it.'

Chapman chuckled. 'I believe you'll find –'

'Shut it, Chapman!' Reg roared. 'Just because I've forsaken every principle I've got to help you and your puppet master, don't ever think I wouldn't slice you from ear to ear for the things you've done!'

Uncle Percy stared at him, confused. 'Then why are you helping them?'

'This is one of those rare occasions when you don't know all the facts, Percy.'

'Then tell me.'

For the first time, Reg's eyes met Uncle Percy's. 'The Box of Eternity and the Golden Fleece are connected in ways you can't possibly imagine.'

'Go on.'

'If memory serves, you'd heard the story the Golden Fleece was a gift from God to the creators of Stonehenge, a reward for their loyalty and craftsmanship, but that's not true. The Golden Fleece is much, *much* older than Stonehenge. Don't get me wrong - Stonehenge is linked to all of this, but not in that way - you see, Stonehenge was built as a shrine to *all* of the Eden Relics, not just the Fleece. That is its true purpose. It's a temple.'

Uncle Percy looked dumbfounded. '*The Eden Relics?*'

'Aye, all five of 'em. You see, Percy, there's a different story, one that states that at the dawn of time, God created five relics, each with unimaginable power, and that he placed them in the Garden of Eden -'

'Oh, come on, Reg,' Uncle Percy interrupted. 'The Garden of Eden?'

'Hear me out,' Reg said. 'The first of these Eden Relics was supposedly the Golden Fleece, in which God supposedly placed all the knowledge of the world, past, present and future. Ring any bells?'

Uncle Percy turned white as he recalled what happened when he held the Golden Fleece in the Red Caves.

'The second was The Box of Eternity,' Reg continued, 'in which he placed the power of resurrection. I don't know anything about the other three, Drake didn't tell me. But I know they're out there, just waiting to be found.'

But Uncle Percy had stopped listening, one word

whirling round his mind. 'Resurrection?' he said in a whisper.

'The Box of Eternity can bring people back from the dead!'

'You mean … as zombies?'

'I mean, for *real*, Percy. It can bring people, back from the dead - better, stronger, healthier than before. Read your bible … You'll get the picture.'

Reg turned miserably to Chapman. 'My fee for working with filth like him is my wife. Drake has promised I shall have my Mabel back, whole, healthy, without that damn cruel illness that stole her from me. That's why I'm doing this … that's why I've sold my soul to the scum of the earth …and that's why I can't afford to care about what you, or anyone else thinks.' His eyes began to water. 'I can get my Mabel back. Don't you see?'

Uncle Percy sighed helplessly. 'Of course. But that doesn't make it right.'

'I don't care about what's right. I only care about being with her again.'

'I know you do,' Uncle Percy said softly. 'But this is not the way.'

Reg dabbed his eyes with his sleeve. 'I thought you'd be the first to understand. Wouldn't you do the same to bring Stephanie Calloway back?'

Uncle Percy looked like he'd been hit over the head. After a long pause, he said in a soft, small voice, 'She's gone. And she would hate for me to ally myself with Emerson Drake, with George Chapman, with Otto Kruger, just to bring her back from what I'm certain is a much better place. No, I shall love her until my dying day, and that is why I would never do what you're doing. Stephanie's time has passed. She accepted that when she was alive. And so did Mabel.'

Reg seemed to consider this for a moment, and then his face turned scarlet. 'BUT I DON'T ACCEPT IT!' he bellowed.

Uncle Percy waited until the shout's echo faded. 'Do you truly think Mabel would want you to help Emerson Drake?'

Reg looked broken. 'Of course not,' he said faintly. 'It's the last thing she would've wanted ... but she's not here to stop me.'

Uncle Percy glared at Reg. 'Then shame on you for ignoring what you know would be her wishes ... and Becky, you may want to give Reg back the ring he so touchingly gave you. My guess is that time machine we heard at the Magpie Inn was Emerson Drake delivering a chrono-tracer, and it's how Chapman's been able to keep up with our progress. Am I right, Reg?'

Reg didn't reply.

Becky looked down at the ring. It gleamed red in her eyes. Looking over at Reg's guilty face, she knew Uncle Percy was right. She had been deceived, misled, an unwitting pawn in Emerson Drake's game. Slowly, she pulled it off, feeling a wave of anger rise within.

Unable to meet her eyes, Reg walked over to Becky, his hand outstretched. 'I am so sorry, lassie. I hope you'll find it in your heart to forgive me.'

Becky was about to hurl the ring at him but, looking at his crushed, devastated face, she couldn't bring herself to do it. 'Forget it,' she said, passing it over. 'I hope it's worth it.'

Chapman stepped forward. 'Now that we have all had

the occasion to air our views, Mister Drake would like to liaise with all of you, so if you'd care to accompany me, we have carriages waiting outside.' Then he withdrew a pistol and pointed it at Bruce. 'I'm afraid, Mister Westbrook, Mister Drake never mentioned you...' And with an earsplitting *bang*, he fired.

Bruce slumped to the ground, blood pooling around him. Becky's scream echoed off the cave walls. Uncle Percy raced over, dropping to his knees. 'Bruce?'

Writhing in agony, Bruce managed to slur, 'Son of a –' before losing consciousness.

Uncle Percy worked quickly. Gently removing Bruce's hand, he studied the wound closely, before bending over and whispering something in Bruce's ear.

Indifferently, Chapman turned to the Associates and said, 'Seize the box! We must leave...' He pointed at Will. 'Mister Doublehook, if you would care to escort Mister Shakelock personally. He can be rather troublesome!'

Doublehook nodded darkly and moved over to Will, hooks raised. A sickening smile curled on his mouth as if eager for Will to try something. At the same time, Four Associates slipped on thick leather gloves and raced to Pandora's Box, heaving it on to their broad shoulders. The remaining Associates surrounded Uncle Percy, Becky and Joe and escorted them at gunpoint out of the cave.

Entering the second tunnel, Becky looked back helplessly at Bruce, who lay motionless, before turning to Uncle Percy, her eyes watering. 'Is - is he dead?'

'No,' Uncle Percy replied. 'And I have no intention of letting him die either.'

But Becky wasn't entirely convinced.

THE TUNNEL FOLLOWED a steep incline of such length it spanned the mountain bottom to top. Becky's heart sank further with each step: not only were Bruce's chances of survival fading fast, but they were unarmed, outnumbered and the Box of Eternity was securely in the hands of Emerson Drake.

The group advanced in a dull silence, higher and higher, until the dim, shadowy tunnel brightened into flickering orange daylight.

Exiting the tunnel, Becky's stomach churned when she saw two large military trucks, sandwiched between thick jungle and a sheer, rocky cliff that overlooked the ocean. Then, all at once, a strange, high-pitched whistle floated over the trees. She stared at the undergrowth but saw nothing unusual. Then, much softer this time, a second whistle came in four short staccato bursts.

At this, Uncle Percy's eyes narrowed for a fleeting moment. 'So what does Drake want with us, Chapman?'

For some reason, Becky felt sure he was trying to keep Chapman distracted.

Chapman didn't notice. 'I'm sure Mister Drake has his reasons,' he replied, before approaching Becky. 'For myself, as long as I'm rewarded, I don't care.' He leaned into Becky's ear and spoke just loudly enough for others to hear. 'I once told you your heart would be mine, child. If only Mary Kelly were alive, she would tell you I mean it ... *literally.*'

Becky shivered when she glimpsed the scalpel in his hand.

His face ablaze with rage, Uncle Percy made to launch

himself at Chapman, but a frantic shake of Becky's head made him stop. 'No, Uncle Percy, I'm fine,' she said desperately.

Then, from the fringes of the group, an unexpected voice spoke up.

'No,' Reg said quietly, his head shaking, eyes locked on the ground. 'No – no – no … I can't have this…not right… sorry, Mabel, but … can't have it...' Then he marched over to Chapman. 'Get away from the lassie, you abomination of nature, or I'll …'

Chapman sneered. 'You'll what, Mister Muckle?'

'Just get away from her.'

'Can I remind you I now possess the Box of Eternity and thus don't require your participation. I would remain silent if I were you.'

'But you arn't me,' Reg snarled. 'Hell, even I've not been me for a long time. But I'm back now...' And with a roar, he hurled himself at Chapman who, although shocked, whirled gracefully to his left, dodging the attack. Then, with a flash of silver, Chapman's hand shot out towards Reg's neck. With a bloodcurdling cry, Reg fell to his knees, clasping his throat, blood seeping through his fingers.

Becky screamed.

'REG!' Uncle Percy yelled, about to run to his side when –

BOOOOOM! A cannon ball tore into the cliff, sending gigantic clumps of rock and earth everywhere. The ground shook angrily.

Chapman glanced at the ocean. To his amazement, Gingerbeard's ship was anchored about a hundred meters from shore, its cannons trained on them. 'Pirates!' he yelled. 'Load the Box into the vehicle.'

The Associates carrying Pandora's Box hurried to the trucks when – BOOOOOM - a second cannonball crashed into the rock face. The ground shook even more violently this time. One of the Associates stumbled, losing his grip. Pandora's Box plummeted to the ground, its lid staying firmly shut.

At once, Becky heard a loud *crack* from beneath her feet. Alarmed, she looked down to see a wide split in the earth.

'Becky ... Jump!' Uncle Percy yelled.

With every bit of strength she had, Becky pitched herself forwards, just as the ground fell away. She landed safely at Joe's side. Then she glanced back in horror. Reg was nowhere to be seen. In that instant, she saw a body dive to the spot Reg had been. Uncle Percy landed heavily, his arm extended over the newly formed cliff edge, clinging desperately to Reg's wrist.

'Percy ... let me go,' Reg rasped, blood leaking from his neck, his legs flailing.

'Not-a-chance,' Uncle Percy grimaced, pain searing his body.

Will appeared at his side. 'Take my hand!' he shouted to Reg, reaching down.

'No,' Reg croaked, struggling, twisting, making it harder for Uncle Percy to hold on. 'Let me go, Percy.'

'No ... Reg ...please.'

Serenely, Reg closed his eyes and a smile curved on his mouth. 'I'm coming, Mabel.' He wrenched his hand away and fell.

Uncle Percy rolled over, distraught. 'Oh, Reg,' he breathed. 'Goodbye, old friend...'

Stunned, Chapman composed himself quickly. He

gestured to the Associates. 'Seize the box. Take them all. Shoot, if – '

Before he could finish his sentence, the crash of musket fire rang out from the jungle. BANG. BANG. BANG. Becky panicked, but it was the Associates that were being targeted. She raced over and helped a distraught Uncle Percy to his feet.

The jungle seemed to come alive. Branches rattled and stirred. Unseen feet trampled leaves. Then three more shots rang out. Associates were dropping fast now, one after the other, their rifles clattering to the floor.

In the chaos, Will's eyes met Doublehook's, who grinned manically back. In an instant, Doublehook charged at him, pitching his right hook at Will's head. Will ducked and scooped a rifle from the ground. Doublehook attacked again, this time with his left hook. Will blocked the swing with the rifle butt, and then drove his knee into Double-hook's stomach, winding him. Then he smashed his fist into Doublehook's chin, and the pirate's eyes rolled white.

At that moment, a man's voice filled the air. 'FER THE BLACK HEAD, ME BOYS!' One-Toe Tom yelled as, with a spine-chilling yell, a mob of shadowy figures charged, limped and hobbled out of the jungle, cutlasses held high. Only Jim and Blind Hugh remained behind.

Becky gasped with relief. The Black Head's crew had come for a fight, piling into the remaining Associates with a terrible fury.

Chapman's eyes seared with rage. In seconds, he knew the battle was lost. He scanned the area as his long fingers found his wristwatch.

'It's over, Chapman,' Uncle Percy said somberly, his mind still clearly fixed on Reg. 'You've lost.'

'Perhaps.' Chapman pulled something small and thin from his coat pocket. 'But so have you.'

Uncle Percy was shocked to see a thin stream of light curl around Chapman's wrist, snaking its way up his arm. Then, with horror, he spied the syringe in Chapman's hand.

With a cruel grin, Chapman's eyes locked on Becky. Then he charged at her, the light enveloping his entire body with each long stride.

'NOOOOO!' Uncle Percy cried, but it was too late.

Chapman seized Becky and plunged the syringe into her neck. Then, in an explosion of light and a piercing *snap*, he and Becky disappeared.

32

JACK'S BACK

When Becky regained consciousness, she didn't have to open her eyes to realize where she was. She could smell the same sickly odor that made her run out of the kitchen in Blackbeard's shack just an hour earlier; but this time, she recognized it: Chapman's cologne. To her horror, she was lying horizontal on the kitchen table, unable to move, thick leather straps cutting into her shoulders and legs. Heaving her head up as far as she could, she saw the kitchen looked quite different. The far wall was completely undamaged, unlike the last time she had seen it; tankards, bottles, jugs and shelving were all still very much intact and in their proper place. At once, she knew they had travelled back in time, but there was no way of telling just how far back.

Before she had the opportunity to think all of this though, she heard soft footsteps to her rear and George Chapman walked in, moving slowly but elegantly like a tiger. 'Welcome back to the land of the living, Miss Mellor,' Chapman purred. 'I always knew we'd share an intimate moment like this, but hadn't planned on it being quite so soon.'

Becky squirmed against the straps. 'Sorry to disappoint you.'

'I'm far from disappointed. True, I'm saddened the Box of Eternity is momentarily out of reach, but I'm certain Mister Drake will make alternative arrangements. Through the advent of time travel, he may already have done so and we're not aware of it. No, for now, I suggest we enjoy the here and now.'

Becky glared at him. 'If you're going to kill me just get on with it.'

Chapman stood at the foot of the table, looking down at her and nodding eagerly. 'Well, Miss Mellor, you certainly are a courageous little thing. Most of the others just begged and screamed and sobbed and prayed. I'm pleased you're not going to humiliate yourself in such a way.' He licked his lips, moistening them until they glistened. 'However, I do have something of a problem. Mister Drake has left very strict instructions for you to not be harmed. Apparently, he wants to involve you in some dialogues with your father.'

For an instant, Becky forgot just where she was and whom she was with. 'What do you know about my dad?'

'I know he's alive,' Chapman replied, 'and from what I gather, his research into the Eden Relics is really quite extensive and therefore invaluable. Other than that, I really can't say. I never encountered him in person. Apparently, they transport him through time most frequently.'

Becky's heart pounded. 'Where to?'

'I don't know. And I think that's enough talking for now, don't you?' He raised the scalpel into the light. As he turned the gleaming blade towards him, studying it closely, his calm, composed exterior transformed into something monstrous. 'You know ... the authorities never came close to apprehending me for what they consider my *real* crimes. Not the ones that furnished me with that ridiculous sobriquet: Jack the Ripper.' He looked directly at her. 'Did you know they said I killed my victims and then just stopped, just relinquished my blades and vanished into the night? How very naive of them. Why would I stop? It was far too enjoyable, too diverting.' He moved round and whispered in her ear. 'But my new position as time traveller, well, that will allow me to indulge my whims over and over again, throughout the leaves of history. Isn't that just delicious? And here's one final morsel for you, something no one else has ever known. The history books only ever credited me with five victims ... I'll let you into a little secret, shall I? Twenty-six ladies came under my knife ...' Chapman smiled as he traced the blunt edge of the blade softly against her cheek.

But Becky didn't feel it. Every bit of her was numb with fear. She wanted to die now. And she wanted it to be quick. But then, suddenly, a strangely familiar feeling swept through her; a sensation she'd had twice before. The top of her skull felt like it had been dipped in water. Swiftly, the watery sensation spread into her eyes, before moving down, filling every inch of her body. Then her eyes shot open - white, blank, emotionless eyes. She didn't look like Becky anymore.

Chapman stared at her, shocked. 'What the –'

'GET AWAY FROM ME!' Becky roared.

Then, as if seized by the throat by invisible hands, Chapman was hoisted into the air. He dropped the scalpel. Choking, kicking wildly, he was hurled powerfully against the far wall; wood, glass, pottery shattered under his weight. His body slumped down the wall, still conscious, but in a deep state of shock. Confused, he scrambled to his feet. Then he spied the scalpel. Picking it up, he glanced fearfully at Becky and said, 'W - what are you?'

Then another voice filled the kitchen. 'She's my niece...'

Uncle Percy's fist smashed into Chapman's jaw, pitching him headfirst into the wall again. This time, he was unconscious before he hit the floor. Frowning, Uncle Percy massaged his knuckles. 'Thumping people really does hurt,' he muttered.

At once, Becky's eyes returned to their normal colour. Swiftly, Uncle Percy grabbed up the scalpel and cut through her binds.

Slightly dazed, as though just waking from a deep sleep, Becky launched herself into Uncle Percy's arms.

'Thank God,' Uncle Percy said, his voice quivering. 'I – I ...' He couldn't finish the sentence.

Becky trembled uncontrollably. 'Uncle Percy, it's happened again. Remember outside the Red Caves, when the Golden Fleece flew through the air and came to me, and we all thought in some way, it had chosen me. Well, I don't think it did ... I think I made it happen... I think I can move things, move them with my mind. What's it called when you can do that?'

Uncle Percy hesitated. 'Telekinesis.'

'That's it,' Becky replied. 'Telekinesis. Well, that's me. I'm telekinetic. Just before you got here, I threw Chapman against that wall without even touching him.'

Uncle Percy inhaled, but didn't respond.

'You don't believe me, do you?'

'I believe every word you ever tell me, Becky.' He

thought for a moment. 'However, I think this is a matter for a future discussion, we do, after all, have a certain Jack the Ripper to deal with.'

Becky nodded, but then something else occurred to her. 'How did you know where and when to look for me?'

'I remembered your little turn this morning, and the curious damage we saw in this very kitchen. I was also aware that Chapman's Portravella was too small to be anything other than a very short-range device. I put two and two together and fortunately, I was right... which reminds me...' He bent down, detached Chapman's watch, and stamped on it. 'No more travelling for you, George.' Then he dragged Chapman's limp body over. 'Well, maybe one more trip...'

'What are you doing?' Becky asked.

'I think it's time Mister George Chapman paid for his horrendous crimes against humanity, don't you?'

'You're not going to kill him, are you?' Becky replied, shocked.

'We don't kill people, Becky. We're the good guys....' Uncle Percy delved beneath his shirt and pressed something on the Tracker pack. His chest gleamed white as electrical charge crisscrossed his Portravella. 'Take my hand...'

Confused, Becky complied, and watched as Uncle Percy grasped Chapman's ankle. A second later, the three of them were encased in a shimmering globe of fizzing blue and white light. And then they disappeared.

———

A MOMENT LATER, Becky found herself staring at a familiar, but completely unexpected landscape. Her mouth fell open.

Glancing round, she saw a beautiful stretch of silvery white sand and a thick wall of palm trees that merged into a cloudless sapphire sky. Then her eyes were drawn directly above. With a piercing screech, an enormous winged creature soared overhead, its colossal leathery wings flapping in a consistent rhythm, making a deep whooshing sound.

'Ah, a Pterodactyl,' Uncle Percy noted. 'Very common in the late Jurassic era. Becky, can I assume that you remember this place?'

Becky grinned. 'London. One hundred and sixty two million years ago.'

'That's correct,' Uncle Percy replied, looking over at the unconscious Chapman. 'Unlike George here, my Portravella can hold considerably more Gerathnium than his, which means it can travel the same distance as any well-stocked time machine.'

'But this isn't the same place as last time though, is it?

'Er, no,' Uncle Percy replied. 'Last time we parked at what would be Piccadilly in the twenty first century. We're about three and a half miles from there at the moment. Any ideas where?'

'No.'

'Shall we see if George recognises it?' Uncle Percy marched over to Chapman and kicked him firmly in the ribs. 'Wake up, George!'

Chapman groaned. 'W-where am I?'

'You don't know it then?' Uncle Percy said coolly. 'I am surprised. George, this is your old stomping ground - this is Whitechapel, the scene of some of your most despicable acts.'

Chapman looked disorientated and rubbed his eyes. 'I don't understand.'

'Well, you wouldn't, would you?' Uncle Percy said. 'Anyway, I thought I'd leave you here; it's rather pretty, isn't it? Much more tranquil than you deserve.' He pulled out Chapman's scalpel and threw it on the sand; it landed with a soft thump. 'Here, you can have your little toy back. You never know, it might come in handy for gathering food, building a shelter, even, perhaps, for self-protection. I mean, you never know what you might find lurking round here.'

Fear flashed in Chapman's eyes. 'W-when am I?'

Uncle Percy stared at him with disdain. 'A time when you can never hurt anyone, ever again.' He inputted something into his Portravella. 'Becky, shall we depart?'

Becky nodded. 'Absolutely.'

Uncle Percy held Becky's hand as twisting branches of light enfolded them. 'Any last words for Mister Chapman, Becky?'

Becky grinned. 'Say hello to Harold for me, will you?'

33

THE MARITIME MAUSOLEUM

B ecky and Uncle Percy reappeared on Mary Island to be greeted by a mass of dumbstruck stares and gaping mouths. The crew were still evidently struggling with the idea of people disappearing and reappearing at will. Becky's gaze shifted downwards to see the Associates huddled in a circle on the ground, bruised and bleeding, hands bound, defeated. Scowling, Doublehook was pinned to a rubber tree, his hooks driven firmly into its trunk. Then, from the side, she saw someone step nervously towards her.

'You're okay?' Joe asked as if he couldn't quite believe his own words.

Becky saw Joe's eyes were puffy and red.

'Course,' Becky said. 'Have you been blarting?'

'No,' Joe lied, mopping his eyes. 'But shoot me if I was getting a bit worried about you. I mean, you were abducted by Jack the Ripper.'

'No biggie,' Becky replied.

'So what happened? Where is he?'

'Right about now, I reckon he's having lunch with Harold in Jurassic London. Better still, he might be lunch.'

Joe looked impressed. 'You fed him to a Megalosaurus? Excellent.'

'Not exactly,' Becky replied. 'But hopefully it won't be too long before -' Suddenly, an explosion of light erupted behind Joe's shoulder, replaced by a loud *popping* sound. Panic rushed through her. *Pandora's Box had gone.* Fortunately, Will's voice calmed her at once.

'Worry not, miss, your uncle has left to assist Bruce, to lay his friend to rest, and take Pandora's Box to - '

Before he finished the sentence, a loud *crack* heralded Uncle Percy's return. Clean-shaven and grinning from ear to ear, he was wearing a cream linen jacket, white shirt and tie, combat shorts, leather sandals and was holding three large black bags.

'Phew, haven't I been busy?' Uncle Percy said. 'Reg has finally been reunited with Mabel, and I am delighted to say that Bruce is alive and well. He did lose a bit of blood, but he's had treatment and is now recuperating nicely in the most wonderful hospital in Bristol, and – ' His smile morphed into a chuckle, which soon became a laugh. 'Well, you wouldn't believe it … it's so precious, it really is.' Then he turned to the pirates and did a strange thing: he bowed deeply and said, 'Bravo, Gentlemen. Bravo!'

Everyone looked at him as though he'd lost his mind.

'What're ye speakin' about, Halifax?' One Toe Tom asked, confused.

'Have yer been on the grog, son?' Will Turnip asked.

'Actually, no, Will,' Uncle Percy said. 'I'm just in a strange mood.'

'So where's Pandora's Box now?' Joe asked.

Uncle Percy composed himself. 'I'll show you soon, Joe. Meanwhile, I've brought some clothes for each of you so you might want to change for our return trip to the twenty first century.' He threw a bag to Becky, Joe and finally Will, and the three of them left to get changed, returning a short while later to find that Uncle Percy had summoned Beryl. Then he approached Blind Hugh.

'Hugh, what can I say? Thank you and your shipmates so much, for everything. Your rescue was - well, it was timed to perfection. I really don't know what we'd have done without you all.'

'Aye...' Blind Hugh gave a toothless smile. "I 'ave ter say I wish I could've seen it with me own eyes, but I'm guessin' me buckos did me proud.'

'They certainly did,' Uncle Percy replied, before turning to the crew. 'And, as I promised, you are now all exceedingly rich men.' He gestured to the tunnel entrance. 'If you take that path into a sea cave, you'll find a second tunnel. In there, you'll find three caves overflowing with more wealth than any man could spend in a hundred lifetimes. There's also a ship moored down there, The Winchester Man, that would certainly benefit from a new crew.'

Celebratory shouts rang out, as the pirates jumped up and down, danced jigs, hooted loudly, and then broke into a loud, vigorous rendition of 'The grand Black Head.' Amidst the jubilant faces, there were two that weren't smiling - Blind Hugh and Jim.

Uncle Percy placed his hand on Blind Hugh's shoulder. 'I'm assuming that now you're all rich men, you'll want Jim to stay with you?'

'Then ye assume wrong, Mister Halifax,' Blind Hugh

replied sadly. 'Jim is too good fer this life, and the richer we be, the more chance they'll be scallywags wantin' a slice of it. Jim, as a rich gentleman, is in more danger than he is as a humble powder monkey. No, Mister Halifax, we still be requirin' that you take the boy. Take the boy and show him a proper, decent life.'

Jim tried desperately to hold back the tears. 'But Mister Livsey -'

Blind Hugh knelt down, his fingers gently stroking Jim's cheek. 'I'm sorry, boy. But surely yer must understand ... me and the rest o' these salts will be dead soon enough. And who'll protect ye then from the bilge rats that'd slit yer throat for a single doubloon, never mind a fortune. We're doin' this because we love ya, boy... I love ya... I love ya with every beat of me old heart.'

Uncle Percy gave a strange smile. 'I respect what you're saying, Hugh. However, I don't think it's fair on Jim if -'

'Hang right there,' Blind Hugh cut in angrily. 'We had a deal, Mister Halifax. If yer about ter tell me that – '

'If you'd let me finish,' Uncle Percy said. 'I was going to say that I don't think it's fair for Jim to make the journey alone. I'd like you to come, too. I've already set up lodgings for you both at a wonderful house with a splendid lady, a place I know that Jim can grow up well loved, well educated and comfortable for the rest of his days.'

Blind Hugh's lip trembled. 'I can come, too? I get ter go ter the future?'

'A hundred and thirty eight years into the future. What do you say?'

Blind Hugh's face exploded with joy. 'Yes, sir... a thousand times, yes.'

'Good,' Uncle Percy replied. He leaned towards Becky and Joe and lowered his voice so only they could hear. 'To be quite honest, I knew he'd say that.'

Blind Hugh was too thrilled to notice. He turned to the other pirates and roared, 'I'll be voyagin' to the future, me boys. The ultimate voyage!' Then he wrenched Jim close, and the two of them remained locked in each other's arms for an age, beaming, as loud, boisterous cheers surrounded them.

Becky, Joe, Uncle Percy and Will watched as Blind Hugh and Jim were inundated with messages of luck and support as the crew bade their farewells.

'So what will happen to them?' Becky asked, looking at Blind Hugh and Jim.

'They're going to live at 16 Heriot Row, Edinburgh, in 1857, with a lady called Hilary Chambers, the widow of a time traveller friend of mine. She moved there after her husband died. The thing is, she and her late-husband, Arthur, always wanted children but couldn't have them. She was delighted when I told her about our situation and insisted that Hugh and Jim come live with her...'

A short while later, a very nervous Blind Hugh and Jim trailed Becky and Joe into the time machine. Will sat with Uncle Percy up front. Becky watched as Blind Hugh's fingers probed every inch of the taxi's interior, his face igniting with child-like wonder at the new materials, textures and smells in his reach. She thought he already looked ten years younger.

Uncle Percy rolled down Beryl's window. 'Oh, and one last thing, gentlemen, after you've collected the treasure, would you be so kind as to go to that cabin over there?' He pointed in the direction of Blackbeard's Hut. 'There's a little parrot with a penchant for rum that would make a fine mascot for your next ship.'

Short Jack Copper chuckled. 'Consider it done, matey. I've always wanted a parrot for me shoulder.'

Uncle Percy smiled, and inputted the new coordinates into the time panel. Jim's hand tightened anxiously around Blind Hugh's. Then the time machine shuddered slightly, as streams of blue and white light spilled from the dashboard.

'Tell me what it looks like, boy,' Blind Hugh said to Jim.

Jim watched spellbound as the light twirled and looped before his very eyes. 'It be like shooting stars, Mister Livsey, sir,' Jim panted. 'It be like flying through a night sky filled with shooting stars.'

Becky couldn't have put it better herself.

***

BERYL MATERIALIZED on a long street of large grey stone terraced houses. Facing south, they overlooked a large park, its borders guarded by trees and tangled hedges. A thick, dewy fog had settled all around, hiding the sky and giving the scene an eerie, otherworldly air.

'So when is this?' Becky asked.

'3.30am, December 1st 1857,' Uncle Percy replied. He leapt out, opened the rear doors and pointed at the adjacent house. 'Hugh, Jim, welcome to your new home.'

Jim helped Blind Hugh from his seat and on to the street. Then he looked up at the house and his eyes bulged with astonishment. 'And this be where we'll live?'

'That's right, Jim,' Uncle Percy said.

'I ain't ever seen anywhere so grand,' Jim added quietly, as Blind Hugh's arm curled around his shoulder.

Uncle Percy smiled. 'Now, Hugh, you'll be staying with Hilary, an old friend of mine, for as long as you want, and I have established a bank account that will give you a very handsome income should you wish to move, although I don't think you will.' He cast Becky a very curious look. 'Anyway, we must be going soon so I think it's about time you met Hilary, don't you?'

Becky, Joe and Will said their goodbyes and watched as Uncle Percy helped Blind Hugh and Jim up the dozen or so steps to a large front door, which he rapped twice. From within, a light flickered to life and the door opened to reveal a tall, attractive woman of about sixty years of age. Wearing a broad, kindly smile, Hilary Chambers gave Jim and Blind Hugh a welcoming hug before ushering them into the hall. Then she turned and whispered something in Uncle Percy's ear, pointing to the house next door. Together, they began to laugh. Uncle Percy was still laughing when he returned to the time machine.

Becky looked baffled. 'What's so funny?'

'Oh, it really is amazing. I just didn't see it coming.'

'What's amazing?' Becky asked impatiently.

'Well, throughout our trip, I've noticed curious parallels with a certain adventure story about pirates. The most famous pirate story of them all, as a matter of that.'

'You mean *Treasure Island*?' Joe asked.

'I do indeed, Joe, yes,' Uncle Percy replied. 'I mean we've had Blind Hugh instead of Blind Pew, Short Jack Copper instead of Long John Silver, Mister Flint instead of Captain Flint. There have been plenty of these little coincidences.'

'So?' Becky asked, intrigued.

'So, Hilary has just informed me that Robert Louis Stevenson, the author of *Treasure Island* lives just next door at number 17. He's only a young boy at the moment, but apparently Hilary has been invited to dinner at the Stevenson's house tomorrow night. What's the betting that our Jim and young Robert become good friends?'

Soon, they were all laughing, too.

'So *Treasure Island* happened because of us?' Joe asked.

'It happened because Robert grows up to be a truly gifted writer with a remarkable imagination, but I think we can take a modicum of credit, don't you? Anyway, would you like to see where I've buried Pandora's Box? As luck would have it, we can visit Bruce at the same time. He's been there for three weeks now and is feeling much better.'

'Yes, please,' Becky and Joe said at the same time.

Uncle Percy smiled widely. 'If you think the Treasure Island connection was unexpected. You just wait until you see this ...'

BERYL REAPPEARED IN A DARK, deserted alleyway, flanked on both sides by gigantic walls. Everyone clambered out quickly and Uncle Percy triggered Beryl's invisiblator. Then he moved towards the passage's entrance and the gardens beyond.

'Where are we?' Becky asked, struggling to keep up with his long strides.

'Bristol,' Uncle Percy replied.

It was when they emerged from the alleyway, however, that Becky's eyes widened with surprise. The adjacent building made Bowen Hall look like a garden shed. Elegantly designed in silvery-white Portland Stone, it had a copper roof, a succession of towering spires and a lengthy marble portico that provided covered entrances to its hundreds of doors.

'What is this place?' Becky gasped.

Uncle Percy pointed to a large sign on his right. 'See for yourself...'

The Hugh Livsey Hospital and residential home for injured Seafarers, Established 1721

'I – I DON'T UNDERSTAND,' Becky stammered.

A wide smile formed on Uncle Percy's face. 'Isn't it amazing? Apparently, the Black Head's crew, along with Battle-Axe Beattie and Stinky Mo shared Blackbeard's treasure equally, but it was so much they didn't know what to do with it. In the end, they barely spent any of it on themselves. They returned to England, and set up a charity in the name of their absent friend, Blind Hugh Livsey. They employed the finest architects of the day and built a number of magnificent hospitals for injured sailors across Great Britain and Europe. In short, they made sure that Blackbeard's treasure would forever be used for good.'

'That is brilliant,' Becky said.

'Cool,' Joe said. 'Isn't it, Will?'

'Indeed.'

Becky was about to laugh, when she heard a familiar voice. 'And I can certainly recommend the medical care. There's a lovely lady nurse called Poppy that can skin my hump anytime ...' Bruce limped round the corner, gripping a walking cane and wearing a leather biker's jacket over his blue and white checked pajamas.

'BRRUUCCEEE!' Becky and Joe shouted simultaneously, racing over to him and giving him a gentle hug.

'So, Perce, are you gonna show 'em where you've buried Pandora's Box? That's the best bit.'

Uncle Percy smiled. 'Of course, Bruce. Are you coming?'

'No,' Bruce said, leaning into Uncle Percy and whispering, 'I think I'll go and find nurse Poppy. I could do with another bed bath.'

'Ah,' Uncle Percy nodded awkwardly. 'Very well. Everyone, follow me.' He turned a sharp right and proceeded down a footpath. Soon, they were all trudging across well-maintained lawns, passing dozens of patients, some sitting on benches, others in wheelchairs, all of whom were enjoying the morning sun.

'Where are we going?' Becky asked, 'and why exactly did you bury Pandora's Box here, at a hospital?'

'You'll see,' Uncle Percy replied. 'And strictly speaking, I didn't bury it at the hospital.'

A short while later, Becky received something of a shock. They had exited the hospital grounds and were walking along a narrow tree-lined road to a sprawling cemetery, which they entered through a rusted iron gate; headstones, old and new, peppered the landscape. And still Uncle Percy showed no sign of stopping. For a further few minutes, they walked the length of the cemetery until Uncle Percy finally came to a halt at the top of a hill. 'And that's where I've buried Pandora's Box ...' he said, pointing ahead.

Becky's mouth fell open.

At the far edge of the cemetery, dwarfing the horizon, stood a gigantic marble statue of The Black Head, about a third of the size of the real thing, but resplendent in its detail.

'Isn't she wonderful?' Uncle Percy said to a stunned silence.

'I-I don't get it,' Joe said, confused.

'It's a Mausoleum, Joe. The Black Head's crew are buried beneath her. One Toe Tom, Hairy Harry, Jedidiah Quint, Windy Pete ... all of them. In fact, there are only two crew members not with them.'

'Blind Hugh and Jim,' Becky offered.

'That's right. They're buried in their family plot in Edinburgh. Would you believe it, Blind Hugh married Hilary and they legally adopted Jim. Together, as close any family could be, they lived long and very, very happy lives.'

Becky felt her eyes well with tears. 'That's good,' she said quietly.

'Let's have a closer look, shall we?' Uncle Percy said.

Uncle Percy led them over to the Mausoleum. With each step, Becky didn't know whether to laugh or cry. It was the most remarkable, lasting monument to friendship she had ever seen. Reaching the base of the statue, she saw a silver plaque that read:

> *'Aye we're the crew of the grand Black Head*
> *And proud ter be now we be dead ...'*

Becky read it again and again. Then she found herself laughing. 'That is so cool.'

'I couldn't agree more,' Uncle Percy replied.

'And Pandora's Box?' Joe asked.

' - Is buried way, way down beneath her, far away from Emerson Drake's clutches, and protected for all time by the bravest crew of pirates to have ever sailed the seas.'

'Awesome,' Joe said simply. 'What do you think Will?'

Will smiled back at him. '*Awesome*, indeed.'

'Anyway,' Uncle Percy said. 'I think it's time we returned to Bowen Hall. I think we've all earned a jolly nice rest, don't you?'

'Maybe,' Joe said. 'Or maybe we start looking for the other Eden Relics?'

'Yeah,' Becky agreed. 'Actually, I've had some thoughts on that.'

Uncle Percy couldn't help but smile. 'I'm sure you have, young lady.' He glanced at Will and the two of them rolled their eyes. 'I'm sure you have...' He curled his arms round Joe's shoulders, as Becky linked arms with Will, and together, the four of them walked back to the time machine.

And just then, Becky could understand why the Black Head's crew had remained together in life and beyond. Friendship. Family. A sense of belonging. These were the things that mattered. Not money. She glanced over at Uncle Percy, Will and finally Joe and knew deep down that spending time with them, sharing adventures, making sure they were all safe - these things meant more to her than all the riches in the world. Of course, she also knew she would never tell them that, particularly Joe. After all, Christmas was just around the corner and she really did want a new pair of trainers.

The End

IF YOU ENJOYED THIS BOOK, then continue the *HUNT* with 'The Time Hunters and the Spear of Fate.'

Made in the USA
Las Vegas, NV
03 September 2021

29508093R00156